NOVELS BY ERIN MAINE:

Bittersweet Justice

Masquerading Justice

Mystique River Justice

W9-CYB-296

~~~ Chapter 1 ~~~

"Don't take it personally," she said as she saw the last flicker of life fading from his eyes. Not wanting to prolong what had already been a boringly long death, she tightened the garrote around the neck of the man pinned beneath her. No longer fighting, she smiled as she watched his chest rise for the last time. Almost immediately, she relaxed her hands, stood and walked silently over to her sink to warm her hands under the spray of the scalding water. "Suppertime," she mumbled as her hands started to burn, quickly snapping her back to the last task of the evening before meal time.

(20 years earlier)

"But Uncle Joey, I don't like this game," she pleaded as she found herself backed into the corner of her tiny bedroom. "Please don't, please stop. It hurts when you play your game and I don't like it," she begged, already knowing it was useless to whimper, cry or beg. Her uncle grinned the most malicious smile she'd ever seen, and she knew she hadn't won the battle again today. "At least," she thought to herself, "Rebecca is safe tonight since she's at a friend's sleepover." She squared her shoulders in one last ditch effort to ward him off, but knew it was useless.

"Shhh honey. Remember what I've told you and your sister. This game is a special game, between just the three of us. It's our little secret and terrible things will happen to your momma if the sorcerers hear that you've told anyone, understand?" he said, as he stroked her long blonde hair as if petting a dog. He smelled of body odor, cigarettes and booze and each time he kissed her, touched her, or penetrated her, she felt her skin crawl. She wasn't quite twelve but understood far too much about the dynamics between she, her sister and her so-called uncle. She'd spent too many nights covering her ears when daddy made the same guttural noises in her parents' bedroom. Funny, she thought now, she only heard those sounds when daddy had their neighbor over to show her some of the projects that he'd completed. Momma and the lady neighbor were great friends in church but she never came over to visit her mother, only her dad, when momma had to go into work early. The pretty lady always wore a flower in her hair and always smelled like baby oil, she thought now as she felt her uncle's hand leave the safety of her hair and move farther southward. She hated those nights when the lady came over. Those were the nights that she and Rebecca, her little sister, were forced to go to bed early, even when it wasn't their bed time, and sometimes even before supper if daddy had forgotten to cook something because he'd stopped at the Pub on the way home from work. Jasmine had never understood why she was old enough to take care of her little sister when momma went into work early and daddy wasn't home from the Pub yet, but she wasn't "mature" enough to be allowed to cook something for them to eat. She didn't understand what double standards were yet, but she knew that going hungry wasn't fair. None of what she endured at the hands of her "Uncle" was fair, and the worst part about it was that she couldn't tell anyone because she firmly believed that something awful would happen to her momma if she did. And momma was the only one, other than her sister, who ever paid her any attention or showed her any form of affection. Her momma sang to her, and combed her long blonde hair, and told her and Rebecca wonderful fairy tales of unicorns and knights in shining armor and castles in faraway lands. Staring into the eyes of the devil, she calmly responded to the man who had her cornered with his hand already caressing her tiny breast.

"I understand completely Uncle Joey," she said as she quickly willed her tears away and allowed anger to fill her instead of fear. She had always tried to be brave and not cry when her Uncle wanted to play his games, but as his excitement grew, so did the pain. Jasmine did not like her Uncle and did not like his games. And now that he was including her little sister in his special games, she did not like her parents for allowing him to come to their home to visit. And she hated that the visits were becoming more and more frequent ever since she started looking more like her mother and all the grown up ladies at church. She'd tried to hide it and conceal the obvious changes but her attempts had been in vain. Her body had blossomed, as her mother called it, almost overnight. The changes frightened her; all of the boys in school seemed to take notice of the way her blouses now looked. Unfortunately, the boys at school weren't the only boys who noticed and her Uncle started making comments about how "womanly" she had started looking, his comments repulsed her to no end. She almost wished that she still looked like the boys in her class so everything would go back to normal and everyone would leave her alone!

(12 years earlier)

"Welcome to the Marines," he whispered as he held her down, sliding his hand inside her fatigues and finding the spot that he was searching for. "You fucking women come here all high and mighty, thinking that you're as tough as us, as dedicated as us, and think that you deserve the same chances and fucking rights as the plebes we get in here from all over. Fuck that," he said as he drove his fingers inside her, shoving them roughly as far into her as he could with a sense of satisfaction flickering in his eyes as he saw the flash of pain show in her face, though just for a second. He gave her credit for not screaming or calling out. Maybe she realized that no one would hear her or even if they did, no one would come to her aid. Or maybe she realized that if she did cry out, it would only prove once and for all that she wasn't nearly as tough as she wanted everyone to think she was. Either way, he didn't care. He wanted this particular soldier to know that she and her kind weren't wanted here. The military was and always would be a boys-only club and anyone with tits didn't belong.

"Broads were put on this earth for cleaning house, fucking, and making babies with; he certainly didn't think that were his equal," as he struggled to unbuckle his uniform while keeping a tight grip on her throat as he straddled her. Knowing what was coming, she tried to slow her heart rate and find her happy place; the place in her mind that she'd been escaping to since childhood whenever she needed a safe haven.

Her eyes didn't show the fear that she felt as she willed herself to remain calm and let the Major get his rocks off one way or another. Luckily for her, she knew that he had a little issue with premature ejaculation so it wouldn't take long for this evening's nightmare to be over. She refused to surrender to the mental and physical assault that had become all too common an event since she'd started her tour out here in the desert. She'd seen his kind all throughout her military career, from the drill sergeants during basic, (during the 54 hours of hell that was affectionately named "Crucible,") to some of her fellow serviceman. She'd worked her way slowly up the ladder to E-4, and even though she'd worked twice as hard as than her male counterparts, the rank of Sergeant or E-5 still eluded her. That still pissed her off. Everyone was out to prove that they could handle the responsibility that came along with being called a Marine, and she guessed that the men set out to make the women in the unit look bad just to prove that they were superior. Maybe it was simply to take the pressure off of them to excel. Either way, she'd seen how many of the women were treated, or mistreated for that matter. All of them kept their mouths' shut for fear of retaliation, and because they knew that the military's "Zero Tolerance Policy" wasn't worth the paper that it was printed on. But at the moment what pissed her off the most was the ox on top of her.

In her mind, she soared, higher and higher on her black unicorn as he plunged deeper and deeper into her; laughing all the while he raped her. She felt the tearing before the burning started, but never flinched. She'd been trained and conditioned to ignore pain, and what she was currently feeling was more of an inconvenience than actual pain. She would survive this and soon, as with all the other times before this assault, it would be over. She'd be threatened, and then he'd let her up. She'd return to her barracks, shower and go back to her normal routine as if nothing had happened. She refused to let him break her. Deep down she knew that infuriated him, which ultimately made her the winner. But tonight, as he finished, she silently vowed that he'd pay; someday he'd pay with his life.

~~~ Chapter 2 ~~~

(12 months earlier)

"Oh honey, why do you have to work late again tonight?" she asked, somewhat breathlessly. Having just finished her workout, she had so looked forward to washing up, putting on something sexy and making Nathaniel his favorite meal since it was one of the rare evenings that she expected him home before dark. Now everything was ruined because he, yet again, had to meet a client after work. She knew that it came with the job, but at the moment she didn't like it one bit. She missed her husband, her rock, her everything and even though she realized that every new client meant a substantial paycheck, all she wanted was some quiet quality time with the most important person in her world.

In the eyes of everyone who knew, Jasmine and Nate had a storybook marriage. They were the envy of many of their friends. At Nate's insistence, Jasmine, a Registered Nurse by degree; had left the hospital the week before their wedding. Her only job now was decorating their 7000 square foot home. Nathaniel, or Prince Charming as she called him, didn't want his wife to be stuck working weekends and holidays and unavailable when he was home from the office. That suited Jasmine just fine. She enjoyed volunteering her time, going to the gym to work out (even though Nate had had a professional gym installed in their home for that very purpose), and making sure that their home looked immaculate for her husband when he returned from a long day at the office. Nate had scolded her more than once for cleaning as they had a housekeeper, but Jasmine took pride in the upkeep of the beautiful home that her husband had provided for her.

It was truly fate how two people from opposite sides of the tracks had met, let alone ended up together. As luck would have it, Jasmine had been on a four-day work stretch when Nathaniel's appendix had ruptured. She was the first face he'd seen and remembered after waking up from surgery. He'd never known if it was the great anesthesia or truly her image, but he had told everyone for years that he fell in love with the blonde angel at first sight.

Jasmine on the other hand hadn't been nearly as taken with him, or happy about his family's first impressions. Having come from nothing, money and affluence were just things that other people had, so his mother's splashy, almost circus-looking attire didn't impress her. Jasmine had always known that money doesn't buy class, and the woman who'd given birth to her husband didn't have one ounce of class in her polished pinky, let alone the rest of her body. She was definitely one rich bitch, and made sure that everyone around her knew who she was and what her net worth was. Nathaniel wasn't like his mother in that sense. He wasn't snobbish or flashy. While in the hospital he ate the hospital food that was served, jello and all; despite his mother's scathing objections and insults about the dietary department within the facility. Nathaniel didn't treat her or the other staff members like second-class citizens or look down upon them like his mother did. Jasmine never could figure out if her mother-in-law did it consciously or simply had her nose so high in the air that it came naturally. His gratitude for the little things that the staff did for him seemed genuine. His sincerity was probably what caught Jasmine's attention more than his looks or his family's wealth. Over the course of the four days that Jasmine took care of Nathaniel, she spent more and more time in conversation with him, quickly realizing that they had more in common that she had ever thought possible. They both had an affinity for nature and the mountains, both enjoyed tent camping, despite Nathaniel's family having second homes in Tahoe and on the Cape; and both were fanatical about eating healthy and being in the best physical shape possible. Without gawking or being obvious, Jasmine had already discovered that fact for herself when she had initially cared for him following his surgery. Hospital gowns didn't leave much to one's imagination, and from what she had seen, the man was an excellent specimen of health, sans the wound on his abdomen from his recent emergency surgery.

He'd asked her out just prior to being discharged from the hospital and much to her own surprise, and his mother's disapproval, she'd said yes. The first date had turned into a second, and a third, and now here they were, married for over five years, living a life that made others envious. They had traveled extensively, with Nathaniel taking Jasmine to the places that she'd only read about, including Dubai for their honeymoon. They'd stayed in the Royal Suite of the Burj Al Arab and he had spared no expense. He'd given her an exquisite sapphire and diamond pendant with matching earrings on their first night in Dubai, and equally beautiful jewelry each subsequent night of their weeklong stay. Jasmine had nearly fainted when she realized that her new husband had shelled out $24,000 a night in order to fulfill one of her dreams. No, she had never cared for he or his families' money, but even she had to admit; wealth did have its perks!

But right now, all she wanted was to spend time with her husband, her rock, the man who would always be the love of her life. She had such amazing news to tell him and couldn't believe that after nearly five years of trying, her dreams were all coming true. Nathaniel was going to be ecstatic, she thought to herself, and maybe, Nathaniel's mother would accept her now that she was providing her with the first grandchild to carry on their name and legacy. She understood completely that work had to come first in order to continue to live the life that she had grown accustomed to, but sometimes, like tonight, she just wished that she could capture his attention the way his court cases, or his clients did. She missed his company so much lately that she'd even offered God their money in exchange for more time with the man she'd married. Knowing that it was futile to dwell on it, she asked him to make his meeting as brief as possible and told him that she'd see him when he got home.

"I love you Nate, and I'll see you soon. Honey," she said as she subconsciously rubbed her still flat and toned belly, "I have something to tell you when you get home, so hurry. Let me know when you're on your way and I'll warm your supper for you."

"Oh Jazzy, you're so good to me. I don't know what I ever did to deserve such an amazing woman," he said as he quickly packed up his briefcase while loosening his tie. He grabbed his suit jacket and flung it over his shoulder and lowered the blinds in his corner office, ending their phone conversation.

"Baby, you know that I'll be home as quickly as I can, and we'll spend the rest of the evening together, okay? You be a good girl and don't pout. Have a drink or two, and be wearing something sexy for me because I have a little something for you my love. But I have to be at my appointment in fifteen minutes so I need to run. Remember baby, I'll come home to you and only you as soon as I can. I love you Jasmine."

Not sure why she felt the hair on the back of her neck rising, she whispered back, "I love you too Nate."

~~~ Chapter 3 ~~~

"Harder!" she demanded, feeling her sweat mingle with his. All too happy to oblige, he pushed deeper inside her, with each thrust making her want more. He'd had many lovers over the years, but Mandi had been the best, and was certainly the most willing to try anything that he'd thought of, dreamed about or read about. The scenes in 50 Shades of Grey paled in comparison to some of the ideas that they both had come up with and experienced with one another. Her sexual appetite was insatiable and she never hesitated to try anything he suggested. Her body was slightly overweight, and maybe not quite as toned as he would have liked it to be, but her melon-sized breasts and tight pussy more than made up for her lack of discipline in the gym. "And her mouth," he thought as he was driving it home, "The things that woman could do with her mouth." He nearly came at that moment, just looking down at her as she licked her lips in ecstasy as he continued pounding her as hard as he could, just the way she begged for it. He watched her boobs bounce up, down, and sideways as she enjoyed their latest position, and he sometimes wondered how she didn't knock herself out with the way they swayed.

Nearing exhaustion, he finally filled and collapsed beside her.

Closing his eyes momentarily, his mind wandered to his wife who was waiting faithfully at home. She'd sounded so disappointed on the phone when he'd, yet again, told her that he had to work late. She'd even said that she had a surprise for him when he got home, though he had no idea what she was talking about or what she could have possibly bought him this time. Knowing his Jazzy, she'd probably seen some tie or cufflinks somewhere when she was out shopping and picked them up for him. Originally he'd found it endearing when she started showering him with gifts that she thought were cute. But now, this far into their marriage, he found them more of an annoyance since it meant that he had to take the time to reciprocate. As he lay there, and for the first time since he'd started his fling with Mandi, he felt guilt, genuine guilt. "She's done nothing wrong and has been nothing but a devoted wife and companion. She doesn't deserve a husband who can't keep his zipper shut," he thought to himself. "Maybe it's time to end it with Mandi and remain faithful to my blonde angel."

Before he could open his eyes or mouth to say anything to the woman lying beside him, he felt a sensation on a certain tired extremity. And all he could think of immediately was "Oh my god, that tongue." Every sane thought that he'd been having about his wife and life in general went out the window when she took him, all of him, in her mouth. And they moved on to round two.

~~~ Chapter 4 ~~~

It was well after midnight when Nathaniel finally made his way into their home. Jasmine was fast asleep after finally giving up on him around ten. He felt a twinge of guilt for the second time that evening when he saw the beautiful centerpiece and table setting that she'd obviously taken the time to prepare for him. As he made his way into their bedroom, he walked silently so as to not wake her. His guilt was already starting to consume him and even though he knew she'd never challenge him or give him the third degree, (she never had in the five years that they'd been married), he certainly didn't want her to tonight.

He'd found her asleep in their bed with her book still on her chest. She looked so beautiful even in sleep with her long blonde hair covering half her face. As he reached over her to lift the book from her chest, he caught a whiff of the perfume she was wearing. Knowing she insisted on wearing it only on special occasions because she'd been astonished when discovering that he'd shelled out over $500 for the quaint 2 ounce bottle, his guilt grew exponentially. She had said that she had a surprise for him. Having no idea what it could be, he now realized that it must have been something really important for her to make a fancy meal, get all dressed up, (as evidenced by the dress lying over her dressing table chair), and be wearing his favorite perfume. Gently he leaned in and kissed her, and suddenly felt the need to take a shower to hopefully wash away any remnants of his evening's adventure. As he let the spray hit his crotch, which still throbbed from the workout it had endured earlier that evening, he wondered why he kept going back for more. It wasn't that he couldn't get great sex at home; hell, Jasmine had always been willing to try whatever he asked her too despite her occasional reluctance. Early in their relationship Jasmine had disclosed everything about her past and the horrors she'd endured as a child and while in the Military. Even though deep down he didn't think that she'd told him everything that had happened, he did not want to know. He'd been saddened, angered and slightly repulsed by the idea of anyone harming a child, let alone a family member abusing her and her sister. Once their relationship had become serious, Jasmine had wanted him to know that she considered herself damaged goods, as she put it, and before they took it any further, she had wanted Nate to know everything and then decide if he still wanted her. Maybe it was her openness that he had first fallen in love with, maybe it was her crystal blue eyes which still held a hint of naivety or fear and always reminded him of the innocence of a baby fawn, or maybe it was the inner strength that she had; strength enough to overcome so many horrible events that would have broken most of the women he had known in his life. Whatever it was, his blonde angel didn't deserve a husband who kept stepping out on her; and as the water scolded his tender and swollen groin, he decided then and there that he would never cheat on her again.

Drying off, he silently slipped into bed beside his love, and snuggled up to her as if he'd been there for hours. Unbeknownst to him, compliments of the Marines, Jasmine was an extremely light sleeper and had not only heard him enter the house, but feigned sleep as he entered their bedroom, and then left her to shower. She'd felt his presence standing above her even though her eyes were shut, she'd smelled him even before he'd approached her, and even though she'd willed herself to shut off her brain, she'd known the smell. He'd smelled of fresh sex, and knowing that it hadn't been with her, her heart broke silently as he showered away the scent of whomever he'd been with. Yes, she'd known betrayal and mistrust all her life; but had never thought that her one true love could or would ever do the same to her. She kept telling herself that she was mistaken, that she was simply tired and not being rational, but deep down she knew better. Refusing to convict the man without proof, she slowly rolled over to face her husband, as she pretended to just be waking. She slowly opened her eyes to see Nathaniel gazing deeply into her, with a somber look on his face.

"Love you," he said as he gently touched her shoulder and back. "It's a little after twelve love, we really should sleep," he said as his lips came to hers. He no longer smelled of anything but his body wash, deodorant and toothpaste. His eyes were clear and looked so sincere as he smiled at her, that all the paranoia that she'd felt just moments before disappeared when she looked into them.

"I love you too Nate."

Seizing the moment, he gently cupped her exposed breast. "You said that you had a surprise for me," he asked with every ounce of boyish charm that he had.

Subconsciously rubbing her belly, she smiled and reacted to his touch. "I do. But it can wait." She leaned in to him for another kiss as he pulled her closer. And as he made love to her, she forgot completely about her insecurities and dismissed them as being her overactive imagination.

~~~ Chapter 5 ~~~

They woke in each other's arm, with both feeling slightly tired after a few hours of love-making in the middle of the night. Jasmine remained in bed as Nathaniel shaved and showered. Luckily, the queasiness that she'd experienced for the last eight weeks had finally subsided and she finally felt like her old self. As she stood to slip on her robe, she caught her reflection in the mirror and knew that she'd have to tell him soon. Her breasts had grown at least another cup size. Even though she'd always been a very healthy B bordering on C cup, it was now quite apparent that they'd grown even more. She gazed at her abdomen which was still rock hard and flat as a washboard, but knew that it was just a matter of time before that too started showing the changes happening inside her. They had talked briefly about having children someday but had never really dwelled on the topic with Nathaniel always saying that they had plenty of time to start a family. Well, it looked like the time was sooner rather than later to start that family, and she'd have to tell him this evening when he returned home from the office.

They ate breakfast together like they did every morning with Nathaniel having his poached egg, two pieces of wheat toast and yogurt. Jasmine still wasn't ready to stomach any version of eggs quite yet; the morning sickness was finally starting to wane but she didn't want to jinx herself. They ate in relative silence as they did every morning, she with a book and her husband with the NY Times and Philadelphia Inquirer. He certainly wasn't a bore or pompous in any way, but his choice of reading material bored the daylights out of her. Jasmine on the other hand preferred self-help books, anything to do with living the minimalist, self-sufficient life style or anything to do with the outdoors. She'd always loved being outdoors, and even though her childhood didn't afford her many organized vacations, she and her sister could always be found exploring the woods, streams and mountains which surrounded their childhood home. Between that, and living in a tent in a god-forsaken desert for so long while in the military, she was used to doing more with less. Even though she wanted for nothing since marrying Nathaniel, she preferred utilizing only the barest, basic necessities.

She'd grown up in the southern Adirondacks of Upstate New York in a little podunk town that didn't even have a red light and whose claim to fame was the fact that the number of cows outnumbered the humans two to one. It was simply a blip on the map and no one had ever left there and become anything of importance. Most people who grew up there married and stayed, continuing the cycle of mediocracy. Jasmine and her sister had always envisioned getting as far away from home as possible. She'd spent hours in the woods, making believe that they were warriors and unstoppable. As adults, they sometimes chuckled when they spoke on the phone, as they did almost daily, about the make believe lives that they'd created so well as children that they almost seemed real back then. Maybe it was their way of escaping the reality of what their childhood had been. Maybe it had been something that every child had done as a kid, but either way it didn't matter, as she and Rebecca had always had very vivid fantasies. Being able to use their imaginations to detach from reality was how they'd survived into adulthood.

When Nathaniel had finished with his breakfast and his papers, he looked up at his wife and smiled as he excused himself and carried his dishes to their kitchen. He felt like he was dancing gingerly around her, waiting to see if she was going to ask him anything about last evening. She'd certainly acted like everything was fine, and their lovemaking was as good as it had always been. He assumed that if she'd had any hint of how'd he'd spent his evening she wouldn't have warmed to his advances so quickly, or at all for that matter. He loaded his dishes into the dishwasher and rejoined her as she sat in their dining room. He couldn't help but think about how beautiful she looked there in her pale blue robe which made her eyes look even brighter, bigger and darker than what they were. She was beautiful, simply beautiful he thought as he looked at the women whom he'd married nearly six years earlier. She felt his stare and looked up from her magazine and smiled.

"I promise to be home tonight long before dark Jazzy, okay?," he said. "And I can't wait to hear what your surprise is. I certainly hope you didn't go through much trouble Jasmine, because I just want you to be happy. Making you happy is better than you surprising me with something. You know I love you right Jaz?"

Looking at her husband, she smiled an innocent but sincere smile. "I promise Nathaniel," she said softly, "I didn't go to any trouble. I just hope that you like my surprise."

"Baby, anything you give me will make me happy and I'll love it."

He leaned over and kissed her gently on the lips, grabbed his coat and headed for the door. She couldn't help but feel as she heard the door quietly shut, that he'd just walked out of her and her baby's life. She had no idea why she felt such a sense of foreboding but still did. She tried to shrug it off but the feeling lingered, so much so, that she no longer felt hungry. She forced the last few bites down, if for no other reason than to give her unborn child a little more nourishment, got up and cleared her dishes. Needing to concentrate on something to clear her mind, Jasmine decided to go for a run, followed by a good workout in their home gym.

It took two hours, but after a good run, and an even better workout, she felt relaxed and rejuvenated at the same time. Her muscles were fatigued but her mind was at ease. She'd come to the conclusion somewhere between working out on her punching bag and elliptical that her hunches and worries had just been her insecurities working overtime. True, she had never understood why a man in Nathaniel's position would be interested in an average looking middle- class hourly worker like herself, but after nearly six years of marriage, hadn't she proved that she was a good companion, excellent housekeeper and cook, equal partner in bed and decision- making, much more intelligent than she'd given herself credit for, and truly was his equal in many ways? Sure she hadn't been raised with the same silver spoon that he had, but she'd made something of herself in spite of it, even though she'd come from nothing. She didn't think of herself as a Phoenix rising from the ashes, but damn it, she'd risen and overcome when others would have given up and accepted the cards that they'd been dealt. Many never would have tried to achieve more. Not she, Jasmine had decided back when she was merely a child that the horrible cards that she'd been dealt were not her destiny and would not be the building blocks that determined her future. She was not to blame for her father's alcoholism and adulterous ways, her mother's absence, her Uncle's pedophilic incestuous ways, or the dumb fuck Officer she'd had to deal with during her Military career. No, their issues were their issues and it was neither her circus nor her monkeys. They were the ones with the problem but she unfortunately had been the one caught in their crossfire. But Jasmine had always believed that what goes around comes around and though it was very unchristian of her, she admitted only to herself, and once to Rebecca, that she'd actually laughed when she'd heard from their foster mother that their Uncle had died in a car accident when the brakes in his truck had failed while going down Route 28 near Blue Mountain Museum. She knew it was horrible to think, but remembering back to her childhood, she had silently hoped that when the accident happened, he didn't die instantly but was in pain and suffered until his last breath. She hoped, just hoped that maybe right before he died, he'd think about his little niece who was so proficient around cars, especially that he had taken the time to teach her how to replace brakes. She'd always loved tinkering on the poor excuses of trucks and cars that filled their driveway during her childhood. She had been a quick study and unbeknownst to her father and uncle, she absorbed and retained every bit of instruction that she'd been given way back then.

Drying the sweat from her face, she felt so much better about all that had been worrying her. She'd shower, go shopping and grab a couple of steaks and cook another special meal that they'd share when he got home. Then everything would be back to normal. She'd tell him about her surprise and they'd laugh and cry together and determine when they'd tell their families and friends, and if they'd find out the sex of their unborn child. Yes, she thought, finally they were going to be a family and the one thing that they'd been missing, that money could not buy, was finally within their reach. In six short months a baby would enter their lives and they'd have a complete family.

She showered and dressed for the day. She'd thought about starting a load of laundry before she headed out, but always erring on the side of caution, she left it in the hamper and decided it could wait until she was back from her errands. As she was about to walk out the door, she noticed that Nathaniel had left his briefcase behind. Immediately worried that there might be something in it that he needed for his day, she grabbed it and put it in her SUV. She'd give him a shout on her way into the city and if he needed it, she'd swing by and drop it off to him. Besides, she was wearing one of his favorite dresses and it gave her an excuse to see him during the day.

As she drove, she decided that instead of calling him, she'd just stop by the office and surprise him. She had only been in his office a time or two since he'd taken the job at the new firm a few years back. She tried to recall the receptionist's name as she parked in the parking garage, but it wasn't coming to her. She remembered the other partners in the firm and Nate's paralegal's name; for some reason, the receptionist's name eluded her even though she'd spoken with her on the phone on several occasions. She checked her makeup and lipstick and when satisfied, exited the truck and made her way inside. It was a stunning building, a young female architects' vision brought to fruition. It was just one of many new buildings helping to revitalize the city's downtown. Once a thriving city made famous for its' textile plants and printing companies, it had fallen onto hard times when companies left to produce their products abroad. The printing companies had been replaced with computer companies all located in Silicon Valley. When Jasmine was a child, she remembered going downtown with her mother and sister to go shopping. It was before huge malls existed, and family owned businesses could be found on every city block. By her teenage years, where there had been thriving businesses, lie graffiti covered abandoned buildings, flophouses and burnt out shells of what once was lined the streets. As she looked around now, she smiled as she viewed a few new high rises, clean, litter-free streets, the return of a few mom and pop stores and boutiques, phase 2 of the condos that were being built in the area announcing their grand opening, and Nathaniel's majestic building standing regally in front of her. Every time she saw the building it was like seeing it for the first time. Where one was standing determined the hue it gave off. Sometime the reflection from the sun made the exterior color of the building appear to be silver, other times almost pink. Regardless of what shade or color, its clean lines and seamless appearance made it more a work of art than simply a building. It had been the young architect's first major project and although there were many skeptics while it was being erected, once the final product was revealed, her popularity, referrals and business grew exponentially. The entire building was heated and cooled using solar power. The rooftop panels were invisible to the naked eye, and working in conjunction with the side facing panels along the east side of the building, they produced enough electricity for the owners to receive a monthly stipend from the Power Authority. That suited the owners' just fine.

She made her way past the security guard positioned at the front door, greeting him cordially, as he held open the door for her. The Carrera marble glistened in the lobby as she walked across the spotless floor toward the elevators. Once inside, she held the doors ajar for a few others, and then pushed #6 for her husband's law firm's floor. They took up the entire 6th floor and she was the only person who got off when the massive doors opened to allow her passage. Entering his office, she was greeted by the receptionist, and smiled in return to her warm greeting. When she asked if her husband was in a meeting with a client or available to see her for a brief moment, she swore she saw a quick flash of panic in the woman's eyes. The secretary recovered almost instantaneously and instructed her to take a seat and said that she'd see if he was available. She was offered coffee and tea, to which she politely declined, before the secretary left the room. Finding it odd that she didn't simply call Nathaniel on the phone, Jasmine chastised herself for being paranoid again, and forced herself to physically relax her tense body. She had no sooner taken two slow deep breaths to slow her heart rate when she saw the secretary returning, informing her that her husband would see her now. Quickly she got out of the chair and walked briskly toward his corner office. As she entered, she saw him in deep conversation with his paralegal and realized that her barging in on him in the middle of the day was not only insensitive of her, but disruptive to his work. Even though his mother owned the firm in which he was employed, it wasn't fair to her husband to have her interrupting his schedule that way.

He looked up and saw her. Initially shocked, he smiled and stood. His paralegal also straightened up and made her departure, barely acknowledging her boss's wife.

"Hi Mandi, God you smell good."

"Hello Mrs. Brownstein. Thanks," she said, somewhat self-consciously.

Smiling, Jasmine quickly blocked her exit. "You don't have to leave on my account. I won't take up but a minute of my husband's time and then you can have him," she said smiling.

Nathaniel stepped around his desk and embraced his wife before his paralegal could respond.

"What an awesome surprise Jazzy. But what are you doing here?" he asked as he spun his wife in a 360 so that he could make eye contact with Mandi. Glaring at her, his eyes said what his voice could not. Mandi took his cue and made a quick departure, but not before Jasmine felt the tension rise within the confines of her husband's office.

"Hey baby, what are you doing here?"

Still holding her love, she looked up at him and kissed him. "I brought you your briefcase. I thought you might need it today and you left in such a hurry this morning that you forgot it," she said innocently.

His knee jerk reaction was to snatch it from her the second he saw what she was holding but he controlled his initial reaction and thanked her but didn't take it from her. When she extended her arm towards him, he gently took the briefcase from her and thanked her for going out of her way to bring it to him. Once in his grip, he pulled it near his body as if to guard it with his life. He promised to wrap his afternoon up early and be home by six at the latest, to which her face showed her pleasure. She kissed him one last time and exited his office as quickly as she'd entered, but not before he noticed Mandi was back in her own office, attempting to look as if she was concentrating on whatever she was holding. Jasmine couldn't help but feel as if she was being watched as she crossed the lobby and exited towards the elevator. So happy that her husband had promised to be home at a reasonable hour that evening, she shrugged it off and went about the rest of her morning.

When she finished her errands, she returned to their home to do a little housework before starting to make her husband a wonderful meal. She vacuumed, dusted, and did their laundry; then decided to take a nap to ward off any fatigue since she certainly wanted to be very awake for when she announced her wonderful news to her husband. She made sure everything looked perfect, the table was set for the second time in two days, and everything looked in order. She knew that he'd be so incredibly happy when she told him about the baby, and even though she was bursting with excitement, she forced herself to head upstairs to rest.

<center>~~~ Chapter 6 ~~~</center>

"Well that was interesting," she nearly purred as she reentered his office, shutting the door loudly behind her.

Concerned about the attention that she was causing, Nathaniel got up to make sure that no one was in the hall near his office. Then he rounded to her, giving her his attention and disdain as she stood in front of him, arms crossed.

"It's over Mandi," he said as sincerely and candidly as possible. "It should never have happened and it needs to stop, effective immediately." Trying to convince himself that he meant it, even though his eyes happened to land on the very abundant cleavage spilling out of her low-cut blouse, he felt an almost immediate awakening in his crotch. "People are starting to talk and I can't take a chance on Jasmine finding out, so it's over. We can continue to work together but "we" are never happening again," he continued, almost sounding convincing.

She knew that this was just a knee-jerk reaction to the fact that his wife had made an appearance at his office, which she rarely did. She'd heard his spiel before but he always came back for more so she wasn't all that concerned that he was ending it, so to speak, again. She'd give him a day or so, and then they'd be back into their usual routine of screwing each other's brains out two or three times a week, like they'd been doing for over a year. She knew that what they offered each other couldn't be replicated at either of their homes. She also knew that he was as addicted to the sex as she was, whether it was morally or ethically wrong or not, and as long as no one found out, no one would get hurt. Mandi smiled as he continued on about how they could be friends and continue to work together, but needed to end any further extra-curricular games. When he finally stopped talking, she smiled again, said nothing but walked up to him, nearly pinning him up against the wall. She leaned into him with everything she had and kissed him deeply on the mouth, inserting her tongue immediately. His kiss started out reluctant but almost immediately warmed into a tongue tango with hers. She allowed his mouth to mold with hers as she started stoking a certain part of his anatomy and his response was immediately evident. Before he could say no, she slipped her hand inside his Armani trousers and took what she'd claimed as hers, and held it as it grew in her hand. He couldn't help it, there was something about the way Mandi touched him over which he truly had no control. She turned him on like no one ever had and even though every brain cell in his head told him to stop it before someone walked into his office, he couldn't formulate the word. Instead he simply leaned back against the mahogany wall and enjoyed. Knowing she'd won, yet again, Mandi took advantage of the moment and dropped to her knees. He almost gasped as she took him all the way into her mouth, in one swift movement, and at that very moment, he knew he'd never end it with her.

~~~ Chapter 7 ~~~

As promised, he pulled into their drive before six with a bottle of very expensive Chardonnay and a dozen pink roses, her favorite, and quickly parked his Escalade next to hers. He took a deep breath, again feeling like a heel, and entered their home to greet his wife with his surprise. He entered their kitchen to the most amazing aroma that he instantly knew was coming from the oven and was homemade lasagna, his favorite and his wife's specialty. His guilt grew tenfold as he set his briefcase down, and called for his wife. As he set it down, he remembered what he'd left in it and felt his face flushing. "Oh my God," he thought immediately. Jasmine had driven all the way from their home to bring him his briefcase and obviously hadn't opened it. He quickly called her name again, as he headed from their laundry room, and when she said she'd be right down, he took the moment to dash to their laundry room and throw the contents of his briefcase into their dirty laundry hamper, then rushed back to the kitchen to greet his wife.

How would he have explained to her his change of clothing tucked in there when he'd met Mandi the night before he thought as he heard her heels on their marble floor. He tucked the roses behind his back and tried with everything he had to look like the devoted loving husband she thought he was, and deep down he wished he could be.

As soon as he saw her, he smiled and pulled the roses out from his back. God she was beautiful, he thought to himself as he watched her approach. She wasn't tall and thin like the runway models that graced the pages of magazines, nor was she short and stout. She was compact and so incredibly muscular. Her military training, along with her self-imposed conditioning made her a perfect example of what a woman looked like who was in great shape and health. She looked awesome but he also knew that her muscular physique wasn't just for show; she was incredibly strong and could bench press almost as much as he could, and thanks in part to her love of boxing, her biceps were stronger than most men he knew. He noticed that she seemed to glow as she walked tentatively towards him. She had on a very short, tight fitting sheath-style dress which definitely showed off her toned legs and petite frame. When she got within reach, she all but flung herself into her husband's arms, holding him tightly. He was the most important person in her life, and other than her kid sister and the child she was carrying, there was no one in the world that she loved more.

"You made it home!" she said as enthusiastically as a child receiving a prize. "You said you would and here you are," she said, holding him tightly, never taking her eyes off of him.

"Of course, Jazzy," he said, again feeling very guilty for this past indiscretions. "I said I'd be home and here I am my love. Separating himself from her embrace, he held up the long stemmed roses. "Beautiful flowers for a beautiful woman."

Taking the bouquet, she brought them to her face to sniff them. He was always so thoughtful about bringing her flowers and jewelry. She had more bracelets and necklaces than any woman should ever own, but he always seemed so happy to see her expression when he brought them home. She graciously accepted every gift, secretly knowing that she'd give away all of them if he would simply carve out more time in the day to spend with her. All she had ever wanted was his love and attention, not the trinkets that he showered her with constantly.

"Honey, they're beautiful. Thank You."

"Anything for you Jasmine; you are my life and I hope you know that. Even when I disappoint you and hurt you, know that I never mean to and I love you with every ounce of my being."

Thinking his wording was a little peculiar, she looked up into his eyes and quickly dismissed it. "I love you too

Nathaniel. You are my heart and soul and I have never wanted anything more than to make you happy." Seizing the moment, she grabbed both of his hands and drew him closer. "And I hope that my surprise makes you so happy. Nate, we're pregnant!" she exclaimed, nearing bursting inside as her eyes filled.

He'd heard what she had said but somehow it wasn't sinking in completely. She said that they were pregnant, meaning that she was pregnant, meaning that they were going to have a baby. As he processed the words, a million emotions ran through his head simultaneously. She waited for what seemed like an hour for him to say something, anything.

"A baby; you're pregnant Jazzy?"

Afraid that maybe she'd misjudged what his reaction would be, she studied his facial expression. She was very good at reading faces but looking into her husband's, she couldn't tell if he was happy or mad. She didn't have to wait long to get her answer.

"A baby, Oh Jazzy; we're going to have a baby? Oh honey," he said hugging her again and then looking down at her, "How are you feeling? Are you sick or tired? Here," he said, grabbing the closest chair, "Sit down baby and put your feet up. You should rest."

Pushing him back, she laughed. "Nate, I'm pregnant, not sick silly. I feel fine; actually feel better than I ever have in my life."

"Are you sure? Oh my God," he said, raking his hand through his hair, finally absorbing the depth of her proclamation. He knew now that it had to be over with Mandi, and he'd have to make sure she understood that it was absolutely final. He was going to be a father and his cheating days needed to come to an end. "How far along are you? Do we know if it's a boy or girl? Wow, is my mother going to be excited! Who knows so far? And, how come you didn't tell me the second you knew baby?"

Laughing, she kissed him again. "One question at a time Nate. I'm approximately 13 weeks and no, we can't find out the sex for another month or so. And regarding your mother," she said tentatively, can we possibly hold off until we know if it's a boy or girl?" she asked, wanting to prolong the inevitable. She just didn't want to deal with his mother's disdain if the sex of her grandchild didn't meet her approval. Continuing to answer his questions, she kissed him again. "You are the first person to know Nate. You're this baby's father and I wouldn't tell anyone before I told you my love. And in answer to your last question, I didn't tell you at first because I wanted to make sure that nothing was going to happen. From everything I read, the first trimester is the most crucial so

I wanted to get through it before I told you. But," she said as she saw an instant look of concern flash over his face," the doctor says that I'm absolutely in perfect health and that it should be an easy pregnancy since I'm in such great shape and have no underlying problems. And," she added in almost a whisper, "Issues from my past should have no bearing on carrying this baby to term. Nathaniel," she said as she watched his face for any changes in expression. It didn't take a rocket scientist to figure out what she meant by that. She'd told him about the abuse she endured as a child and again as a young adult while serving her country when their relationship started down the path to being something serious. She'd been brutally honest, telling him every horrid detail, not to try and scare him away but because, that if he chose to take their relationship to the next level, he would do that knowing that she had no secrets. She'd told him of the incest at the hands of her uncle and of the physical but not permanent damage caused by the repeated rapes that occurred during her stent overseas. She'd told him of the VD that she'd contracted because of it, and showed him the thin scars at the base of her throat from where he'd held a blade on more than one occasion as just another form of intimidation.

He absorbed everything that she had just told him, and she found his eyes looking down at her abdomen. She laughed when she realized what he was doing, and before he could say a word, she reached behind her head and silently unzipped her dress, she allowed it to drop to the ground, revealing her still perky but definitely bigger breasts and a still very firm, flat abdomen, which is what she knew he was wondering about. His eyes said what his mouth did not as she viewed her in her stiletto heels, black lace underwear with thigh-high stockings and garters. She truly looked stunning standing there with just enough lace covering only a few inches of her that he felt himself getting hard within seconds. When he pulled her to him, she didn't argue, simply said, "Enjoy my love before I get big and fat." And for the second night in a row, Jasmine's beautifully planned dinner went uneaten.

~~~ Chapter 8 ~~~

She felt so happy, so loved and so content when he leaned in and kissed her good bye the following morning as he got ready to head into the office. They'd made love half the night with Nathaniel being kind, gentle and very attentive to her needs. They'd talked about the prospect of bringing new life into the world and speculated as to when she might have gotten pregnant. They'd laughed and cried and fallen in love all over again. She rolled over in their kind-sized wrought iron bed and stretched, looking up at the beautiful blue sky outside her window. When she got up, she immediately felt the very frigid fall temperature in the air in their room. Knowing that it was just a matter of time, she decided that maybe it was time to replace their sheets with her favorite cotton flannel ones. She showered, picked up their room and made their bed after with clean sheet and a plush blanket. Carrying her towels and the sheets, she made her way to the laundry which was located on their main level and dumped them on the floor. Suddenly feeling ravenous, she decided to eat breakfast before continuing with any cleaning or laundry.

Nathaniel made his way into the office attempting to avoid Mandi as much as possible. He greeted his receptionist with a smile and told her that he really didn't want to be disturbed for the morning and asked him to push his late morning meetings back to the afternoon. He grabbed the cup of coffee that Monica, his secretary, had prepared just the way he liked in and made his way into this corner office, shutting the door silently behind him. He turned and walked right into her, spilling half his coffee down his designer shirt in the process.

"What the hell Mandi!"

"And good morning to you as well my love," she retorted back, somewhat sarcastically.

"I'm not your love Mandi. I'm not your anything," he snapped, now very irritated with the invasion of his personal space. "I'm just the guy you like fucking. You're not in love with me nor I with you; so don't delude yourself into thinking anything along those lines. We both provided each other with what we needed at the time. But like I said earlier, and I think that I made myself perfectly clear, it's over. It will NOT happen again Mandi, so get used to that fact."

"Nice speech Nathaniel. Calling you "love" was simply a Freudian slip so relax. We both know what we had. Last I knew we were consenting adults, so no harm, no foul Nate," she said never making any attempt to touch him or enter his personal space as he held his ground despite the fact that his shirt was half drenched.

"I heard what you said and I agree with you to a degree," she purred. "We aren't in love with each other honey, and I never professed to be. I just love fucking your brains out Nate, then sending you home to your cute little lady. It's comical that she has no clue about how extreme, shall we say, your tastes are. I can't see her wanting you to stick it in her,"

"Shut up" he snapped. "Leave Jasmine out of this, she's got nothing to do with us" he practically yelled. "You stay away from her and leave her alone!"

Chuckling when she realized just what an Achilles' heel Jasmine truly was, she smiled and responded to his command. "I'd say she has everything to do with this Nate, but I'll keep her out of it as you wish."

Actually believing that she was serious, he smiled for the first time since he'd entered his office and found her there. "Thank You, Mandi" he said sincerely. "Your husband is a good man and maybe if you were spending less time with me and more time with him, you'll realize that as well."

"What the hell did he know about her husband," she thought to herself but didn't respond that way. She looked at him and in her most convincing voice replied, "You're right Nate. We should each focus on our own lives and make them work. I hope that we can still remain friends and co-workers Nate, since we do work very well together." What he didn't realize at the time was that she had no intention of ever letting go of the best sex that she'd ever had. She would say what he wanted to hear at the moment, but was already plotting about how she'd get what she wanted, and she wanted Nathaniel permanently.

Jasmine finished her breakfast and decided to start the laundry before she went for her morning run. She loaded the sheets and towels in the wash and automatically looked in the hamper to see if she'd missed anything from the day prior. She was surprised to see one of her husband's dress shirts, socks, and underwear in what she thought was an empty hamper. Thinking nothing of it, she picked them up and tossed them into the wash with the other things, shut the door and leaned over to put the liquid soap in. The whiff of her husband's shirt confused her. It didn't smell like his deodorant but she knew that she should know the smell since she'd smelled it on numerous occasions, she just couldn't place it. Dismissing it, she realized that it must be one of the colognes that he only used occasionally. And then it hit her! She nearly dove at the control to shut off the water. Once the washer unlocked, she grabbed the clothes and pulled his shirt out as quickly as possible. She drew it to her face and sniffed. It definitely smelled of her husband's deodorant and body odor but also of that very distinct cologne. And she realized that it wasn't cologne that she smelled, but perfume. She felt her heart breaking because it dawned on her that she now knew where she'd smelled that perfume before.

Back in her office, Mandi paced. She didn't want to deliberately hurt Jasmine; she seemed decent enough. But damn it, she wasn't letting go of something she'd enjoyed for almost a year now, and in her mind, it was innocent enough. They both provided each other with something that they both needed. They filled each other's insatiable need for sex and neither was fazed by the other's somewhat perverted fetishes or desires. They'd been nothing but compatible in the sack for months now, and she was not letting him go that easily. She knew what she would do to convince Nate that they needed to continue what she had decided was essential to surviving. She casually looked up Nathaniel's home address and placed a call. Hanging up, she smiled smugly and knew Nathaniel would be beyond furious if he ever found out but all was fair in love and war so to speak. She knew how a woman's mind worked, as after all, she was one.

Jasmine hung up the phone after speaking with Mandi and was perplexed. Why was she calling her asking where Nate was? she wondered. She thought that Nathaniel was at the office working, but now she wondered where he could possibly be in the middle of the day. Her first instinct was to rush down to his office and see for herself but she knew that that was a silly idea, especially if his own paralegal was calling inquiring about his whereabouts. And why wasn't he answering his cell phone? she wondered. Refusing to buy in to her own paranoia, Jasmine, who had already rationalized as to why her husband's shirt had smelled of his paralegal's perfume, knew that there must be a logical simple answer to all of this. Once she spoke with her husband, she'd know what it was and feel much better.

She forced herself to go for her morning run just like she had planned despite the phone call and discovery in the wash. She refused to allow herself to get upset or draw any conclusions until she spoke with her husband face to face. Her run was part of her morning routine and was not only a jump start on getting her workout completed but also cathartic in the sense that the fresh air always cleared her mind.

She ran the same route that she'd done for the three years that they'd lived in the neighborhood, and today was no different except that she cut almost two minutes off of her usual time. She wasn't sure why, but for some reason her pace was much faster despite the brisk temperature.

Once back inside, she felt so much better. She showered, dressed and decided to surprise her husband again today. The more she thought about it, the more she knew that she didn't want to wait until he came home. She thought what better way to resolve her concerns than to see her husband in his element? And in the environment where the woman whose perfume she smelled on her husband's shirt was. She drove downtown still not convinced that there was anything to worry about and now more than ever determined to prove that her intuition was correct.

Monica looked up from her desk surprised to see the boss's wife for the second time in two days, but she quickly reigned in her surprise and greeted her warmly.

Jasmine tried to read the woman's expression but saw nothing but a young woman who greeted her in the same bubbly manner whether she was on the phone or in person. Knowing that her husband was notorious for leaving his phone in his truck, on his desk or unattended, she hadn't even attempted to call to let him know about her intentions for lunch. Of course, she also thought that it wouldn't hurt to walk into his office unannounced and see what was what. Before Monica could offer to page her husband, Jasmine waved her off and headed toward her husband's office. She walked right through the closed door, not knowing what to expect. She coughed gently when she saw her husband leaning over the conference table with his paralegal sitting there, cleavage spilling out everywhere. From her vantage point, she realized that her husband's position in relationship to Mandi's afforded him spectacular view of her very pronounced assets. They both looked up simultaneously with Nathaniel immediately walking over to his wife. Mandi on the other hand seized the moment to look smugly at his wife and allow a feeling of understanding to pass between the two of them. Not one to back down, Jasmine put what emotions she had at the moment aside, and hugged her husband, embracing him in a move that normally she'd reserve for the intimacy of their own home. Both women were attempting to establish what they considered to be their territory and as they stared at each other, with

Nathaniel oblivious to what was going on in the room, both Jasmine and Mandi realized that they were in for the battle of their lives. Jasmine's whole demeanor changed in that very instant. Mandi had no idea what she was up against but, Jasmine thought silently, she'd find out soon enough.

Separating from the embrace, Jasmine smiled up at her husband and held out her hand.

"Come on honey, I thought we could go out to lunch to celebrate. What do you say?" Seeing the smile on her face and wanting nothing more than to get her out of the same room as his lover, he immediately smiled and agreed with her, picked up his suit jacket which was carelessly thrown over his chair and put his arm around his wife, directing her toward the exit of his office.

Not quite sure how to act, Nathaniel started to relax when, over lunch, Jasmine gave him no cause for alarm. She acted absolutely like she always did, bubbly and in a great mood. They'd talked at length about the baby with Jasmine finally conceding that he could tell his mother tonight about their pregnancy, providing she could call her sister. Knowing that her sister would be ecstatic, she wondered how her mother-in-law would react, especially if their baby wasn't the sex that Meredith would prefer. Her mother-in-law was not only intelligent, she was a cunning business woman and downright ruthless when it came to getting what she wanted. Their law firm prospered not only because of the attorneys whom she oversaw and controlled to a degree with an iron fist, but also because Meredith Brownstein was ever present to add her input and direction to every situation. She was known to walk into any and all offices, unannounced, at any time of the day and was known to be in the office as early as 5am, sometimes staying late into the night. She knew, and wanted to know about every nuance of the office and every detail about the people who represented her family's name. It had been she who hand-picked each and every attorney, paralegal and secretary on the payroll. Although her only son was a partner, it was Meredith who had the ultimate say regarding anything related to the growth and prosperity of their office.

His mind wandered as he listened to Jasmine daydream about their baby. He hoped that his mother would approve and hoped that Mandi would keep her promise and move on, or better yet, rekindle her relationship with her husband. He honestly thought that he could maintain a platonic relationship with her, and no one could deny she was an excellent paralegal with a brilliant mind. With an unbelievable body, he found himself thinking, quickly chastising himself for allowing that thought to enter his mind. He wondered how his mother would take the news, and couldn't help but think that maybe this pregnancy would be the leverage that he could use to make Mandi realize that it really was over. As he sat across from his bride of five years, he realized that maybe today was a great day after all.

Jasmine knew he was distracted over lunch but wasn't sure why. Maybe he was still in shock about their upcoming new arrival. Maybe he was just distracted because of his overwhelming workload at the office. She knew from the long hours that he was putting in, and how exhausted he looked when he'd finally come home at night, that his schedule was taking a toll on him. She'd already convinced herself that everything would slow down and get back to normal once the baby came. As she sat across the table from the love of her life, she decided that they needed a getaway, a romantic vacation before she was too pregnant to travel or before the baby arrived. "That's it," she thought to herself, "we'll go back to London where we conceived this baby and everything will be as it should; and he'll be out of Mandi's grasp for a few days," she added silently.

Angry that she actually thought she was a match for her, Mandi stormed back to her office the second Nate had dismissed her and left with his smug wife.

"We'll see who's smiling later, you little bitch" she said under her breathe, slamming her office door shut. Her explosive temper didn't go unnoticed by Monica or some of the others in the vicinity. She immediately went to her computer and started searching for what she was looking for. She scanned the videos one by one and edited where she needed to, then created a second video from the clips that she wanted to save. It took her only 20 minutes to create another, shorter video from the original, and when done, she sat back, watched her monitor and smiled. "That bitch wants to play games with me does she? Well she's in for a rude awakening. Though she knew that she'd

probably already lost Nathaniel, she really didn't care what his reaction was going to be when she sent the altered video to his wife. He would flip out if he'd known that she'd secretly videotaped several of their rendezvous, but after editing out her face in the scenes, was sending a synopsis of what he was really doing all those late hours he "worked." Sure Jasmine would probably realize who the woman was in the video but at this point it didn't matter. Mandi knew that by exposing Nathaniel for the snake he truly was, she was probably jeopardizing her career at the firm. At the moment, she just didn't care; she was furious and wanted to get even with both Nate and Jasmine for thinking they could simply dismiss her.

Mandi finished reviewing the altered video and allowed herself approximately two seconds of guilt before sealing the Fed Ex envelope, addressing the front label to the recipient, sliding the package into her oversized purse and heading to the nearest Fed Ex shipping center. She purposely went to the one on the other side of the city, parked two blocks away, and slipped on a long black coat that she'd borrowed from her sister the last time they'd gone out on the town together. She'd tucker her hair up, covered it with a bandana and wide brimmed hat. Knowing that no one would be able to recognize her from any security cameras, she walked smugly toward the office, putting on her sunglasses only when she was about to enter.

The young girl manning the counter barely looked up as Mandi approached. She was too busy reading the magazine spread out in front of her to pay any attention to the details her customer's appearance, which suited Mandi just fine. Just to be safe, Mandi spoke with a very distinct French accent and normally boisterous and loud, she spoke in barely a whisper.

"Can I help you," the attendant asked without looking up.

"Oui, I mean yes, thank you. I need for this package to make it to the recipient before six PM this evening. Is that possible?"

"Yeah, no problem; but it'll cost $29.95, plus tax.

"Oh," she said, feigning concern. "Yes, yes that's alright I suppose. My boss said that it absolutely positively has to arrive there. If I knew how to get there, I'd deliver it myself, but I don't know what buses I'd take. Oh golly, $29.95 you said. Oh my, that's a lot of money," she repeated, just for good measure. "Oh I hope that he gave me enough cash for that, and my goodness, you'll be able to give me a receipt right? I mean, wholly molly that's a lot of money but okay, here it is," she said, all the while acting like it was the most amount of money she'd ever held in her hand at one time. The young attendant stopped snapping her gum just long enough to weigh the envelope, and do the necessary processing before taking Mandi's money. Once the transaction was completed and the confirmation was printed, along with her tracking number, Mandi took both, thanked her in French, politely corrected herself, and scurried out. She knew that she shouldn't draw attention to herself and that they'd obviously have cameras everywhere, so she had padded the coat, and walked slightly hunched, with a shuffling type gait; hoping people would be reminded of her, the timid and scared rabbit looking woman. She stifled her laughter until she was back in her car. "Scared rabbit my ass! We'll see who feels intimidated and threatened when she opens her present."

Nathaniel and Jasmine finished up their meal, having truly enjoyed each other's company. Not wanting the moment to end, he promised to be home by six or seven at the latest. He also told her to go ahead and let her sister know about their great news and they'd call his mother together once he got home. Jasmine truly felt as if everything she'd ever wanted, hoped for and dreamed of was coming to fruition with the arrival of their child, and she couldn't be happier. Her only regret was that her mother wasn't still alive to see her first-born grandchild come into the world. Even though her father told her and her sister repeatedly that their mother had run off with another man, neither had ever believed it. They both had been old enough to understand the horrible life that she'd been forced to endure at the hands of their father. He was a drunk and a wife beater, plain and simple. Her momma would never admit it, but Jasmine had always suspected that her Uncle Joey was probably dipping his wick into her and Rebecca's momma when their daddy wasn't home as well. Her mother had been a saint to put up with the beating for a long as she had, and her leaving to escape was the smartest thing that she ever did. As a child, she often wondered why her mother hadn't taken she and Rebecca with her when she'd disappeared, but they'd never held it against her for doing so. Her momma had hated that shack of a house, hated what had gone on for years inside the walls and most of all, hated that she couldn't provide her girls with a more stable environment. But in a way, Jasmine thought now, her mother's leaving had ultimately saved them all.

It happened less than a week after her momma left. Her father was beyond consoling once he realized that his wife truly wasn't coming back. He took his anger, frustration, and downright rage out on both she and her little sister, with Jasmine sustaining a broken arm trying to stop his assault on Rebecca. He had been drunk already, but went back to the pub for a few more rounds with his buddies from work as soon as he had beaten them black and blue. The fire marshal's official report stated that the cause of the fire was her father's lit cigarette. He'd returned home and passed out in his Barco-lounger, but not before popping open another beer and lighting a cigarette. Her father never knew what hit him; with the bastard burning up right in his favorite chair, propped in front of the TV. The timing, she remembered, couldn't have been more perfect for the "accident" to happen. Her uncle had been out of town, and she and her sister were in the back of her house, nursing their injuries. When she'd smelled smoke, both she and Rebecca grabbed the backpacks that they kept stored under their beds in hopes of their mom coming back for them, along with a few of their prized possessions, and ran out the back door to the neighbors to get help. But it had been too late for their father. His cause of death was listed as smoke inhalation with burning to death secondary. Jasmine had always thought it was an appropriate end for a horrible person. What no one knew, and what she'd take to her grave was that her father hadn't been the one who lit that fatal cigarette.

After their home burnt to the ground with their father in it, the girls were placed in a foster home and eventually taken in by the same family. They prospered in the safe environment, flourished and came out of their shells. Gone were the girls who tried to be invisible and go through their days unnoticed. With the support, love and encouragement of their foster parents and the six children already living in the home, some biologically theirs and some adopted in the same manner they had been, both Jasmine and Rebecca finally had a loving home and blossomed because of it. They went from barely passing to becoming honor roll students in school with Jasmine surprising everyone, herself included, when it was determined that her IQ score came back at 130. She now loved to learn and forever had her nose stuck in a book or was researching something on the internet. They participated in after school activities and joined clubs and went out for sports teams. The day their father died opened the door allowing the girls to finally live. They never heard from or saw their disgusting uncle again. The both finally felt safe. Both graduated with their respective classes and continued their education at college. Jasmine never knew why she went into nursing but halfway through her first year, her psychology teacher, who became her mentor, advisor and friend had explained it in the most simplistic way possible. Maybe Jasmine went into a profession where she could help people when she hadn't been able to help her little sister, her mother or herself for so long. Rebecca didn't follow the same path; she pushed herself as hard as she could, eventually gaining entrance into the male-dominated Police Academy which sky-rocketed her self-esteem and confidence. She was now one of the leading snipers on the city's SWAT team and had been credited with assisting in not only numerous extractions but also had numerous commendations for her bravery and fortitude in saving the mayor's life when a psychotic killer set his sights on him. Rebecca often teased her big sister, telling her that they were yin and yang; one killed and the other healed. Jasmine always laughed and agreed with her baby sister's ribbing but deep inside knew that the two of them were more alike than Rebecca would ever know.

~~~ Chapter 9 ~~~

She made her way back home, stopping along the way at the mall to pick up a few things. The day's weather had turned to be amazing with the cloudless sky allowing the spring buds to blossom as they made their arrival known. She truly loved this time of year when everything looked so bright. The cool nights allowed for a great night's sleep but the days still teased about what summer would be offering soon enough. She carried her packages back to her SUV and thought about what she'd make for their supper. Her mind wandered from meal preparation, to baby shopping and several areas in between. She thought about camping, and hiking with the baby, and how maybe she and Nate should think about buying a place of their own to vacation in when the baby came. The Cape was great but how practical was it to drive five hours with a baby for a weekend getaway? She'd always had an affinity for the Adirondacks and, with them practically being in their back yard, and with Lake Placid less than three hours away, she thought that maybe they should think about buying a condo or townhouse on a lake somewhere in the mountains. The more she thought about it, the more that sounded like an excellent idea. Nate worked hard and could certainly afford to buy her any one of the homes that she desired, but she wanted to do something for him, surprise him instead of him always treating her. Once she got home, she looked up the 401K portfolio which she'd established while working in the hospital, retrieved the rep's number and gave him a call. After their conversation, Jasmine was surprised and elated to know how much she could withdraw from her account without too much of a penalty. She knew immediately what she was going to do to surprise her husband. He'll be shocked when I show him our new vacation home, she thought, smiling. She pulled into her garage, brought in her purchases and once unloaded, grabbed a cup of tea and set down with her laptop to begin her research.

~~~ Chapter 10 ~~~

Nathaniel dreaded walking back into the office after lunch, knowing the look that Mandi had given him when he'd left for lunch.

"Damn it," he thought to himself, "I can go to lunch with my wife if I want to." Knowing that Mandi would be on the lookout for him, he attempted to sneak in unnoticed but only got as far as the lobby before he heard his mother's commanding voice.

"Nathaniel," she called, summoning his attention. "We have an issue and I need you to come into my office," she said, already turning her back and entering her office, not allowing him to refuse her request. He knew he had no choice but follow her into her massive office and deal with whatever she wanted to say head on.

"Hello mother, what's up?" he asked tentatively.

Not one to mince words, she cut to the chase; "I need you to head out to Kingston in the morning to meet face to face with Charles Beckwith and his son James. I've told them that you'll be there for a 2pm meeting with dinner at the country club after as it will most likely carry over into the evening hours. I've reserved the Manor Room at the club for you to meet with Charles and James, and I've booked you a suite at the Marriott for the night. You should be able to wrap everything up in one day, but I've told Theodore at the club that you might need the room for the following morning and I've had Monica clear your morning appointments just in case." She allowed her info to sink in, but only for a second. She then instructed him to sit down so she could discuss what the issue was and how she expected him to handle it. Knowing it was useless to argue with the woman, he only half listened to her; instead trying to figure out how he was going to tell Jasmine that he was leaving in the morning, especially when she'd just given him the most important news of their lives. But knowing that his mother was always all-business, he turned back to the topic of conversation and started taking notes. His mother highlighted the concerns and issues that needed to be addressed and halfway through, pushed the button on her desk summoning Monica who immediately came running.

"Get Mandi in here so that she can hear the necessary information," she dictated.

"Yes Mrs. Brownstein" and she scurried off.

Practically whipping his head around and suddenly at attention, he shook his head. "Mother, I do not want nor need Mandi there for this meeting; I can handle it on my own."

"Nathaniel, she is needed and knows how to convince both father and son to see things our way and trust in our company. You've worked well with her for years now, and I expect that you'll put your personal issues aside for the sake of the business." When he looked at his mother perplexed, she smugly added, "Of course I've known about your, shall we say, indiscretions. It's my business and therefore my obligation and right to know everything that goes on around here. And whether you're still seeing her on the side or not is irrelevant, and I certainly don't expect it to get in the way of business. Do we understand each other?"

Not believing what he was hearing, he simply nodded silently.

Just to make sure her point was made and her opinion known, she added somewhat sarcastically "I certainly would have thought that you had slightly better taste in women than her though. I thought you scraped the bottom of the barrel when you married that hourly worker, who came from nothing, but at least she was moldable and trainable; Mandi on the other hand might have a great head for business, but she is and will always be nothing but a gold digger and downright trailer trash."

Mandi stood outside of her employer's door and heard the entire conversation. While she was thrilled to be spending two days in a hotel with Nathaniel, she was seething about his mother's unfair, mean remarks. Sure they might be true, but they were mean and unnecessary, especially when she planned on becoming the witch's daughter–in-law someday. She took a deep breath, put on her best bullshit smile and knocked lightly before entering the senior partner's office. Once sitting next to Nathaniel, she listened to her directives, nodding when appropriate, but all the while planning on how tomorrow night in the hotel would go with Nate. As he listened to his mother and sat next to his associate, he felt his stomach turning in knots. He already knew that Jasmine had concerns about Mandi, and now that she was pregnant, hormonal and definitely emotional, he wondered how she'd take the news. Ultimately he decided that ignorance was bliss and she'd be upset enough to know that he would be gone for two days. She didn't need to know that Mandi would be there as well. Maybe it was wrong not telling her everything, but since he knew in his heart it was definitely over with Mandi, why stress his wife out about it? At least that was his rationale when he reviewed all the possible outcomes in his head. When she was finished with her directives, they were dismissed as quickly as they were summoned, and they walked out together silently and into their respective offices. Monica observed the tension between the two of them but watched in silence as their body language conveyed far more than any words could. She'd known that they were partners in more than just the work environment but who was she to judge? She secretly couldn't stand Mandi and her cocky, arrogant attitude. Since she needed the job and he was the boss's son, she kept her mouth shut and did the job that she was paid to do.

Back in his office, Nathaniel put his head in his hands and sighed. He knew that he was between a rock and a hard place and knew that he couldn't reveal to his mother or his wife why he was so very uncomfortable traveling to Kingston with Mandi. He had very much enjoyed screwing her brains out and her sense of adventure when it came to the bedroom was beyond anything he'd ever experienced; but that part of his life was over. It needed to be over now that his wife was pregnant and they were going to become a family and no longer just a couple.

Knowing that Jasmine certainly wasn't interested in monetary things, Nathaniel knew that he wanted to bring her something to ease the blow of him being away for a few days, but wasn't quite sure what to get her. Then it hit him and he smiled, realizing that he'd just thought of the perfect gift. He packed up his briefcase and locked up his office, exiting the building and setting off for his destination.

Jasmine spent the rest of the afternoon researching real estate sites specializing in Adirondack listings from

Old Forge all the way to Wilmington, New York. She saw several that intrigued and amazed her and couldn't wait to investigate the info more thoroughly. Remembering that she hadn't grabbed the mail out of her mailbox yet, she stepped outside to retrieve today's bills. When she stepped out onto her front landing, she noticed the Fed Ex package sticking out of her mailbox. Not sure what her husband could have ordered, and knowing that she hadn't ordered anything. The package was addressed to her with no return address, she tucked it under her arm, retrieved her mail and headed back inside. She ripped it open as soon as she set everything down, with her curiosity getting the better of her. Inside she found one unlabeled DVD with a simple note attached. "I provide him what you can't. See for yourself."

Her hands dropped the DVD like it was on fire and suddenly she found herself shaking uncontrollably. She felt ill. Knowing what the DVD was going to show, she didn't want to watch it, but knew that she had to. She felt like vomiting right there on her marble floor but being the ever-sensible woman that she was, knew that becoming emotional over something that she had no control over wouldn't do her any good. Instead she took a deep breath, walked over to their flat screen TV and inserted the DVD in and turned on the power. It took her less than 5 seconds to have her biggest fears confirmed. It was very apparent that the man on the tape was indeed her husband, and even though the face was blotted out, she had no doubts as to who the voluptuous bimbo was that seemed to really be enjoying getting laid doggy style. It made her sick watching her husband fuck somebody else but Jasmine found that she couldn't look away or turn it off. She watched the entire clip, saying nothing nor shedding a tear. Her father had instilled in both she and her younger sister the notion that tears couldn't save them, wouldn't get them sympathy nor solve anything and they only showed weakness. She was not weak so not a single tear fell as she watched it in its entirety. She felt numb as she removed the tape from the player and tucked it into her purse, not sure what she was going to do with it but knowing that she didn't want Nathaniel to discover it. She paced and paced around her family room, subconsciously holding her abdomen and chest. It felt like her entire world was crashing in on her again and she'd be damned if that woman was going to destroy her happiness. Besides, it could all be a hoax, she convinced herself. It could have taken place before she'd married Nathaniel. It's not like either of them were virgins when they'd met. He'd had several significant relationships and she was pretty certain that he'd been involved with Mandi back then, so for all she knew the tape could have been old.

"Yes," she thought quickly, trying to convince herself, "She wants him again and he must have told her that I'm pregnant and that pissed her off so this is her way of trying to get rid of me. Well, Mandi is in for a rude awakening," she thought as she went to the kitchen to grab a bottle of water.

He parked in the driveway so that she wouldn't hear the door opener. He wanted to come in the front door with his surprise. He hoped that what he'd found would be enough to offset the fact that he was going out of town in the morning. He'd dropped a bundle in the specialty store. He'd had no idea how expensive everything was when it came to babies, but he spared no expense when purchasing a few items for his future son or daughter.

She'd heard him pull in, and found it odd that he hadn't pulled into the garage; but Jasmine refused to speculate as to why he hadn't. She'd been jumping to too many conclusions lately and intended to give him the benefit of the doubt. He came in with his arms full. She met him in the foyer. The second he saw her, his face lit up and he set down the bags, took her into his arms and kissed her on the lips, melting into her like his life depended on it. His passionate kiss took her breathe away and made her heart race. Forgotten were her doubts and fears; he was hers and no one was going to separate them. When the kiss finally ended, he smiled, instructed her to wait there, close her eyes and keep them shut. She did as he said, and within a minute or two, she heard him coming back into their house, clanging something on the door jamb as he entered. Once she heard something get set down on the tile, she felt his arm go around her waist and he instructed her to open her eyes. She did so and gasped. In front of her was the most beautiful bassinette she'd ever seen in her life. It was both modern and contemporary with its straight lines and minimalist design, but the inside looked so dainty and intricate, like something out of a storybook. Inside was a neutral colored silk coverlet that featured pink and blue elephants on this surface. The floodgate opened when she saw that their last name was scrolled into the wood as if it had grown into the tree that way.

"Do you like it Jazzy?" he asked, still afraid to make direct eye contact with her.

"It's the most beautiful thing that I've ever seen in my life Nathaniel."

"If it's not what you had in mind for the baby, I can return it and we can pick something out together. Oh," he said excitedly, "I picked up just a few other things for the baby; I hope that you don't mind."

She looked at the man in front of her and knew what genuine love was. He not only loved her but also the life that they'd created together; and she was now more certain than she'd ever been that any emails, calls or stupid tapes were from his past. That is where they'd stay, in the past. She wasn't even going to bring any of her concerns up. They were going to have a baby, she'd finally have a family and nothing else mattered.

~~~ Chapter 11 ~~~

They spent the evening together, laughing and planning for what life would be like once their baby arrived. He waited until the timing seemed perfect to break the news that he had to travel to Kingston in the morning to meet with a client. He promised her that he'd do his best to wrap everything up that day and return back late that evening. Neither believed for a minute that he'd be able to accomplish that feat but both were riding high on all the talk of the baby. Both wanted to believe that they'd be in each other's arms by nightfall. She helped him pack as they continued their conversation in the bedroom. The wheels were already turning in her head, having already made up her mind that she'd call her cousin Louise who lived in Delmar and meet her to go shopping in Albany for the day. If Nathaniel told her that he couldn't make it home for the night, well then, she'd just continue on down the thruway to him and spend the night with him. It's not like Kingston was that far away, especially if she was already in Albany when he gave her the news. They retired early but not before making love on their couch while watching TV. He all but carried her up to their room afterward, with both giggling like children. Once in bed, they made love again and fell asleep in each other's arms. They both slept peacefully, each of them content in their own dreams.

Mandi threw back a few stiff drinks and silently swore as she packed her overnight bag. Her husband Clive ignored her, like he always did; too fixated on whatever was playing on his big screen TV. Story of her life she thought, he didn't give a shit if she was traveling for work for one night or ten, or running away with the circus for that matter. She'd given up long ago trying to compete for his attention, and almost daily she wondered if he'd even care if she left for good. She showered, shaved her legs and another area, in hopes of surprising her lover. She made sure that she packed the sexiest negligee that she owned, and one that he hadn't seen before. She picked out the suit that showcased her assets the best and made sure to pack Nathaniel's favorite body lotion. And just as a precaution, she packed a tiny envelope containing a sure fire way to convince Nathaniel to be with her. She didn't think that she'd need it, but a little La Rocha couldn't hurt if he wasn't necessarily a willing participant. He would be if she slipped him a roofie. He truly had never been able to resist her before, and who was he kidding, he always came back for more; but she figured it was better to be prepared in case she met any resistance with his new-found conscience. It pissed her off that he had become so self-righteous. What they had between them had been so right, so special and now here he was saying it was over. "We'll see about that," she said to herself as she zipped her bag shut.

At first he had refused to have her ride down with him, but even he saw how ridiculous and suspicious it would look if they drove separately. He reluctantly told her that he'd meet her at the office at 10AM and they'd head down from there. She just needed to get a good night's sleep and once they were together tomorrow, everything would work out and get back to normal.

~~~ Chapter 12 ~~~

Morning arrived and while Mandi was ecstatic about the day, Nathaniel was dreading it. He really didn't want to be stuck in a car for three hours with Mandi but knew that it was inevitable. He also felt guilty about omitting the fact with Jasmine that he wasn't going alone but in his heart he knew that it would only upset his wife and there was nothing to worry about. Why stress her out if he didn't need to? Yes, he knew it was a cop-out but it made him feel better, and it made him accountable to himself to make sure that nothing happened between he and his paralegal while they were away from their respective partners.

He pulled into the firm's parking garage fifteen minutes early and found her already there. She was dressed casually with camel form-fitting slacks; a tan lace camisole under a fuchsia colored cashmere sweater. Her riding boots made her otherwise short legs look elongated and gave her an overall appearance of being taller than she really was. Her ever present MK bag was slung over her shoulder with a matching travel bag at her feet. For a brief instant he looked at her and felt a twinge between his legs. He immediately shifted position and suppressed any thoughts of how sexy she looked standing there waiting for him. She smiled an actual genuine smile when she made eye contact with him and waved as if greeting an old friend. For that moment, she looked like a school girl, or maybe a college friend, a colleague that valued his friendship; in essence, she looked innocent enough. But while he couldn't help but admit that she was beautiful, in a sexy, glamourous, Va-Va-Voom type way, he also knew that she was like a pit viper and wouldn't let go of something that she wanted. He only hoped that he'd made himself perfectly clear, and she realized that it was over between them.

The drive down was surprisingly more comfortable than he thought it would be. They discussed the marketing strategy that they'd sell to the old hoot and his son at the meeting later in the day, they laughed and made small talk, and even found themselves signing along together to classic rock on the radio. Neither mentioned a word about the physical relationship that they'd shared for so long; they just enjoyed the moment and each other's company. Once checked into the hotel, both set about getting ready in their respective rooms. Though they were adjoining, neither gave it a second thought that only a deadbolt lock separated them. They each mentally rehearsed the speeches and arguments that they'd use on the two men they had been sent down to persuade. Both knew their jobs very well and while they might not necessarily agree with his mother, both knew that she had a strong business sense and was ruthless until she got the end result that she desired. They both knew what was at stake.

Jasmine stayed up after helping Nate get out the door and on the road. She went for her run, showered and ate breakfast. She retrieved the overnight bag that she'd packed for her surprise rendezvous with her husband. She had packed a cute little teddy, along with necessary essentials but also knew that she could pick up something new at the mall when she met her cousin for lunch and shopping. Nate would be so surprised she thought to herself. She'd show her ID, get a key and surprise her husband. It wasn't Dubai, but she was anticipating the night almost as much as the first night of their honeymoon, and she couldn't wait to see the expression on his face when she let herself into his room.

She set off on the road late morning, and made it to Crossgates Mall just before one. Her cousin was already waiting in a corner table at the restaurant. They caught up on each other's news, made small talk, gossiped and enjoyed a wonderful meal, then set off to shop their hearts out. Jasmine hadn't revealed that she was pregnant but it became quite evident when every store they entered, she found herself meandering around until she found the kid's or baby section. This pregnancy had somehow become the most important thing in her life, besides Nathaniel, and she found that it was all that she could think about. It wasn't until they made their way into Victoria's Secret that Jasmine started thinking about herself. She walked up and down the store aisles looking for something to blow her husband's mind. She wanted something above and beyond sexy, and she wanted to step out of her normal comfort zone. She knew she would know it when she saw it, and it only took a few minutes of browsing to find what she was looking for. It was black, lace and leather, and was comprised of very little material. It covered just enough to intrigue and entice, and she knew with her recently enhanced cleavage, that it would look amazing on her. She tried it on and was shocked when she saw how bold a statement it made on her. Staring at the woman in the heels and black lace and leather, she felt empowered, and snickered when she thought she looked like a dominatrix. How funny, she thought now; staring back at her was the girl who once was so shy that she never made eye contact with people. She was still that same girl, only without the insecurity. She ultimately had her foster family and the Marines to thank, for forcing her to come out of her shell, and for making her self-confident and tougher than she looked. Gone were the days of being pushed into a corner. With the outfit she currently was totting, she felt as if she could dominate the world, or at least her husband's hotel room for the night.

While Jasmine was daydreaming about how romantic the evening was going to be, Mandi was also speculating about how she was going to get into Nathaniel's room. She knew once they were alone, and in a room with a king-sized bed, he'd become a puppet. She knew exactly what strings to pull to get her way and ultimately give them both what they wanted. His little "It's over" routine was getting old and she knew that he needed what she brought to the table just as much as she needed him. They'd go a few rounds in the plush looking bed, grab a nightcap, spend the night in each other's arms with a few more rounds mixed in with sleeping and by morning, everything would be back to normal. They'd be back to their weekly meetings at the condo that she'd been smart enough to maintain even after she'd married. Her husband just assumed that it was rented out and never thought to ask why he never saw an income from it.

Mandi had originally kept it as a fall back incase her impulse marriage to Clive hadn't worked out. Her marriage, such as it was, was still intact but she refused to give up the one thing that was solely and individually hers. Clive never inquired about the place, Nathaniel's wife didn't know about it; and in the end, it was a hell of a lot cheaper for her to keep it than to have them paying for a dirty hotel room weekly. "Yes," she thought as she zippered herself into the form fitting sheath- styled dress, "after tonight, everything will change." With that, she picked up her jacket and stepped outside her room to meet Nathaniel.

~~~ Chapter 13 ~~~

The afternoon meeting, though arduous, went as expected and by supper everyone had come to the same agreement. The partnership would be beneficial for all parties involved, and with Charles Beckwith and his son felt as though they were the true victors in the end. He had to give Mandi credit, she certainly had a way of making men come around to her way of thinking. Whether it was her discreet sex appeal, flashy smile, or her incredible way of presenting a sales pitch; she had both father and son eating out of the palm of her hand. Once the business part of the meeting concluded, they relaxed and had a celebratory drink, which turned into two. Not one to drink heavy liquor, Nate found himself really enjoying sipping on Gentleman Jack. He exclaimed that the last time he'd had Jack Daniels, he'd been about sixteen and vaguely recalled it tasting like turpentine. Beckwith Senior laughed and poured them all another round from the very ornate and expensive bottle. It didn't take long for everyone to start feeling the effects of the alcohol; with the Beckwiths finally excusing themselves and leaving for home. Not one to walk out on a party, Mandi convinced Nathaniel that they should head back to their rooms and order room service since it was getting so late and she felt a migraine coming on. Knowing that she suffered terribly from them, he quickly agreed. Unbeknownst to him, she had no more a headache than he did; she just wanted to get him out of there, get him alone, and with a little luck, get him naked. They made their way outside, both leaning on each other for balance and support. The doorman flagged down the next available taxi and within moments, they were on their way back to their hotel. Seizing the moment, she pretended to lose her balance as the taxi made a sharp turn, and as she leaned into him, her hand purposely landed on a certain part of his anatomy. Initially shocked, he neither reacted nor shifted positions, nor did she. She didn't move her hand; she kept it completely motionless, waiting to see what his physical response would be. It didn't take but a few seconds for it to become very evident what the natural response was. It was only then that she looked deep into his eyes and apologized, slowly removing her hand. When he didn't say anything, she didn't know how to react and didn't know what he was thinking. He remained silent as he allowed his hand to travel over the soft texture of her dress, making its way eventually to the area that he was seeking. As usual Mandi surprised him by having no restrictive underwear for him to maneuver around. He easily found what he was searching for, and found her not only hot but very wet. He teased with just a lone finger, all the while looking forward and remaining silent. She almost wondered what he was thinking, but ultimately didn't really care, as long as he kept touching her that way. She knew they'd continue whatever little games he wanted to play once they got inside his room, and as he continued to rub and tease, she found the anticipation was getting the best of her. She wanted him inside her and inside her at that very moment. She hadn't even realized she'd done it, but in the course of the ride, she'd unzipped his trousers and allowed him freedom. They might have considered going at it right in the back seat of the taxi, but much to the taxi driver's relief, their hotel came into sight and their ride was over. Nathaniel tipped the taxi driver very well and as he shut the cab door to walk inside, he saw the driver simply staring at Mandi's ass as they made their way toward the door.

They barely made it inside his room before they started ripping off each other's clothing. At the moment, she didn't care that he was probably destroying a very expensive and favorite dress. She just wanted his hands on her and she wanted him in her mouth. The majority of their clothing had been stripped away by the time they hit the bed. He took one breast in his mouth and grabbed hold of the other. It only took a few minutes of foreplay before he couldn't wait any longer and dove into her. She took what he offered, opening herself willingly. They screwed forwards and backwards, with each taking turns on top. They finished a bottle of Champagne and toasted with the Gentleman Jack that they had sent to the room. Knowing that he'd probably regret the drinking and the cheating in the morning somehow didn't stop him from doing it. He had to give her credit in the sense that the woman certainly could hold her liquor. Every time he thought that he was filled to the gills, she'd down another shot and hand him one. Though definitely a light weight, he felt invincible at the moment and kept even with her until they both passed out in his completed destroyed bed. Their clothes were strewn all around the room, half the blankets were off the bed, and there were shot glasses, empty bottles and a half eaten pizza lying around but the two people passed out in the bed were oblivious to all of it. They'd finally fallen asleep after round three, with her butt snuggled up to his abdomen; his arm was wrapped around her gripping one of her pendulous breasts as if holding on for dear life. Both were snoring and in their own respective dream states.

Jasmine found the hotel easy enough. Her GPS only took her on one wrong street before she found what she was looking for and pulled in. She brought her overnight bag, leaving all of her shopping purchases in her SUV. She made her way to the reception area and was met by a cheerful young clerk. She explained her situation and asked in what room her husband was staying. At first a little upset, she understood why they wouldn't simply give her a key to his room. She had hoped they would, but she understood policies and procedures all too well after being a nurse. The young clerk did at least tell her what floor and room he was in and she thanked her. As she was turning away she heard the clerk call her back, saying that since they had the same address, as evidenced by the license and credit card that Jasmine had displayed, she didn't think that it would hurt if she gave her a keycard to her so that she could surprise her husband. Jasmine thanked the young girl over and over, and quickly took the card before she the clerk changed her mind.

Once in the elevator, she took a deep breath, reapplied her lipstick and ran her hand through her hair. She was so excited about her spontaneous idea and surprise and knew that her husband would be as well. She quickly walked down the long corridor and found his room at the end the hall. She smiled, inserted the keycard and entered, and was met by a darkened room and silence. Thinking that he must be taking a nap she silently set her bag down and tip toed toward the bed, but not before noting that she was stepping over his dress slacks. The smell of old pizza, booze and sex hit her like a brick wall as she proceeded into the suite. First she saw the remainder of her husband's attire from his meeting, mixed in with what was obviously not his dress. Her eyes focused in the darkness and she perused the room noting the empty bottles, food and condition of the room. Then she honed in on the bodies lying in the bed and felt her blood turn cold. Quite simply, her heart break in two. Lying cuddled up together her husband, her everything and the father of her child and his assistant. She hadn't liked Mandi from the day that she'd met her, but didn't honestly think that she had anything to worry about when it came to her. She dressed and acted like the classless bimbo that she was; and never in a million years would Jasmine have thought that her husband would be attracted to someone of her caliber. Staring at the two sleeping peacefully in the king-sized bed, she realized now that maybe she never really knew what her husband wanted after all. She would never have believed that he was capable of such deceit if she weren't staring at it with her own two eyes. Yes, she'd seen the video that she now realized must have been sent my Mandi; but until this very moment, she would not have believed that he was capable of hurting her so badly. Something inside her snapped, simply shattered; and while most other women would have broken down, it wasn't heartbreak she was feeling but hurt, betrayal and the very strong desire for revenge. She now knew what he was capable of given the opportunity, but he had no idea what she was capable of. He would soon find out though. She'd always wondered about the argument that her college psychology professor had brought up in the debate about nature vs. nurture. She now knew the prevailing trait that humans possessed. Soon enough Nathaniel and his assistant would find out as well. She took one last look at the man whom she'd loved with every ounce of her heart; the man who held the key to her happiness and obviously now, her heartbreak. She knew their marriage was officially over. Now she just needed to clean up the pieces, and that she knew how to do very well. She had had years of practice beginning with her father, and then moving to her uncle and lastly a certain Marine officer who had hurt her just one time too many. As she left the room as silently as she had entered it, she was already formulating her next move. Nathaniel would never know what hit him. Most importantly, she would make certain that he'd never see the child he'd help create, he'd never get an opportunity to watch their son or daughter grow nor would he enjoy living to a ripe old age. Her first inclination was to simply have him killed, but the more she thought about it, the more she realized that he wasn't the only guilty party involved. As she pulled out of the parking lot and turned toward the Thruway, it came to her. She gazed in her rear view mirror and the person looking back was one she didn't recognize, a stranger to her. In that moment, she could feel herself reverting to her most primal instincts. All that she could think of was destroying them before they destroyed her. Just how to do it was the question.

~~~ Chapter 14 ~~~

He woke before the sun was up, temporarily confused by his surroundings. It only took a second to realize that the breast he was grasping did not belong to his wife. The memories of the previous night were a blur and as he started to lift his head, he felt like someone was stabbing him with spears along both sides of his temples. He forced his bloodshot eyes to focus and, as he looked down at the brunette sleeping peacefully beside him, like she belonged there, he felt his stomach start twisting in knots. Suddenly the events that transpired the evening before all started rushing back. He remembered the meeting, which had gone very well, he remembered celebratory drinks and oh my God, he thought now, he remembered that he did the very thing that he'd promised himself would never happen again. And he had done it multiple times in multiple positions. And the proof was lying next to him! He spontaneously withdrew his hand from her breast as if she were toxic and rushed into the bathroom, grabbing his phone along the way. He felt sick, genuinely sick, with his heart racing as he checked his phone for messages from Jasmine. He saw that she'd called once and felt even worse when he listened to her voice message. She had always been so supportive of his job and her message from the previous night had been no different. She'd also texted him, saying that she was going to bed and that she loved him and couldn't wait for him to come home. He read the text and now felt like vomiting. How was he going to face her, after what he'd done? He knew that this time he'd gone too far and if she ever found out, the damage would be irreparable. He got into the shower and hoped the scolding water would wash away any memories of the previous night, knowing full well that it wouldn't. He looked at himself in the mirror, and felt ill all over again when he noticed the scratch marks on his chest, back and a few other locations. Realizing that Mandi must have been in one of her "wild" moods the night before, he silently thanked God that it all was a blur and he couldn't remember much of it. But as the water pelted his skin, he made a vow then and there that he'd go to the grave trying to make it up to his wife, and he'd die before he'd ever reveal what a cad he really was.

It had taken Jasmine a half hour longer than it should have to make the drive back to the Utica exit; partly because she found her mind continuously wandering, plotting and overanalyzing. As the three-hour mark of being on the road passed, she already knew how she would take care of her problem. She was working out the details as she pulled into the drive. Knowing she should get some sleep, but still too wound up and upset to go to bed, she turned on her computer and set about finding a new home. One far away from Utica, and one far away from people was what she wanted. Funny how things came full circle; she knew in that moment that in the mountains was where she was meant to be and where she belonged. Sometime halfway through the night, she found it. It was small, simple, secluded and perfect for what she needed and wanted. She'd tell her beloved husband that she was going to go visit her sister and scope it out in person. Not wanting anything associated with her name or cell number, she would have to make a few necessary arrangements. What Nathaniel didn't realize was that both she and Rebecca had been given new names and identities when they'd been adopted out of foster care. For some reason, that person didn't exist in her mind anymore, so she'd never told him that her real name was Trista Marie Carpenter. From now on, that is who she would become again. But gone was the shy introverted child who took abuse and injustice after injustice. The new Trista was definitely stronger and tougher than even she realized or imagined.

She managed to get a few hours of sleep and before sunrise, she was up, showered and back on the computer. She'd emailed the listing broker, from an account that she'd created during the night with her new name. She made it clear that she was a qualified cash buyer who wanted to preview homes within the next few days and purchase one if what she was looking for was out there. She provided no phone number since she knew she'd need a different phone if she wanted to have any conversations with the agent prior to her arrival date. Satisfied with her progress thus far, she was at her bank as soon as the doors were open at 9am. She withdrew the amount of their most current Visa bill, which was seven thousand, two hundred dollars and change. It was something that she did about every other month and wouldn't raise any red flags when it showed on their bank statement. She often withdrew from one account to transfer into another. The only difference this time was that the amount wouldn't make it into the second account. Later that same morning, she went through the drive-through lane to withdraw a few thousand more dollars. Nathaniel knew how much she hated using her American Express to purchase big ticket items so she'd just tell him that she needed additional cash for baby or

Christmas shopping. He'd be none the wiser and certainly wouldn't care. She called her financial advisor to ask about tapping into her 401K and was very pleased to find out how much she could withdraw with minimal penalty. The last call she made prior to the anticipated arrival of her beloved was to her attorney. She had always insisted on having her own council when she'd married Nathaniel. She felt that they each came into the relationship with a few assets, and while Nathaniel obviously had many more than she, she'd felt compelled to have representation. She called her attorney to set up an appointment and was surprised to find that she had an opening right after lunch. Jasmine immediately accepted. She needed legal counsel regarding either forming an LLC or purchasing a home in her former name. She knew that Monique was the person who could answer all of her questions and that confidentiality would be maintained, as with any attorney-client privilege. As she headed toward her appointment, she ignored the repeated calls from her husband and the messages he left. She'd deal with him once and for all when he got home.

~~~ Chapter 16 ~~~

They rode in silence almost the entire way home. Mandi wanted to talk, but Nathaniel had no interest in trivial conversation, nor any type of conversation that related to the previous evening's events. He prayed that she didn't remember much about what had transpired in his hotel room, but he knew better. Mandi definitely could hold her liquor better than he could and deep down he knew that she probably remembered every detail. In her twisted mind, would think that they were right back to the way they'd been for so long. She kept her husband out of convenience, not love, and she made it very clear that she wanted Nate for their compatibility in bed. She never really spoke about them ever becoming a real couple, nor did she beg him to leave his wife, like so many mistresses did. She just was in it for the sex, and up until recently, he'd been okay with that. Now, looking over at her, she did nothing but repulse him. Quite honestly, if he had his way, she'd be reassigned so that he'd never have to work side by side with her again. He wanted her out of his car and out of his life once and for all.

Jasmine knew the moment she heard the garage door open that she'd have to put on the performance of her life. She loved and loathed the man who was about to enter the door and knew that she'd have to be very convincing if she was going to pull off what she had planned for him. And that which he absolutely deserved. Correction, she thought, what they both deserved. She was going to love taking care of Mandi, in a way that only she could. Framing her husband made her planning all the more enjoyable.

He entered their mud room and then kitchen, and putting on a smile, he called her name.

"I'm in here honey," she replied, though it repulsed her to sound so chipper and jovial. She knew though that he expected to find his dotting wife happy that her husband had returned. She intended to put on the charade for as long as it took; knowing it would be worth it in the end. He took one look at her and felt like more of a cad that he already did. There, standing in the kitchen, she looked so elegant so regal, but not in his mother's sense. Pregnancy looked good on her, and she seemed to glow when she smiled. Her eyes had always caught his attention, and today was no exception. They were blue, the darkest blue he'd ever seen and with a slight oval shape to them, reminded him on many occasions of a Siamese cat. With her long blonde hair, and still lean body, she still turned him on. If not for the guilt that was tearing him up inside, he'd have taken her to bed that very instant.

"Whatchaa making" he asked as he made his way to her.

"Nothing special," she responded, allowing his embrace. "Just thought I'd make you some peanut butter cookies since I know how much you love your grandmother's recipe," she added, just to push the barb in a little deeper.

"Oh Jazzy, you shouldn't be on your feet for too long you know. I want you to take it easy okay?" he added, with complete sincerity.

"Nathaniel David Brownstein, I'm pregnant, not sick. I feel perfectly fine and am in excellent health so don't go around acting like I'm an invalid." Any other time she would have thought his concern was endearing but now that she knew the man she married was not the same loving Nathaniel from her wedding day, the hypocrisy of it all made her sick. He didn't give a damn about her or how she was feeling and she'd make sure that someday he'd understand that she knew everything. She might not know all the details but she knew enough to understand that he'd traded her, their marriage and everything they'd shared together for some trailer trash piece of ass. "Oh he'll pay, sweet Jesus, he'll pay," she thought as she held him close, like she had not a care in the world.

<center>~~~ Chapter 17 ~~~</center>

The next few weeks flew by, with Jasmine noting that her beloved husband made it a point to be home by 6:30 at the latest every night. He showered her with gifts, not only for her but also for the baby. She accepted them graciously, but deep down resented the fact that he was giving presents to a child that he no longer deserved, nor in her mind, had a right to. He made idle conversation with her morning, noon and night and called her at least twice a day from the office, something he'd never done during the course of their marriage. He followed her around like a lost puppy when he was home in the evening and on weekends. He repulsed her, and it pissed her off that now that she felt nothing for him, he was all over her like a flea on a dog. If only he had been this way before she found out about Mandi. Back then it would have made her the happiest girl in the world, now she just wanted to punch him in the throat. After two weeks of his sucking up, she'd had enough and set her plan in motion. She had everything in order for phase two of her life. She had more than enough cash to start a new life somewhere and had already purchased a new home, such as it was. She was ready to go back to her old identity and start over in a new town. She just needed to rid herself of the two impediments standing in her way.

Jasmine waited until her husband was in the shower. Once she heard the water

running, she quickly turned on his computer, got into his personal email account, (one that he didn't realize that she knew about), and fired off a quick email.

"It's been too long. I was wrong, I need you. No discussion about it while at work, but meet me Friday at seven--- you know where. And wear something sexy. Remember, to build the anticipation, do not mention one word of it at work. Just thinking about it will make it even more memorable when Friday finally arrives. It will be the time of our lives, promise..."

She hit the send button, and as quickly as she typed it. She then deleted the message from his sent and trash files. She didn't even bother to open all the other messages that she saw from Mandi or to her. She didn't care at this point, and there was no use reading them and getting madder. She now had Mandi heading to their meeting spot, but wasn't quite sure how she was going to get Nathaniel there at the correct time. This was going to call for a little more manipulation. Mandi had been easy, and she knew that if the bitch thought she could get laid, she'd show up. "She is definitely going to get something Friday night, but it isn't going to be enjoyable," she thought to herself as she watched her husband enter their bedroom wearing nothing but a towel. Any other time, she would have found it tempting but tonight, she just wanted to sleep. He had thoughts other than sleep on his mind, and though the thought of him touching her now made her ill, she knew that this would be the last time that he ever made love to her. In her mind, she found herself once again, riding her black unicorn through the night sky; just the way she so often had when she was a child and young marine. "It'll be over soon," she kept repeating in her head. "Keep flying on your unicorn; it'll be over soon."

Mandi couldn't believe her eyes when she saw the email.

"Finally," he has come to his senses," she thought to herself. He'd made her wait almost two weeks. After their last night at the hotel, she hadn't wanted to wait twenty-four hours, let alone two weeks. She'd run by the condo after work this week, and make sure everything was in order. "Maybe it will be a bondage night," she thought to herself, feeling her thighs tingling at the thought. They definitely were compatible when it came to experimentation and maybe they needed a few ropes and chains to get them back on track. Secretly, she loved being tied up and feeling defenseless. When he blindfolded her while she was tied up, she was nearly over the edge before he even laid a hand on her. "Yes," she thought, "that is definitely what we'll do Friday night." She turned her attention back to Clive who was oblivious, watching TV in his Barco-lounger, drinking beer. "The man is such a loser" she thought as she looked at her husband of nearly ten years. She'd been barely eighteen when they'd married and if she hadn't been pregnant, compliments of their senior ball, she'd never have settled. Back then, he'd been both the rebel and the jock; tall and dark with a wild side. He'd been the football hero and a D-3 pick, until a torn ACL ended his football career and his dreams for the future. He dropped out of school and was content taking an entry-level job at a local factory. Sadly, he remained at that entry level position ten years later.

Thinking back now, they both settled. She should have left him after they lost the baby but for some reason she stayed. Now, years later, she had a career and he had an addiction to beer and reality shows. He was okay with working for next to nothing and they had a home that reflected that fact. She made good money but it only stretched so far. Maybe it was time to let Nathaniel know that she'd waited long enough for him to realize that he needed her and that she should be by his side not that simpleton he'd married. She'd show him the time of his life when they met on Friday, and then she'd tell him what they both needed to do to achieve their respective goals. "Yes" she thought now, "once we're officially together, what a power couple we'll be!"

In the two weeks since their business trip downstate, Jasmine had been able to learn more than she had ever wanted about both her husband and his business associate. Mandi, when not screwing her husband, lived a very simple middle-class lifestyle. Her home reeked of suburbia and her husband reeked of beer. And she didn't have any extravagant pleasures, other than taking what wasn't hers, but that would end soon enough. She had less than $10,000 in her bank account and still had a mortgage and car payment. Jasmine didn't think would be fair to saddle Clive with that if Mandi were to have an accident. She knew she'd have to figure out a way to help out with that, should the situation arise; which she knew would, sooner rather than later. Nathaniel also had a few secrets that she discovered once she started digging. His life insurance policies didn't have her listed as a beneficiary, but rather his mother. That fact in itself pissed her off. His mother had more money than God and at her husband's insistence, she had given up the job she had loved, when they'd married. "And now if something happened to him, she'd get nothing? How was that possible?" she wondered to herself as she slammed down her laptop lid. "We'll see about that."

Once upstairs, she went to her jewelry box first, then to her husband's armoire, and lastly, to the safe that was in Nathaniel's walk-in closet. Once she had the items that she was looking for, she made her way to their dining room. She scanned the room, looking for anything that she could pawn quickly and found a few ornate antiques that should fetch a decent price. She spread all of the collected items out and did a quick estimate of approximately what their sum total should be. She had two pairs of diamond earrings, one pair studs, another pair of hoops with sapphires intermingled. She'd collected six designer bracelets; two Rolex watches, one his and one hers; another three watches, two of which had diamond inlays. She'd found not 3 or 4 but 7 pairs of cufflinks that she knew her husband would never miss, ten tie clips of various shapes and sizes, and at least a dozen 24-karat Italian gold necklaces that she'd collected or he'd given her over the course of their relationship. She took whatever coins they had in their safe, knowing that Nathaniel had never gotten around to having them registered or recorded. She retrieved several designer purses that she thought would sell, along with numerous rings that she could care less about. All of the gifts that she'd been given over the course of their marriage had meant so much at the time, but looking at them now, she found that they meant absolutely nothing. Having never been a materialistic person, she realized now that it hadn't been the item that had brought her joy, but the man who'd loved her that had made her happy. And now, he meant nothing to her.

Even she was satisfied that she should be able to walk away with at least $40,000 once everything was pawned, and that was after the stores lowballed her, which she knew they would. She continued to walk around their home looking at all of their collected mementos and furniture now viewing them in a new light. She no longer thought of when and where the items had been purchased, and the loving memories behind each. Instead she scanned the rooms for what would sell or could be pawned the quickest, easiest and for the most money. She'd already done her research and realized that there were nearly a dozen pawn shops between Rochester and Utica. If she mapped it out correctly, she should be able to hit all of them in one day or two at the most.   Using her birth name, she had already made reservations to pick up a rental for the following day. With the newly created license reflecting her real name, Jasmine found herself slowing transforming back to being Trista Marie Carpenter sans the shy, introverted personality. The woman taking back her birth name was nothing like the weak child she'd been so long ago.

Jasmine did a mental inventory. The items that she was going to sell, between the jewelry and antiques should generate more than enough profit. She had emailed them a detailed list of what she was bringing to the various dealers and knew that they were salivating in anticipation. She'd also scheduled an appointment at a very high-end consignment shop and sent the owner an inventory of some of the designer suits and dresses that she'd like to bring in. They too had been all too eager to have Jasmine bring her items in to sell. Jasmine knew that everyone would try to low-ball the little old lady who was going to the various stores and shops in the morning. While they would think they were dealing with an elderly widower, they would in fact be dealing with an extremely cunning and business-savvy woman. She simply considered it her trial run and wanted to see how well she could pull off being a totally different person. She had a blast trying on wigs, and makeup to change her appearance and had finally purchased three different wigs for both tomorrows charade and for her new life once the loose ends were tied up here in Utica.

She'd given considerable thought to each step of tomorrow's adventure, even going so far as to dig through their garage to find a set of old license plates that had belonged to their mother's car before she'd left and their father had sold it. Rebecca had always thought that it was kismet that they'd stumbled upon them one day while playing in the barn. Jasmine had wanted no memories of their childhood or their childhood home but had hidden them anyway for her only sister. Finding them now, covered with dust in her garage had been a stroke of luck. In the morning she would pick up the rental car, switch the license plates, change her attire and set off on her merry way to hock everything she could. Still feeling slightly worried about Mandi's husband's well-being after what was to transpire over the weekend, she thought about how she was going to make sure that he was well cared for. Then it hit her.

The realtor had called to update her on the progress of her purchase. She said that the all the papers were back from re-date and should be over to her attorney by week's end. Everything was coming together nicely as Jasmine tidied up the house, knowing that she'd be gone all of the following day. She loaded everything into totes in their garage, throwing a tarp over the items.

One nice thing about having a sister on the police force, she'd learned more than she'd realized over the years by listening to he, and also quizzing her on occasion. Now those lessons were paying off, and Jasmine felt confident that she would be able to pull it off without any complications.

As she drove to her destination, she still was trying to figure out how she was going to get Nathaniel to fall for the bait and come there. Neither of them had any idea that Jasmine in fact knew about Mandi's condo. Knowing about it, and getting him to go there at the exact time that she needed him to enter the building were two different things. Hacking into his computer had been easy but how was she going to coerce him into going, she wondered as she pulled down the entrance road to the former park, her designated area for her transformation. No longer state-maintained, the road was more dirt than crusher run, with weeds and grass tall enough to hit the undercarriage of her truck as she made her way in. "Yes," she thought to herself, "this will do." As she sat in her truck looking out at nothing but wooded forest, she figured out how to get Nathaniel to Mandi's condo. It was a simple, but ingenious idea and even Jasmine couldn't help but chuckle as her plan completely came together.

~~~ Chapter 18 ~~~

She pretended that she was sleeping in when Nathaniel got ready for work but the second she heard the garage door go back down and his truck pull out of the drive, she set her plan in motion. She was at the car rental agency as they opened their doors. As soon as she had the car, she drove back to her home, and pulled into the driveway unseen. She had remembered days before to disable the security camera positioned on the house overlooking their driveway, and felt confident that no one had seen her generic-looking Honda CRV pull in. She always had vehicles of every shape and size coming and going from her home, and since she'd been in costume already, she doubted that anyone would remember the vehicle even if they'd seen it pull in. With the precision of a professional burglar, she paid attention to the time as she loaded the vehicle, keeping the items segregated based on where they were going and organized based on which destinations were first on the list. She had always been a very meticulous person and the military had taught her efficiency. Once loaded, she set off on what was destined to be a very interesting and profitable day.

She drove the speed limit on the Thruway, made sure she paid the toll in cash, and had the privacy setting indicating her location on her phone shut off. She had placed stuffed animals across the dash of the vehicle, conveniently covering up the vin number, and had altered the numbers of the vehicle registration on the sticker, just to be safe. Looking at herself in the rear view mirror, she didn't even recognize herself. Kudos to Party City for having such an awesome assortment of Halloween make-up in their store. Thanks to their store, she no longer looked like a thirty-year old athlete but more like an eighty-year-old grandmother. "Oh what a fun day we're going to have Trista," she said to herself as she hummed to the music coming from the radio.

Once in Rochester, she easily found the first shop. Twenty minutes later, she walked out of the store empty-handed, with a wad of cash in her tattered-looking purse. She repeated the same scenario at the second, third and fourth stores in Rochester and the surrounding suburbs. She couldn't get over how easy the process was, and thought to herself that it was no wonder that petty thieves were able to stay in business when anyone could simply walk into a pawn shop, present a fake ID and sell merchandise for cash on the spot. She thought of it as dress rehearsal for what was to come. In one store, she was the adorable Irish widow whose brogue was so thick that she could hardly even understand herself. In the next, she was the little Jewish spinster getting rid of her late brother's possessions, and so on. She was fluent in Spanish and French and enjoyed conversing with the young Latino store clerk in his native tongue. He was very generous with what he offered her for her merchandise and treated her with respect and dignity. She appreciated his demeanor and didn't haggle the way she had in the previous stores. By the time she made it back to the last pawn shop in Rome, she had only a handful of items left to sell. They were mismatched and not of any significant value. As anticipated, the antique stores had snatched up the few small trinkets that she thought would sell quickly and easily. None had any distinguishable numbering to link them back to her home. All in all, it had been a great morning and as she neared the exit to get back onto Route 49 and head back to Utica, the clock on the rental dashboard said that it was only 1:39pm. She made a split-second decision and made a sharp right hand turn to exit onto East Dominick Street and eventually onto Route 365, heading toward Holland Patent, and Route 12 North. The mountains were calling her and she wanted to drive by what was going to become her new home.

Claudia was surprised to see Trista pull up as she sat in her real estate office working. She was definitely one odd duck but who was she to question a cash buyer? In her line of work, she knew never to judge a buyer and as long as their cash was green, they could have all their quirks and idiosyncrasies. Trista had changed out of her little old lady costume and now was donning what was going to be her new look. Her eyes popped with color when she wore the black wig styled into a bob. Her outfit accentuated her now very well endowed chest and though she tried to hide her figure with her loose-fitting ensemble, anyone who wasn't blind would see that she was fit and trim.

"Well hello Trista," she said cheerfully. "What brings you to this next of the woods?"

"I was just wondering if it would be alright to go see the cabin again. If you're busy, and it's okay, I can just walk around outside?"

Claudia had just washed her Beamer and really didn't feel like taking it down the long dirt road that led back into the camp that Trista was purchasing. She knew it bent the rules but also knew that the owners had moved everything out that they were taking and there was nothing there to be stolen that wasn't already coming with the place. In the Adirondacks, as with other rural settings, it was quite common for the home or camp being sold to be sold fully or partially-furnished with the exception of the seller's personal items and mementos. Camps in the area ranged in size from one room, unheated cabins to mega-Mansions, with everything in between. The one that she was purchasing was not large by any means but had everything that she'd need to start her new life. The road leading into it was unmarked, unpaved and easily missed if someone wasn't looking for it. The barn that came with the property was almost as large as the house and would house the animals that Trista intended to get as soon as she was settled. She was excited that her agent was allowing her to go to the house unaccompanied as she wanted to take the time to absorb more of the details about the home and its surrounding land. Knowing that she'd have to make some type of arrangements for when the baby came, she would need the realtor's assistance in finding a midwife and down the road, a reliable babysitter. She made mental note after mental note as she drove down the numerous side roads off of Route 28 before she finally came to her destination. She parked the CRV and quickly got out. Using the lock box code that Claudia had reluctantly provided her, she gazed around at her new home and fell in love with it all over again. The wide stone hearth was the focal point of the cabin and the other rooms all flowed off of the great room. The kitchen was tiny but efficient and the two bedrooms provided more than an adequate amount of space for her and her unborn child. "Maybe I'll get a dog or two," she thought as she gazed around the space. She finished inside the house, locked up and made her way out to the barn. After surveying it, she nodded to herself in satisfaction, then headed back to her car to make the journey back to the car rental agency and then home before dark. As she was heading out of town, she noted the help wanted sign in the restaurant/bar and memorized the number as she drove past.

~~~ Chapter 19 ~~~

It was finally Friday and Mandi was beyond excited. She tried to read Nathaniel's expression as the day wore on, but she didn't notice anything different in his demeanor. He was jovial enough to her but still wouldn't allow himself to be in his office or the conference room alone with her. She chuckled to herself while thinking that he was playing such a good game of cat and mouse for everyone's viewing pleasure at the office, when she knew what they'd be doing in less than four hours. She had decided to leave the office early in order to get to the condo, shower and get ready for the evening's events. She'd told Clive that she had a late dinner meeting with a client out of town and may or may not be home that evening. Clive barely nodded as he continued to watch the fishing channel. Sometimes she wondered if her husband would even notice if she walked around the house bare ass naked. She had already placed her overnight bag in her car. She gave her husband a quick peck on the cheek and hurried out the door, smiling all the way to her car.

She entered the condo and found it odd that her security system didn't beep when she opened the door. She rushed in anyway so that she could get ready and set the stage for the night's adventure. Unbeknownst to her, she already had company. Jasmine watched from her vantage point as the homeowner lit some candles, poured herself a large glass of wine and drank most of it in three large gulps. She remained silent as she watched the woman head toward the bedroom, and moments later reappear wearing next to nothing. The room filled with the aroma of perfume that she always wore, the same scent that Jasmine realized now was what she'd smelled on her husband's shirts on more than one occasion. Her blood boiled as she watched "the other woman" strut around as if she had a right to her man. Although she wanted to eliminate the threat right that second, her training had taught her that a well-executed plan was far more successful than one done in haste. She continued to watch the bimbo set the stage for what she thought was going to be a lustful and sex-driven evening. Jasmine waited until the right moment, and after checking her watch, slipped out from her hiding spot. Up until that moment, she hadn't decided if she wanted Mandi to know her killer and who was behind her demise, but after watching her set the stage for her romp with her husband, she knew that she wanted her nemesis to understand completely what was going to happen to her. Checking one last time to make sure her gloves were secure, and that her hair was firmly covered under the stockinet, bandana and wig, she approached the woman from behind. She knew that she could end it right then and there with one well-placed blow to her throat, but chose instead to cough to gain her attention. Mandi heard her and spun around in the direction of the noise.

More startled and shocked than afraid, she looked at the face in front of her, down at the blade in the intruder's hand, and back up at the eyes that seemed to pierce through her. She didn't recognize the woman, and Jasmine found that extremely comical.

"What the fuck! Who are you? And if you want money, I've got some; just don't hurt me," she said, quickly losing her bravado.

"Oh, I don't intend to hurt you Mandi," she said in a monotone voice that showed no emotion what so ever. "I have much bigger and better plans for you." And with that simple statement Mandi knew that she was doomed.

Still not quite ready to give up hope, Mandi quickly scanned the area that she'd been backed into for something that she could use to fend off the very large knife that the psycho who'd broken into her house was holding. "You won't get away with this" she said trying to make herself sound brave and self-assured. "My security camera outside would have caught you entering and I have cameras in here that are recording us right now."

"You mean these Mandi?" she said as she held up the three tiny recorders that she'd found in the bedroom, bathroom and living room. She'd found it sick that Mandi had planted one in the bathroom but knew that she must have intended on a romp in the shower sometime during the course of the evening. She watched the woman's color drain from her face and smiled smugly. "You see Mandi, I know all about what you've been doing, who you've been screwing and what lives you've been destroying. It stops tonight." Finally seeing the light of recognition show in her eyes, Mandi looked at the woman standing just feet from her. When she really looked closely past the wig, makeup and skin-tight spandex jumpsuit that Jasmine was donning, she recognized the woman who'd broken into her home.

"Jasmine, are you crazy?" she asked once she realized that it was in fact only her lover's wife. In her eyes, the little mouse was harmless and obviously just pissed because she finally realized that her husband needed more than the mediocre sex that she occasionally provided. But as she looked into the woman's eyes, as she waited for an explanation, she felt her blood turn cold and the hairs on her neck rise. The person in front of her might be Nathaniel's wife, but something wasn't right and she wasn't acting or sounding like the quiet reserved woman she'd known. Mandi looked into the eyes and soul of the person who would be the last human she encountered before her death and knew something was gravely wrong. It was her but it wasn't. She quickly tried to backtrack and rationalize the situation.

Hands up, she tried to smile and act sweet, suddenly feeling very naked and dirty. "Hey look Jasmine, I'm sorry. We never meant for you to find out. He loves you and will never leave you, nor would I want him to. It's just," she stammered, still staring at the knife, "We both needed something that neither you nor Clive could provide us. Nate was afraid that if he asked you to indulge him in his, shall we say, unusual tastes, that you'd be repulsed. He loves you Jasmine, only you; this is about satisfying needs, and has nothing to do with love. Please understand, I never wanted you to find out, and neither did he."

"Shut up!" She screamed. "Just shut the fuck up!" Calming herself by breathing, as she'd been taught so many years ago, she cut the dumb bitch off. Mandi obviously thought that she had a chance of saving herself. The idiot had no clue. "You never wanted me to find out you say?" she continued, still in a non-emotional, almost soft-spoken voice. "And I suppose the video that you sent me was simply for my viewing pleasure and not because you wanted me to know that you were screwing my husband at every opportunity that you could?"

"Oh, about that," she said, feeling her face blush, and suddenly wishing that she had more on than the skimpy bra and panties that she'd exited her bedroom in; "I was furious because Nathaniel wanted to cut me off and stop what was a very good thing. As I said before Jasmine, what I have with your husband has nothing to do with love, it's simply sex, deviant, perverted, but very satisfying sex. I'm sorry that you found out, and I'm sorry if the fact that your husband's affair with me has hurt you. I'm no threat to your marriage Jasmine, you have to believe me."

With that last statement, Jasmine burst out laughing. "Honey, you're no threat to my marriage or to me. You have no clue about who I am or what I'm capable of, but you will very shortly." When she'd spoken, her voice sounded like it had come out of someone else's body. Mandi now knew that this situation was not going to end in her favor if she didn't do something proactive and do it now. She lunged toward the side of her counter where her butcher block of knives was but before she could reach the counter, her legs were kicked out from under her. As she fell to the cold tile below, she became fully aware of the gravity of her situation. She tried to stop her fall but within a second was on the floor and straddled by the woman who'd invaded her home. She saw Jasmine lift the blade and expected to be knifed, but instead felt the hard metal come crashing down on the side of her head. As it hit she heard her cheekbone pop and the taste of blood in her mouth was almost instantaneous.

The blow had only been to get her attention. Jasmine stared down at the woman and felt nothing. She no longer meant anything to her, and this had become a job; nothing more, and nothing personal. As the military had taught her, you eliminate the threat; that simple. She watched as the woman's breathing changed as the fear set in. She couldn't help but feel slight satisfaction now that the bitch was no longer smug and self-righteous. She noted how much of her cleavage was falling out of the tiny push up bra she'd forced her overly large breasts into and in one swift move brought the knife down to cut away the thin piece of material. Shocked and startled at the same time, Mandi didn't move and hadn't realized that she had been holding her breath. Before she could say anything, Jasmine had sliced the thin panties and ripped them away from her as well. Now totally naked and feeling very exposed, instead of being scared, Mandi found herself just wanting to cover up. Jasmine found the irony of it; trapped underneath her thigh was a woman who couldn't wait to get her clothes off whenever she was around her husband, but was begging her to allow her to put some clothes on at this very moment. Knowing that emotional rape was almost as painful as the physical act itself, Jasmine laughed as she ignored the woman's pleading. She plunged her gloved fist into her crotch. Shocked, she screamed out, but didn't dare move when she saw the blade lifted above her chest, and saw the eyes of a madwoman staring back at her. Jasmine pushed her fist as forcefully and roughly as she could as far up into the woman crevice as possible, saying nothing. She pushed it from side to side, feeling the tearing that was occurring. When she was satisfied, she withdrew her blood covered hand, and wiped the contents on Mandi's stomach. She stood, and told her to get up. Seeing her hesitation, she leaned in, grabbed her by the hair, and yanked her to her feet in one swift move. Once standing, she punched her hard in the abdomen, doubling her over with one blow.

"When I tell you to do something Mandi, you'll do it. Remember, you like rough sex games; so we're going to play some. Let's go," she said, signaling toward the bedroom.

Wondering what type of sadistic freak Nathaniel's wife was, she once again tried to reason with her, rationalize with her, and beg for her life. Jasmine didn't even register the words that were spewing from her husband's lover; she was focused on the mission at hand and completing it within the time frame she'd allotted herself. Once they were in the bedroom, Mandi tried to whip around and slam the door shut. This did nothing but piss off Jasmine, and gain her another punch to the flank area.

"Lie down on the bed, face down," she commanded. Seeing her hesitancy, Jasmine shoved her onto the bed. Before she knew what hit her, she was flipped over onto her stomach with her left arm pulled into a slip knot and

111

secured to the side of the bed. It took her less than ten seconds to secure the second arm as well and before Mandi realized what was going on, she was tied to the bed, face down. Before she even had time to turn her head, she felt the burn from the riding crop hit her back. The blow had been delivered with such force that it drew blood and welted up almost instantly. Mandi screamed in agony and braced for the next blow. There wasn't one. Jasmine realized after one strike that she'd have to silence the wimpy thing before they could continue their party; otherwise the neighbors might hear. She withdrew one of her husband's monogrammed handkerchiefs from her bag of goodies and gagged her, making sure it was secure in and around her mouth. Sitting up, she gave the plump ass staring up at her a hard slap, she got up and walked out of the room to give her friend time to wonder and worry about what was to come.

The second she realized that Jasmine had left the room, she tried frantically to loosen the ropes holding her hostage. The more she fought and pulled at them, the tighter they became on her wrists, and within seconds she saw the blood flowing from both where they were tearing into her flesh. Jasmine gave her only a few minutes, knowing that everything had to be done quickly as she needed to be out of there within 15 minutes and preferably ten. She'd texted her husband that she was going shopping at Sangertown Mall and she made sure that she parked in a spot where her CRV was under video surveillance. Once inside the mall, she'd made a few purchases, changed into her elderly lady outfit, and rode the bus downtown to where Mandi's condo was located. Once inside her house she'd put a tarp down, and removed her outer layer of clothing revealing the neoprene suit that she was currently donning. Within ten minutes, she'd reverse her actions, and be out of the unit and back waiting for the bus three blocks away.

She returned to Mandi's bedroom, and with the precision of a professional killer, brutalized the woman in ways even she didn't know that she was capable of. She shoved objects in orifices not meant to have things enter and beat her unconscious, then forced her to come to, and did it again. She used the riding crop, and various "toys" that she found in Mandi's dresser drawer. She knew these had been used when her husband had been present and that they were meant to bring pleasure, not pain. She spent only three or four minutes finishing what she started, and before she lifted her head to slit her throat, Jasmine used Mandi's cell to send one last message to her lover.

"Nate, someone's outside trying to get in. HURRY!!!! Get over here now! I'm scared, so scared; please come and please hurry!"

Once she hit the send button, she looked down at the semi-conscious woman one last time. Instead of slicing her carotid in one swift movement, she cut the largest artery in a human's body ensuring that Mandi would never dance again. But at the moment, dancing was not anything Mandi had to worry about. She carefully transferred her husband's thumb print onto the shaft of the blade and placed it in the zip lock bag that she'd brought. Once minute later she had transformed back into the little old lady who had arrived less than an hour before. She exited the condo under the cloak of darkness, walked slowly to the bus stop. She made sure that she kept her pace slow, with a shuffling-type gait all the way to the bus stop. She took the bus to the North Utica Price Chopper, and then caught a cab to back to Sangertown Mall, this time dressed as a gothic teenager. She made her way into the mall, found the nearest bathroom and quickly changed back into the attire that she'd arrived at the mall in, less than two hours earlier. She went into the stores where she had had set aside articles of clothing and a few gifts for the baby, and paid for them. She paid cash for some, and used her credit card for others creating a paper trail. She stayed another hour and then returned home, knowing by then that it was too late for her beloved husband and his mistress.

He had been in the car almost to his home when he received the text from Mandi. He'd tried to call her back, thinking it was just another one of her ploys to get him to come over; but when she didn't answer, he'd actually become a little concerned. Even knowing that she had a tendency to overreact, he drove out as quickly as he could. He really wasn't expecting to find anything other than Mandi up to one of her tricks. He parked his Escalade and entered using the key she'd given him months ago to enter. He saw the half empty bottle and glass on the island; hors d'oeuvres out as if she had in fact expected company, and noted that the music playing was soft and sultry. He called her name and hearing nothing, made his way toward her bedroom. The door was partially closed and it was silent on the other side. He didn't know what was going on but something registered in the back of his mind telling him that he shouldn't be there, and definitely should have called the police instead of simply showing up himself to see what game she was playing. The eerie silence scared him as he stepped into the doorway and pushed the door open. And then he saw it or her to be more precise, sprawled out spread eagle on her bed with her hands tied to each side of the bed. All logic and common sense went out the window as he rushed to her. The blood was still oozing from her leg and in an instant he realized that she was near death. He felt ill, physically sick as he dug into his pocket searching for his cell phone. His shaking fingers dialed 911, and he nearly screamed at the dispatcher to get help for her, even though he knew that there was probably nothing that could be done for her. He tried to hold pressure on her femoral artery, as he struggled to untie the rope that bound her. He knew he was destroying a crime scene but at the moment he only wanted to hold her when she took her last breath. He heard the sirens in the distance as he willed her to live, not realizing that she'd already moved on. They swarmed the condo, after securing the perimeter. Four men, all in military-type gear stormed in finding him still holding her in his arms. Mandi was already turning cold with the gray look of death apparent on what had once been a pretty face. The bruises had taken on a mottled hue and both she and Nathaniel were covered in her blood. Weapons drawn, they burst into the room. For an instant he thought he'd been shot. He did as they said, lifting his hands away from her and putting them in the air. Then in a split second, they had him on the ground, with his hands behind his back, and he heard the distinguishable click of handcuffs being placed tightly on his wrists. One of the officers had immediately gone to Mandi's side, but within seconds of feeling her carotid, shook his head signifying what everyone in the room already suspected. Nathaniel had been hauled to his feet and the officer in charge approached him, as calmly as if he was asking about the weather.

"Mind telling us what happened here," he asked, not really making it a request but more of a command.

"What? I don't know, you're the cops, you tell me. I'm the one who called 911. Can't you help her?" he said, looking back at the younger officer who remained by Mandi's side. Then it dawned on him. "Oh my God, you think I did this?" he said incredulously. "I came here to help her! I work with her, she's my associate, my friend," he said his words breaking.

"Your lover too Mr.?"

"Nathaniel, Nathaniel Brownstein.   And no," he responded, knowing that they were seeing right through him, "not anymore. We work together and we're friends and yes, we were involved but we ended it a while ago," he finished. He didn't even believe his own words so he knew that they would question his credibility as well.

The senior officer didn't show any reaction on his worn, leather looking face.   "So you two were lovers you say. I noticed your lady friend lacks attire but you seem to be completely dressed.   Want to tell me why or what transpired before we got here?"

"I'm telling you the same thing that I've already told you once. I got a text from Mandi stating that someone was attempting to get into her house and that she was scared and for me to get over here. I raced over as fast as I could, and this is how I found her." Thinking how it must look to an outsider, he cringed.   "I know I probably shouldn't have touched her but I didn't know she was close to death when I got here and I wanted to help her. You've got to believe me; my phone is in my pocket, look at it, the message from Mandi is still on my phone. "

The officer in charge wasn't going to let their prime suspect off that easily. He took his time pulling out the cell phone from Nathaniel's pocket, viewing the text and setting his phone down. His moves were deliberately slow and relaxed as he watched the man standing in front of him. His facial expressions revealed nothing, knowing that they had the woman's killer in their custody; but he played the game anyway.

"If you received a text from your friend," he said, emphasizing the word friend, "and she was telling you that someone was attempting to break into her house, why would you race here and not call the police? Are you trained to take on an intruder? Are you a cop? What were you thinking you'd do when you got here if there was, in fact, someone trying to break into her house?"

Flustered and still very distraught, Nathaniel stammered, "I don't know, I just thought that I needed to get to her. I know now that I should have called 911, but at the time, all I was thinking about was getting to Mandi, thinking she needed me. I don't know anything else, and if we're done here, I'd like to have your handcuffs removed now and be released so that I can get home to my wife, and out of these clothes."

"Mr. Brownstein, you're not going anywhere, except back to the station with us."

"Then I'd like to call my lawyer."

"I'd say that's the smartest thing you've said since I met you Nate," the officer quipped as they escorted him outside, still handcuffed, and into the waiting police car.

~~~ Chapter 20 ~~~

The next month was almost a blur for both Jasmine and Nathaniel. She received the call that he had been arrested for the murder of his co-worker, and lover. This made for great press when a snoopy reporter discovered that the accused killer, her husband, was expecting their first child with his adoring wife. He was held without bond, much to his chagrin and his mother's frustration; and after refusing a plea deal in exchange for his confession, his trial was scheduled immediately. The city of Utica seemed to be on edge since the young woman who was murdered met her demise in one of the hippest locations in the newly revitalized part of town. Except for drug related murders, Utica's murder rate was very low compared to other upstate New York cities. The murder of a young beautiful woman in her 20's created a very unsettling feeling for the cities' residents. Jasmine continued to play the role of dutiful wife and was seen every day visiting her husband. She offered "no comment" when hounded by the press, and stayed out of the public scene except when going to church, her doctor's appointment or the jail which housed her husband. Her time with him was not only monitored, but limited; and he made it a point to express his innocence and love for her with each visit. She listened to his every word and appeared to be the heartbroken but doting wife but inside she was hoping the trial and conviction would take place as soon as possible. She tired more easily now, and the emotional rollercoaster was starting to take its' toll on her. She had been questioned on two occasions, been cooperative when the police searched their home and vehicles, and made herself accessible to them, should they need her again. By the second week she was used to sleeping alone in their kind-size bed, and, other than wishing he was there to take out the trash, she didn't miss her husband at all. She'd considered him dead to her as soon as she'd found out about Mandi; and like the other men who'd hurt her along the way, she had already written him out of her life. Now she just waited for the judicial system to convict him, so that she could close yet another chapter in her life.

She woke early, doubled over in pain. The cramping hit her first and the trail of blood on her legs and in her bed second. She forced herself to a stand and went into her bathroom, dripping more blood along the way. Not sure, but having a pretty good idea what was happening, she held her stomach, willing it to stop. She wanted this child so badly. God couldn't be so cruel as to take it from her could he? She wondered as she used the bathroom and saw more blood. When she stood, she almost fainted from the pain. She called her doctor who happened to be on call; and he asked her to get into the hospital immediately, and to not eat or drink anything along the way. Suddenly she felt panicked, and begged whoever in the heavens was listening, to spare her child. She had never wanted anything as badly as she wanted this child and if she lost him or her, she would have nothing she thought. She drove at near record speed to the ER. Once inside, they assessed her and at her physician's request, wheeled her up to maternity, where she met her Doctor. The ultrasound confirmed their worst fear; the baby had suffered fetal demise, and she was miscarrying. With her child having no heartbeat, they had no choice but to perform a D & C and remove the last remnants of what had been her son or daughter. She'd lost everything, her husband and child, all within one month. Her sister had made it to the hospital while she was in surgery and was there when Jasmine returned to her room. Saying nothing, she simply held her sister's hand while they both cried softly. She left a few hours later, with her sister insisting that she spend the night with her. Her sister promised that it would get better soon, but Jasmine didn't believe her for one minute. In her mind, the only way her life was going to improve would be by getting away from Utica, Nathaniel and all of the memories of what her life had been. She, now more than ever, just wanted to start over again, somewhere else.

She didn't know if it was her sadness, despair, or need to talk to someone, but once she left the hospital and was in the comfort of her own home, she told her sister about her desire to leave the area and move north. She didn't elaborate and tell her that she'd already purchased and closed on a new home; Jasmine simply told her sister that it was something that she was considering. She waited to see what Rebecca's reaction would be and although her sister didn't necessarily seem enthused with her announcement, she also didn't seem surprised by her proclamation and need to reclaim her life. The only advice that her sister offered was for her to not make any rash decisions in her present state. Jasmine loved her sister, valued her opinion and respected what she had to say; but she also knew that her mind was already made up and that once the trial was over, she'd file for divorce, put the house on the market and sell everything that his mother didn't want, and that she didn't need. She and her sister spent the remainder of the evening watching TV and drinking wine, even though they had told her to abstain from alcohol for 24 hours following her procedure. The way Jasmine felt, she figured it certainly couldn't hurt her any more than she was already hurting. When they finally retired, Jasmine lay in bed, unable to sleep. She knew that she needed to as her husband's trial was to commence in less than 48 hours. She knew that she needed to be not only in attendance but also there to make a statement of support for her spouse. She knew that both the prosecution and the defense would be counting on her to support their cause. She rehearsed and practiced her statement and knew that each side thought that she was their ace in the hole. Now that she wanted nothing more than to put all of it behind her, she hoped that the trial was fast, unemotional and would end in the conviction of her husband. That simple, she wanted him dead; or at least locked up for life.

She finally drifted off to sleep; she dreamt of her black unicorn and took it as a sign, a sign that she would make her escape soon. When she woke in the morning, she felt rested and ready to tackle what the next days and weeks would have in store for her. She still felt groggy from yesterday's anesthesia, but was no longer in pain, at least not physically. She held it together during her shower and breakfast. It wasn't until her sister brought her to get her SUV and she returned alone to her empty house that she completely lost it. She saw all of the toys for the child who would never enjoy them. Someday she would look back and realize that that was the day that Jasmine truly became Trista. The woman who had been a loving nurse, wife and expectant mother was gone and in her place, was a shell of a person, one forced to revert back to what she'd once been.

The trial was over almost as soon as it began. Despite Nathaniel's very expensive and powerful attorneys hard on his behalf, the circumstantial evidence against him was overwhelming. And though there wasn't one thing in particular that worked against him, when the jury added up all of the evidence they unanimously felt that he was guilty of the crime and cast their vote. Three weeks after it began, the trial was over and her husband was found guilty and sentenced to 20 years in prison.

The papers once again took delight in exploiting Jasmine and her past. They ate up her sad upbringing and the loss of her parents, and now her husband. While it made for great press, it enraged her that they never bothered to consider that she and Mandi weren't the only victims affected by Nathaniel's act of violence. Mandi had a husband. While he was nothing to write home about, he had loved his wife in his own way and now he too was suffering. He'd lost his wife and his primary source of income. He would never be able to survive on what he made working at the local Wal-mart. Even though he'd eventually get the proceeds of the life insurance policy that Mandi had; Jasmine realized that his life had also been turned upside down. Looking at the poor man when the verdict was read in the courtroom, she made up her mind to make sure that he was taken care of. She knew exactly how she could get the money to make it happen.

Once the verdict was read and her husband was sentenced, the press and papers hounded Jasmine for her story. She received call after call, letters and emails requesting her side of the story, with some of the magazines offering ridiculous sums of money. Nathaniel's mother directed her to keep her mouth shut and their family affairs private. Although she refused to take orders or direction from her bitchy mother-in-law, she did agree that some things should be kept private. She would never allow the old rag of a woman to think that she was right, so Jasmine told her soon to be ex-mother-in-law that she wouldn't sell her story to the various rag magazines if she'd give her a check for $50,000. Although she fought the idea vehemently, she wrote the check the very next day. Jasmine cashed it before the ink on the check hardly had time to dry and had a cashier's check made out in Clive's name. She sent it via Fed Ex to him, and inside the envelope enclosed a simple note:

This won't take away your pain, nor will it make up for the loss of your wife; but I hope it helps make your life a little easier along the way. Your mortgage has been paid in full, and your truck loan has also been satisfied. May God bless you and help you find peace and happiness again someday.

Sincerely,

Trista

Jasmine knew that the money wouldn't bring back his wife, but in her mind if it helped Clive make it through life a little easier and with less to worry about, then she'd done her part to help. He'd never know who'd sent the donation and paid off his loans, and that was okay. She wasn't interested in accolades; she was just doing something that she felt was right. Mrs. Brownstein had also lost something dear to her, but that bitch could burn in hell before Jasmine would acknowledge her loss. No one in Nathaniel's family seemed to care about what she'd lost; she'd not only suffered the loss of her marriage and husband, but ultimately wasn't it Nathaniel's fault that she'd lost her child as well? The more she thought about it, the madder she got. Since she knew what kind of person she became when she let her temper get away from her, she focused instead on getting her house on the market, liquidating any and all possessions that her mother-in-law didn't claim and putting her soon to be ex-husband's Escalade on Craig's List. She kept a very detailed account of how much she sold each item for, whether it was big or small. Before she left her home for the last time, she sent the list and a certified check to his mother and her attorney for safe-keeping. She would never have it said that she exploited her situation for monetary gain. And with that, she walked out the door of her mansion, took one last look at what had been her life for the last six years and drove away to start a new one.

Part 2: New beginnings and deserved endings.

Trista left the city and pulled into the car dealership that she'd visited the week before. As instructed, they had her new set of wheels waiting for her. She traded in her Lincoln, though she was really going to miss it, for something more practical for her new journey. The Jeep looked generic enough from the outside; it was black and didn't have any flashy chrome or upgrades, but the inside spared nothing. It had the heated seats that she knew were a must when you live in the North Country, and although she didn't see the value in its fancy navigational system, she knew that she'd probably come to depend on it more than she realized at the moment. What she appreciated the most about the vehicle was not only the on-demand 4x4, but the amount of room that the cargo area afforded if the back seats were folded down. She knew that with the amount of work that her little cabin needed, the fact that she could fit full sheets of plywood inside her truck just made life much easier. She signed what needed to be signed, gave the salesman her bank check, and went on her way towing what few items she was bringing from her old life with her. She purposely wanted to get to her new home during the early morning hours while most folks worked so that she could unload the U-Haul and drop it off as quickly as possible. One thing about small towns that she remembered from her childhood was that country people mind their own business and don't intrude where they're not wanted. Living a small town also meant that nothing goes unnoticed and everyone knew everyone. She preferred to get moved in and organized before anyone found out that the old Carver camp was no longer vacant. She had always been very good at making sure that the people around her only saw what she wanted them to see and knew that presentation was everything. To her new neighbors, she'd be the young writer who moved in to work on her first novel since graduating from college. She looked young enough to play the part and in keeping with character, she'd live the lifestyle of a starving artist. Satisfied with how everything in her life was turning out, she pulled into the Old Forge Post Office to set up her PO Box on her way to her new home. It would be the rare occasion that she received mail, but Trista knew that she needed a way for her sister or her attorney to communicate with her. She met the postmaster and in her newly acquired Irish Brogue, introduced herself as Trista O'Connor, of the County Cork O'Connnors, by way of New York University, where she'd graduated a few years prior. The post master chatted with her as she filled out her information and paid for her box for the next six months. She said goodbye and cheerfully waved as she walked out the door and the two blocks back to her truck. She took notice of the nondescript CRV parked a block behind her with a man sitting behind the wheel. With his baseball cap and sunglasses, she couldn't make out any features. She wasn't concerned about it but made a mental note of his tags anyways. She'd always had a photographic memory and knew that once she read the plate, it would be forever ingrained in her memory.

Her next stop was to pick up the keys from the realtor, along with a cute little plant that served as a house-warming present. She thanked her for her hard work in finding her a perfect little bungalow and promised to refer her to all of her friend. She knew full well that she'd never see nor speak to the realtor again, but didn't want to burst her bubble when she was thinking about her next commission check. Once the keys were in her hand, she exited the building and headed out of town. She made her way through Eagle Bay and Inlet on her way to her new home. She noticed the various Realtor signs on the numerous listings, along with a few for sale by owner signs, but what caught her eye was the small Help

Wanted sign hanging next to the tiny restaurant. It looked to be more of a diner than an actual restaurant, but when Trista pulled off Route 28 and walked back towards the building, she could see that it was much larger than she'd originally thought. She was about to step inside, when she noted the same CRV pass by. This time she got a much better view of the driver, who slowed but kept his eyes on the road and his vehicle moving forward. She noted that he was Caucasian, clean-shaven, and his high cheekbones were nearly touching the lower rim of the reflective aviator sunglasses that he wore. If she were anyone else she wouldn't have given it a second thought, but the soldier in her felt the hair on the back of her neck rise and she was suddenly on high alert. Maybe it was just everything that she'd been through, or her accurate sixth sense, but, either way she would now have to get in touch with her sister to see if she would run the tag for her.

She walked back to her truck, got in, and once she saw that the CRV was no longer in sight, proceeded slowly toward her camp. A few minutes and several turns later, she was parked in front of what would become her home base. She noticed that the five cords of wood that she'd requested were dumped to the right of her cabin, just as she'd instructed them to do, and the fencing from the local Agway was stacked to the left of her home. She'd have to retrieve the name and number of the local teenager that her realtor had said was always looking for manual- labor type jobs. She'd hire him before the week was out and between the two of them, the pens would be finished and all of the wood brought into her cellar within a few days. She knew that they would be delivering her chickens by the weekend, and the two hogs she'd bought were coming the following week. The only thing left to get would be the goats that she hadn't been able to find yet. She wanted them both for milk and to make goat cheese with, but also for an unorthodox type of companionship. She spent the afternoon unloading the few possessions that she'd brought with her, which consisted mainly of things for the kitchen. She'd brought bed linens for the one bed that came with the place, her favorite bath towels, her clothing, one shotgun that had been her favorite when she and her husband hunted together, and her computer, along with a few other personal odds and ends. She had sold, given away or donated just about everything else that she'd once held dear. She'd used the proceeds to pay cash for her cabin, and made sure that her sister's new truck no longer had a loan attached to it. This infuriated Rebecca who while insisting she could take care of herself, eventually and reluctantly accepted Jasmine's generosity. Before leaving the city of Utica for good; Jasmine anonymously sent a check for $5,000 to be used solely on the pediatric unit at St. Luke's, in whatever way their nurse manager saw fit.

Jasmine/Trista knew that her child would never benefit from the care given to the children who were on the unit, but somehow if her donation made one child's stay a little easier; then she'd know her money went to a good cause. The last certified check that she endorsed over was to the Hope House. She wished that it could have been more, but the $17,500 check was what was left of her proceeds once she sold everything. She kept just a few thousand to start her new life. She hoped that her donation to the charity would help many young women finally find a safe haven from the abusive men in their lives. Having been a victim of abuse throughout her childhood, she wished there'd been a place like that when she and her sister, and mother for that matter, needed one.

Once she had unloaded the truck, she realized that the breakfast that she'd started her day with had long since been digested and she was starving. She had a refrigerator full of food but decided to head back out to 28 to check out the restaurant where she'd seen the sign as she'd passed through town. She might as well go in as a customer and scope out the place before applying at an establishment that might not be a good match for her. She noted the friendly- family styled, atmosphere almost immediately upon entering. The colors were inviting and the booths were spread out, giving one space but also intimacy for conversation. The big windows across the rear of the building allowed natural lighting to complement the small wall sconces that were also lighted. She was greeted with a warm smile by the first waitress that caught her eye, and was told that she could sit anywhere she'd like. Scanning the room, she saw that they were doing a steady business, especially since it was the in-between time between a late lunch and an early supper. As she looked around trying to find a small table tucked away in a corner, she made direct eye contact with the man behind the bar. 40's, single and probably one who'd slept with the entire staff, she immediately knew that he would be absolutely off limits if, and that was a big if, she chose to seek employment here. She found the table that she was seeking, and sat down with her back to the wall. Old habits die hard, and she couldn't help herself. She always had to sit in a public place positioned so that she could see everything and everyone who entered and exited. The military had taught her more than just how to kill, they'd inadvertently taught her how to survive as well. She and her sister hadn't had the luxury of going to 4H or Girl Scout Camps when they'd been children. Every survival skill that they'd picked up were things that they'd either learned the hard way or had read about. Their father had never taught them anything other than the fact that he was the meanest drunk they'd ever want to meet. Their mother had tried helping them the best she could but she'd disappeared before either had really been old enough to remember what she'd taught them. The one thing that she had taught both of them from an early age was how to cook. Trista was an exceptional cook and could make something scrumptious out of next to nothing. It had been out necessity more than desire that she'd mastered the art of substituting one ingredient for another one; but no matter what she whipped up, it always received rave reviews. Nathaniel had always loved her cooking, and she'd taken great pride in making things she knew he loved. As she sat at her corner table and thought of him, just momentarily, she couldn't help but wonder how he was enjoying his meals now.

"Welcome to ADK Bar and Grill. My name's Laverne. Can I get ya something cold, or hot for that matter, to start ya off?"

"Yes, please. Could I have a glass of water with lemon and a hot cup of tea?" she responded politely.

"Sure thing honey, coming right up. Are you new to these parts or just passing through?" she asked as she poured a Trista a glass of ice water and handed her a little bowl with sliced lemon in it. "I know you're not local because that last time I heard that kind of accent I was on my honeymoon in Scotland."

Chuckling, Trista decided that she liked the woman towering over her shooting off rapid-fire questions. She didn't find them intrusive, just a good waitress getting to know her customers and in return, getting a larger tip than if she'd been boring and all business. Trista answered her questions, explaining that she was from Ireland not Scotland, and had in fact only been to Scotland a time or two. She loved that she'd always been like a chameleon in the sense that she could take on the accent and identity of someone else by simply listening to them speak for a few minutes. Her Irish brogue was quite easy to perfect though, since her foster mother's mother had been right off the boat from Ireland. After she and her sister had moved in with their family, it was an accent that Trista adopted with fondness. Her foster grandmother had been nothing but wonderful to the scared little girls that her daughter had taken in, and for that Trista had always been grateful. When her foster parents died unexpectedly in a car accident, she'd insisted that she and Nathaniel pay for their funeral expenses. He reluctantly agreed; since he wanted to keep the peace, he opened his checkbook and shut his mouth. Trista had given them the most elaborate funeral service and burial that money could buy and had insisted that they make a contribution to the House of the Good Shepherd in their honor.

Trista ordered a western egg sandwich on rye as Laverne chatted about the weather, the tourists, and at least seven other topics. In the course of her half-hour lunch, Trista learned about six local families, and what new businesses' were in town and how they were doing. Just before she paid the bill and got up to leave, Laverne came out and said what was on her mind. "You know you might not have any experience waitressing or bartending but we could use someone as cute as you to help bring in a good crowd. If you're interested in the job, just say so. I saw you eyeing the sign outside before you came in. I know that's why, when I wasn't asking my questions, you were casually poling around asking your own fair share. I already told Sal over there at the bar that he'd do well by hiring a gorgeous young thing like you."

"But I'm not sure that I want a full-time job," she said reluctantly. "I am here just for the time it takes me to finish the book I'm working on. I can't work full-time and have time to write."

Laverne wouldn't be swayed that easily. She knew that the young woman was looking for something; maybe working at their little diner would provide her new friend with a small amount of spending money, and might also fill in the gaps of what was missing in her life. "Hey Sal, you willing to hire someone part-time if that's all they can offer you at this point in time? Maybe let her start out part-time and add additional hours if she has time every now and then to work a little extra?"

"Laverne, who ya planning on hiring?" he hollered back, knowing full well that the woman in the corner booth was the one that Laverne felt needed or wanted the job. She had a sad look about her he'd noticed, but then again, after being a cop and a bartender, he had become accustomed to reading people. He was usually extremely accurate in his assessment. To him, she looked like a runner. To the former cop, her plain clothes, and the wig she was wearing so that she'd blend in with her surroundings were a dead giveaway to the former cop. He'd never seen her before but had caught a glimpse of the U-Haul as she towed it through town. He had heard that a young girl had purchased the old Carver camp so it didn't take a rocket scientist to put two and two together. He supposed as long as the willowy-looking woman who sat quietly alone at her table didn't come with too much baggage or someone looking for her, he could give her a chance and a job.

"You think that who you're wanting to hire would prefer maybe working a couple evenings a week bartending instead of tying up her days here waitressing?" he shouted back to her, as he saw Trista look up and make eye contact with him. She acknowledged his comment with a slight change in expression which alone told him that yes, she would take the job if offered to her.

"Hey Laverne, you tell anyone who might be interested that I could really use a bartender two or three evenings a week. The pay is okay, but make sure you let him or her know that we split the tips equally around here. During the busy season, they can expect to make between $200 – $250 on average per night. Okay? And if you come across anyone, let them know that I'd like to hire someone within the next week so I can get them on the payroll and start training them before our busy season gets underway."

Knowing that they were talking about her, without directly talking to her, she listened to them banter back and forth and smiled. Maybe here, in this little sleepy town, she'd make new friends and start her new life; and with a little help, she'd be able to stay for more than a few months. She'd love to be able to put down roots and make a new home for herself.

After she finished her meal, she paid the bill and got up to leave, but on impulse walked over to the bartender Laverne had called Sal. Extending her hand, her lips broke into a thin smile. "I bartended in college, so yes I have experience, and yes, I would prefer working evenings over the day shift," she offered as she shook the owner's hand. "And if you're offering me the job, I need to get settled but could start on Wednesday if that works for you."

Sal released her hand, smiled and made just one comment. "The job is yours, providing that whatever you're running from doesn't grace my doorstep. This is a family restaurant and bar and whether the people inside are locals or tourists, I don't want any trouble."

"Not running, and won't bring any trouble to your establishment. Thank you for the chance," she said as she turned to leave, possibly already regretting her decision to work in such a public setting. As she walked out the door, she heard Sal shout, "See you Wednesday; be here by 4." She heard him but said nothing as she continued out the door; she simply lifted her arm in agreement and waved and the door shut behind her.

Wednesday morning came and there was a flurry of activity at her little abode. Her fence had been finished the day before and the chicken coop was already home to seven hens and one rooster. Her pigs were being unloaded, or at least the men who drove them out were attempting to unload them into their new home; but the two biggest pigs had different ideas. After much coaxing and prodding, they were finally in their new enclosure with the gate slammed behind them. Immediately upon entering the mud, they smelled the food waiting for them in their new trough and were in hog heaven, so to speak. Trista paid the men and upon their departure, looked around at what a few days ago had been an old abandoned cabin. It was now full of life, cheerful to look at and very self-sufficient. Her indoor plumbing was marginal at best, but at least it was indoors and the toilet flushed when it was supposed to. When she originally headed to the Old Forge area to find a secluded place to call home, she'd been afraid that if she got too remote, she'd be forced to settle for an outhouse and that idea held no romantic connotations for her whatsoever. She didn't mind roughing it or living a simple life but drew the line when it came to going outside every time she needed to pee. Knowing that it was fairly common for the temp to dip down to -10 or even -20 with a wind chill colder than that, Trista had no interest in heading out to an outhouse in the middle of night.

It took her 20 minutes to get back out onto Route 28 to head toward her new job. She'd dressed conservatively and with her red wig and green contacts, she definitely looked the role she was currently playing. Her accent was perfect and anyone who didn't know her would assume that she'd come from Ireland just last week. She went into the post office and grabbed the few pieces of mail that had made their way to her new address. She noticed one letter from her sister and one from her attorney. She threw the rest of it on the floor of her truck, but ripped open the letter from her attorney first. It was nothing that she hadn't expected and been mentally prepared for. Of course his mother and her attorneys were pushing for a new trial and trying to overturn his conviction. Her attorney also went on to say that the proceeds of the sale of the house had been split equally, with her half going to the various people and organizations of her choosing. She discarded his letter and opened her sister's. Although she wasn't quite sure she wanted to read it just before starting her first day on the job, she read it anyway.

Jazzy:

I still haven't quite figured out why the hell you'd want to move up to the freaking middle of nowhere but hope that you're settling in okay. Please get a new phone soon and call or text me. I hate the idea that you're out there in the woods by yourself without even so much as a dog, phone or gun. I know that you can more than take care of yourself, but you of all people should know that the world is crazy and you have to be ready for whatever life throws at you. Please get a phone soon, and a dog, and dammit, get a gun too! I'll try and come up in a few weeks when I have a long weekend. Keep working on your book but take time for yourself as well. Enjoy the mountains but enjoy the sunshine; don't stay holed up in that cabin of yours. You've been through hell and back sis, and I'm worried about you. Just like when we were kids Jazzy, I still rely and depend on you, whether you know it or not; so don't let anything happen to you okay? Love you to the moon and back Jaz; remember that. I'll always be here for you, no matter what...

Love,

Rebecca

She put down the letter after reading it for a second time and wiped the lone tear from her eye. She sometimes wondered if her sister would still love her if she knew all of her dark secrets. Years of training and mental conditioning in the Marines had allowed Trista to sleep well at night in spite of what she'd done over the years. They'd always told her while serving her country; that it was simply about eliminating the threat. Trista had become very proficient at doing just that.

She gently folded up the letter and tucked it in her visor, checked her makeup again, threw her truck in drive and headed back toward Eagle Bay and her new job. She walked in the door to a smiling Laverne at precisely 3:50pm. Sal was behind the bar, and there was also a young girl waiting tables who hadn't been there the other day when Trista had first entered the establishment. She looked to be young, maybe 18 or 19, and was definitely heavy with child. At first glance, she thought that she looked tired, really tired; but Trista watched her for a few more seconds as she interacted with the family that was at her station, and she could see that she'd been beautiful once, and could be again if she had adequate sleep and different attire than the beat up sweatshirt that she was currently wearing. Without even knowing her name, Trista asked Laverne if she could borrow her phone quick, reassuring her that it wasn't a long-distance call, and made a thirty second call to her sister. She talked only long enough to tell her what she wanted Rebecca to ship to her, smiled to herself, hung up and was ready to start her first day on the job, punching in at 3:57pm.

Though Sal quickly realized what he'd already expected; that their new bartender was an extremely intelligent and educated person. Trista remained very tight-lipped about her personal life and any details pertaining to it. She only offered that she was originally from Ireland, which Sal didn't believe for a minute even though her accent was perfect, and that she'd studied at NYU before moving up to the mountains. He figured she was slightly older than a recent college graduate, but she had the energy of one so he didn't challenge her. She not only knew how to pour beer correctly, but was also very practiced in the art of mixing specialty drinks. Although she had to reference a few of the more exotic drinks, she did so quickly and proficiently while interacting with the patrons. He watched quietly as the shy, introverted redhead came out of her shell, working the crowd of both locals and tourists. The summer people outnumbered the locals nearly three to one in the summer but it was the winter's snowmobile crowd that kept them in the black. Not one to stereotype, and after he would never admit it but he loved the winter season because the snowmobilers were big business for their economy and were much more inclined to partake in an overabundance of whatever alcohol a bar had on hand. He never let any of his patrons get outwardly drunk, anyone who entered knew that he or any bartender working at the ADK would cut them off and call for a ride if they thought that someone had overindulged. He made sure that Trista was aware of that fact as he gave her his orientation speech.

He stood back and watched as she juggled the numerous customers who'd filled the stools at the bar, along with the orders being thrown at her by the two waitresses. Just when he thought she looked like she needed a hand, she turned to him and said in an authoritative voice, "I've proved myself Sal, so now get over here and give me a hand. They're your customers and it's your business, so help out instead of standing there critiquing me!"

"Yes mam sir," he shouted back at her, all the while smiling ear to ear. That was it, he thought, his new barkeep was ex-military. He came to her side, and together they continued all evening long to serve a very boisterous crowd.

When the doors were closed and they were cleaning up from the onslaught of people, Laverne stayed behind to help out. It was only then, during general conversation that Trista asked about Tabitha, the young girl who'd been waitressing that evening. Laverne, who was a lifelong resident of the area, told her that Tabby was only 20 and pregnant with her second baby, having had the first one the summer she graduated from high school. She had had a modeling contract in New York but had to give up her modeling career and all of her other dreams when she'd become pregnant. Laverne went on to say that the loser who kept getting her pregnant was nothing to write home about and barely kept a roof over the young family's' heads. She said Toad, (his name was actually Todd but since she didn't like him, she referred to him as Toad), worked as a mechanic in town; that is, when he decided to show up. He'd been known to decide to go off hunting for days at a time, leaving Tabitha alone with a toddler and no one to watch her when she needed to work. Luckily, most people in town knew her situation and everybody loved the former homecoming queen. Numerous women and a few men stepped in to help her out when she needed it, which was becoming more and more frequent. Trista listened quietly as Laverne ragged about the father of Tabitha's children, and even though she'd never met him, loathed him already. Twenty was too young to be saddled with such hardship she realized, and she of all people knew how hard it was to stay afloat when the odds were not stacked in your favor. As she wiped down the counters alongside Laverne, the wheels in her brain were already turning as she formulated a plan to help her new co-worker.

It took Trista a little longer navigating the dark roads back to her cabin, than it had to get to work in the daylight. The woods took on a different look when it was pitch black out as it was during her drive. Without a star in the sky to illuminate the night, she found the road slow going and hard to follow. But since that was precisely the type of area that she'd been looking for, she couldn't complain as she slowly approached the last turn before her cabin. As she made the last turn, she could see the motion sensor come on as soon as she turned the corner, picking up on the movement of her truck. She'd made it a point to install the most powerful one sold and it had done exactly what she had hoped it would. She had no intention of anyone invading the sanctity of her home without her knowledge; with the motion detectors installed on both the barn and her cabin, she doubted that even the abundant deer population would be able to surprise her when they approached. Once she was parked, she checked on the chickens to make sure they were secure and then the pigs who were now very content in their new surroundings. After she was satisfied that her livestock was cared for, she made her way inside.

It wasn't until she actually took her boots off and sat down, that the fatigue of the evening hit her. She hadn't worked in almost six years and to go back to a job that required her to be on her feet continuously during the shift had tired her more than she'd realized. She'd met a handful of the locals, the hearty year-round residents who braved the cold upstate New York winters, and had also met tourists here for the week. Intermingled with them had been a few summer people, the residents who spent the summer relaxing along the Fulton Chain of Lakes, with most of them having camps that had been in their families for decades. She had enjoyed the banter between the waitress and bartender, as Sal and Laverne continuously tried to one up each other. And she couldn't help but notice the way Charlie, the young bus boy, rushed in to help Tabitha clear each table when the patrons had exited their booths. He could have his back turned to her, but somehow Charlie had a sixth sense whenever Tabitha was about to pick up something too heavy for a woman in her condition. It had warmed her heart to see that chivalry wasn't dead; at least not at the ADK Bar and Grill!

She poured herself a glass of wine and put her feet up. She knew that she'd never be the woman she had once been, but old habits die hard and she had been thinking about that glass of white zin the entire drive home. She'd started a fire in the wood stove before she finally allowed herself to relax, and as she sipped on the wonderful liquid in her oversized wine glass, it occurred to her that this was the first night in her new life. She lifted her glass in a silent toast and continued to enjoy the moment, however brief it might be.

He'd parked his CRV down the road and had watched her through binoculars as she exited her vehicle and checked on her newly-acquired animals. He'd been right about her and thanked his intuition that had told him not to follow her too close or to try to sneak up on her, for fear of being discovered. As he'd watched her home become illuminated as brightly as if it still were daylight, he quickly realized what a mistake it would have been if he had, in fact, tried to approach too closely. From his perch he sat in the silent darkness watching her drink white wine and stare off into space. He noted that she didn't turn the TV on; she just seemed content to be alone with her thoughts. He never took his eyes off his prey.

~~~ Chapter 21 ~~~

The next few weeks flew by while Trista quickly learned the routine and rhythm and flow of a restaurant in a tourist town. She'd seen the same locals occupy the same bar stools time and time again, and had come to learn almost each and every one of their names, their spouse's names and their children and grandchildren's names. She'd learned who lived where, who was sleeping with whom and who owed money to whom. She taken it all in, and politely answered the questions that they'd asked about her, giving them the minimal amount of information possible, a fact that didn't go unnoticed by Sal. He listened but said nothing. That was one thing about small towns, they definitely were different than big cities where neighbors sometimes can share a common wall between their respective homes and never even know each other's names. Here in a town where the average population, excluding visitors totaled less than 5,000, it was inevitable that people would want to know more about her, since it was now obvious that she was putting down roots in their sleepy little mountain town. Even Tabitha, who remained quiet around her, seemed to open up more and accept the friendship offered her. Once Trista had discovered that she was expecting a little boy, she ventured into the Old Forge Hardware Store and picked up the softest yarn they sold and started working on a baby blanket for the mother- to-be. Trista had learned how to knit when she'd lived in her foster parents' home. Even though she hadn't touched knitting needles since high school, she was surprised by how easily it came back and how soothing and relaxing it was to sit by the fire in the evening, listening to soft music emanating from her radio and knit. Since she'd finished up the blanket the night before, when it was time to head into work, Trista wrapped the blanket up in a decorative gift bag and decided to surprise her co-worker. She was proud of the way it had turned out and couldn't wait to see the look on her young friend's face when she gave it to her. She entered the restaurant fifteen minutes before the start of her shift and felt the tension in the air the second she opened the door. Immediately on alert, she scanned the room to see what was out of place, and was greeted by a very somber looking Laverne.

"What's going on Laverne?"

"Oh honey, I just can't believe it," she said while snapping her gum, a habit that Trista had noticed Laverne only did when she was wound up or upset. "That mean, no good, jackass of a man laid his hands on our Tabby," she said in a near whisper, so as to not let the patrons hear. "She came in here a bit ago all disheveled and upset, and Sal finally got out of her what had happened, or at least part of what had happened. She's upstairs resting with her little girl. Oh Trista, you should see her, she's all bruised and missing a chunk of her hair where the bastard pulled it out of her scalp. He's done this type of shit before, but never this bad."

Trista tried to block out the images rushing through her mind as she listened to the loquacious Laverne describe the beating that Tabitha had endured at the hands of her boyfriend. She tried to calm herself as she listened, but to no avail. She asked if the young mother had somewhere else to stay and Laverne quickly reassured her that Tabitha and her daughter would be moving in with her, at least for the immediate future. Remembering that she was still holding the ornate baby blanket that she'd made for her, Trista asked if she could possibly run up and see her for just a minute before her shift started. Sal told her to take her time. Sal saw the look of pure agony on his newest employee's face as she'd listened to the description of the assault on Tabby; and realized that Trista knew more about domestic abuse than she'd let on.

Trista softly entered Sal's apartment above the bar, to find Charlie at Tabitha's side, gently running his hand down her hair. She stood silently for a moment and surmised that the two of them had had a relationship in the past, or at least Charlie had wanted one. She knew love when she saw it and in that moment, Trista realized that their busboy was in fact head over heels in love with the very pregnant woman at his side. Tabitha lay on her side facing away from the door so Trista couldn't see her face. It wasn't until she gently coughed to gain their attention that Tabitha nearly jumped up out of bed, and turned toward the sound of the noise. Charlie had jumped up and appeared ready to take on whoever had entered the room. Trista immediately put her hands up in surrender and smiled.

"Guys, it's me. It's okay, it's just me." Seeing the black circle forming under Tabitha's eye, Trista rushed over to the young woman, instinctively putting her hand on her abdomen, without even asking permission. Looking into the tear-filled eyes of a still shell-shocked friend, she asked the one question she was terrified to ask. "Did he hurt the baby? Have you been feeling him kick since this happened?"

She couldn't formulate the words at first but finally nodded yes. Tabitha summoned her inner strength and then said, "It's happened before but never this bad. In the times before, he's never touched my belly, but this time the fucker was kicking me, trying to hurt my baby," she sobbed, holding her abdomen as if her life depended on it. Charlie took in the words that he'd just heard and took her into his arms.

"Tabby, I'll kill him; I swear I will. If you won't leave him after this, I'll kill him and you'll never have to worry about him again." Knowing that the young man holding the woman that he loved was speaking from the heart without necessarily thinking, Trista interrupted.

"Charlie, our Tabitha needs you now. She needs you and her daughter needs you. Todd will get what's coming to him; but not at your hand. You'll do our Tabby no good if you're rotting in jail, so promise me you won't go after him, okay?" she added in her most authoritative voice.

As Trista finished her plea Tabitha's little girl, had just woke and started to sit up. The second she turned in Trista's direction, it became very apparent that her hunch had been right. Charlie and Tabitha had been an item at one time, or at least had spent enough time together to conceive a daughter. That certainly explained why he was so concerned about her well-being, and that of the child she was carrying. Trying to distract the little girl for a moment or two, Trista offered her the bag which had the blanket inside. She was so thankful that her sister had told her to make sure that she had a few gifts for the baby's big sister and that she'd had the foresight to stuff them inside the bag. When Penelope pulled the tissue paper away, she immediately found the gifts intended for her and squealed with delight. Grabbing her new gifts, she held them tightly as she sat down on the floor to play; allowing her mother to look at the blanket that Trista had created with her own hands. She stared at it, held it up to her face feeling the softness and started to weep softly.

"Thank You," was all that she could manage.

"You're welcome, Tabby. It's going to be okay, I promise. Nobody will let him hurt you ever again." And with that, Trista knew that Todd Herthum would be dead by this time tomorrow.

~~~ Chapter 22 ~~~

News spread like wildfire about the accident. Todd had been running late as usual, trying to get his sorry ass to work on time. He was navigating the narrow road too fast and from all accounts must have missed the hairpin turn, causing his pick-up to careen off the embankment, exploding on impact. He never made it out of the cab, and what was left of him after the fire was put out was scraped into a body bag and sent back to Utica for an autopsy. It took hours before they could haul the burned up shell of a truck back up the embankment as onlookers watched silently. As with all locals, everyone knew him, a few actually liked him, and while nobody felt that even a punk such as himself should die that way, no one was flat out broken-hearted about it. Tabitha had spent the night at Laverne's and learned about it from the Chief of Police himself, who was accompanied by Sal. She'd broken down, partly from sadness and partly, though she'd never admit it, from relief that he'd never hurt her again. She cried half the morning, while holding her daughter and leaning on both Laverne and Charlie. It wasn't until Trista arrived that she was forced to pull herself together. Trista didn't allow her time to wallow, she told her that she had some things for her in her truck and to come down and see what they were. Tabitha and Laverne followed her back down the stairs while Charlie stayed behind with his daughter. Once they were outside, Trista turned and face the young woman and gave her a direct order.

"Dry your tears Tabby; you've already shed too many on someone who never deserved you or your love. He's gone, and there's nothing that will change that fact. I want you to take what I have in these boxes and wear them proudly. I bought them for myself when I was pregnant, but I never got a chance to remove the sales tags and wear them; but that's a story for another time. You are pregnant, and I want you to take these and wear them, and show the world how beautiful you are, both inside and out. A few were given to me, but most are brand new. I expect to see one of these outfits on you tomorrow when you show up for work. You hear me!"

"But I've got to make arrangements to bury Todd," she said allowing her words to drift off as she saw the look on both Laverne and Trista's face.

"We will take care of the arrangements and the cost. You need to focus on three people and three people only, Honey. Focus on yourself, Penelope and your unborn son; let us take care of the rest. And let your friend Charlie help you when he offers," she added for good measure.

In that moment, Laverne realized that she not only had an ally but she'd gained a best friend. Tabitha realized that her co-workers were not only her support system and her friends; they were the family that she'd never had. She nodded in agreement and smiled for the first time that day when she saw her daughter being carried outside by

Charlie. Her Charlie who'd never stopped loving her in spite of the million times she'd rejected him and in spite of the horribly stupid mistakes she'd made in the last three years of her life.

The look on Tabitha's face when she saw Charlie carrying her daughter did not go unnoticed by anyone. Trista noticed and smiled to herself. She helped lift some of the clothing out of the bags and showed Tabitha what she was giving her. There were designer shirts, casual and formal ones, long-sleeved and short-sleeved and a magnitude of colors and styles. Trista didn't want her going through all of them here, but wanted to make sure that she sorted through them at home in the company of Charlie and her daughter. Trista had put "gifts" in many of the pockets, for Tabitha to find at a later date. She had pulled Laverne aside and insisted that she'd take care of the funeral costs for Todd, even though she'd never met him. When Laverne had adamantly fought her, she shut her down quickly and efficiently. When Laverne later told Sal about her gesture, he told Laverne to let her do it, and that maybe it was her way of buying into the community so to speak. Sal made a mental note that maybe it was time to find out a little more about his new bartender.

Sal told Tabitha to stay home for another day or two and that she'd be paid for her time off. Trista offered to fill in for Tabby, even though she conceded that her waitressing skills were quite rusty. Sal took her up on her offer and when she came into the restaurant at noon; he pulled her aside to chat for a minute.

"That wasn't necessary you know. I don't know who you are or what your deal is Trista, but what you did for our girl was very kind, and generous. I insist that you allow me to split the costs with you. Todd might have been a scumbag and a low-life, but his parents have absolutely no money and certainly don't have any extra to spend on burying their child. I'm sure that they'll be very appreciative of the fact that they don't have to take out a loan for funeral expenses.

"So I assume that he didn't have a life insurance policy that our Tabitha will be entitled to?"

Sal almost laughed. "Ah, no. Todd barely had a pot to piss in, and if I didn't pad Tabby's paycheck here and there, they wouldn't even have enough to put food on the table. I know it sounds horrible to say, but she's almost better off without him. Maybe now she'll end up with the one she should have stayed with in the first place."

She reached over and gently touched her boss's hand. "You're a good man Salvatore."

He leaned toward her, and patted her back. "So are you, you know. I don't know what your real story is Trista, but I do know that you're a very generous and kind woman and when someone becomes your friend, that matters to you and you're very loyal. And I'm just speculating here, but I also bet that once someone wrongs you, they're an enemy for life. Am I correct?"

She looked into the eyes of someone who appeared to look into her soul. She took a moment before responding.

"I care very much about Tabitha, Laverne, Charlie and you Sal; even if you are a little rough around the edges," she winked. "I would hate to have anything happen to the people in my life that matter to me," she said slowly, making sure she worded it correctly. "And I wouldn't necessarily forgive anyone who hurt my friends. If something happened to those people, I can't honestly say I'd feel bad for them," she finished, all the while smiling. He took in not so much what she said, but how she said it. He knew that there was more to his new bartender than met the eye; and that he'd look into who Trista really was first thing in the morning.

The evening went much more smoothly than anyone had anticipated. Charlie stayed home with Tabitha and their daughter until her parents made it in from North Carolina where they'd moved to escape the cold Adirondack winters. He'd insisted that he'd take care of her from then on, and Sal knew that no truer words had been spoken. Although a life had been lost at a very early age, he couldn't help but think that Todd's passing had opened up the door to so many others' futures. Trista had been correct in her assessment that her waitressing abilities were a little rusty. By the time supper was in full swing, either everyone was aware of the situation or she'd adjusted to the rhythm because the dinner rush went off without a hitch. She made her way back to her tiny cabin in the woods only after she was certain that Tabitha was okay. She went about her usual routine, which was checking on the chickens, taking whatever eggs they'd decided to give up, feeding her pigs, warming up the supper that she'd brought home from the bar. She entered her house and knew immediately that someone had been inside. Nothing was out of place but the air felt wrong. She knew that someone had gone through her things and although nothing seemed out of order, she went through each and every drawer in her tiny home. She had picked up a new phone the week before, and toyed with calling her cop sister. What would she tell her, that nothing was missing but she thought someone had been there, been inside her home? Knowing how ridiculous that sounded, she kept her thoughts and suspicions to herself, but knew that she'd be purchasing trail cams in the morning to add to her collection of security measures. She ate her dinner quickly, and then called Sal. He answered on the second ring.

"Can we possibly meet for coffee first thing in the morning?"

Though immediately on alert, he kept his voice calm. "Sure. Everything okay out there?" he asked gently.

"Yeah, yeah, I'm fine. Checked on the girls and my boys, and now tucked in like a bug in a rug. Fire's stoked and I'm heating up the care package you sent me home with. I just wanted to talk to you about a few things if that's okay?"

Curious to see for himself how she was living, he cornered her before she had a chance to say no. "Great, I'll grab some donuts and be there by 8."

"Where?"

Ignoring her question, he continued right on talking, making plans for the morning. "Hey Trista, do you like sausage & biscuits? I know it's a southern thing, but our diner makes the best! So if it's alright with you, you provide the coffee and tea, and I'll grab some donuts and sausage & biscuits and be at your place by 8:30 at the latest."

Hesitating for just a moment, Trista countered; "Oh Sal that's not necessary. I live pretty far off the road, and your truck would need a front-end alignment after trying to make it back here. Besides, I doubt you'd find me the way the roads currently are; nothing's marked and there are numerous twists and turns in the road. I just haven't had time to mark them so people can find me," she lied, trying to save face.

"Ah shit Trista, remember who you're talking to. I grew up here. And anyone who did knows where the old Carver place is. Mrs. Carver was our first-grade teacher and was loved by everyone, so yes, I know how to get out to your place. Just because your roads aren't clearly marked doesn't mean you're impossible to find. You realize that now, don't you? And if that's the reason you'd like to talk to me in the morning, the answer is yes Trista, yes I can help. But you'll have to be honest with me. About everything..."

She ignored what he said, but did in fact let it sink in. She also knew that maybe it was time to gain an ally. Her only response was "Yes, I like sausage and biscuits. Guess I'll see you tomorrow morning. But," she added, "if you get your sorry ass lost and my biscuits arrive cold, I'll be pissed; so be on time and don't get too lost."

He laughed. "Good night, Trista. I'll see you in the morning. Oh, and Trista, make sure you lock your doors."

"Always do." She ended the call and looked around her tiny cabin. She knew that she could confide in Sal. Probably could tell him just about anything and he wouldn't judge her nor think less of her; but she knew that she'd never reveal any of the truth about her past. She'd just ask him for assistance in beefing up security around her compound, that's all. And maybe ask if he knew of anyone wanting to sell or give away a puppy or full-grown dog for that matter. She'd take it as long as it was relatively large, young, and trainable. Scary, she thought to herself, she really was starting to put down roots in this quiet little town nestled in the heart of the Adirondack Mountains.

In the short time that she'd been there, she'd managed to climb Bald Mountain which allowed her a bird's eye view from McCauley Mountain all the way to nearly the end of Fourth Lake. Since buying the cabin, she'd learned from the locals that the Fulton Chain of Lakes consisted of Old Forge Pond, the Channel, and then First through Eighth Lakes. Boats were able to go from Old Forge all the way to Inlet, where Fourth Lake ended. Portage was required to continue on to Fifth through Eighth Lakes. The largest share of summer and year round camps were located on First and Fourth Lakes, but both the North Shore (Route 28 side) and the South Shore were lined with camps, cabins, and mega mansions. She'd seen the nightly crowds lined up at the ice cream stand which was strategically positioned across from the Enchanted Forest. When passing through town at 7pm, the time that the water park closed, she didn't envy the poor kids working at the ice cream shop as the lines of people were twenty deep. She'd managed to visit many of the stores in town, and especially enjoyed her time spent in the Hardware Store. She had purchased the yarn to make Tabitha's baby blanket there but also had managed to drop a couple of hundred dollars on things she didn't know she needed. The store had been in the same family for over 100 years, and the family-friendly atmosphere was evident in every aisle. She had enjoyed a cold beer and hot pizza at the local pizza joint in town as she people-watched one Sunday afternoon, and had made it a point to discover various cross country trails to maintain her training routine. Running the ski trails up McCauley Mountain was her favorite thus far.

When she confirmed that everything was locked up and secure she retired for the night, but found that she couldn't sleep. She had Xanax and Ambien but never liked taking anything that would dull her senses. She knew how crucial it was to always be 100% focused. Instead of sleeping, she lay in bed allowing her mind to wander from one topic to another, and for the first time since she'd left Utica, she wondered how her beloved, now ex-husband was making out in prison. He'd been sent downstate and was incarcerated in a maximum-security facility. If she never heard from him or his family again, that was okay. She had heard that his mother and her team of lawyers was still fighting the verdict and seeking an appeal; she didn't care though as long as they left her alone. When she'd moved out of Utica, she'd left no forwarding address; her last few bills were to be sent to her attorney to be settled. She'd cancelled her credit cards and severed all ties with anyone and everyone from her former home. It was more that she needed to, than wanted to. With her husband incarcerated and her life in shambles, it was time for Jasmine to go away and Trista to rise from the ashes, just like a phoenix. She might have been knocked down like she had been in the past, but as always, she got up and came out on top. Sometimes it took people crossing her to have them truly understand what a strong woman she was, and exactly what she was capable of doing.

She finally drifted off to sleep thinking about what she could do to make Tabitha's life a little easier. She had given slight consideration to asking Tabitha to move in with her not only for the company but also to save the young mother from paying rent. She quickly dismissed that idea as she needed to lead a solitary life, and it was better for those close to her to remain at arm's length. She slept soundly, dreaming of black unicorns and fairies. She soared higher and higher on her winged friend and when she woke, she knew that it had been a sign that someone was trying to get too close. That was something that she'd never let happen. She rose before the sun crested the horizon, stoked her woodstove again, and took a quick shower. The cool fall air caught her off guard and she knew that she'd probably have to break down and turn on the electric heat soon. Once clean and dressed for the day, she ventured outside to feed her chickens and Porky and Delilah, the names she'd given her pigs. She was just heading back inside the cabin when she heard the tell-tale sign of someone's truck heading down her road. She glanced at her watch and noted that Sal was not only punctual, but slightly early. She waved as she set down the pail that she'd been carrying and walked over to meet him. He, being a native of the area, appeared unfazed by the sudden drop in temperature, as he stepped out of his truck with a light-weight Carhart jacket, which was unzipped and didn't appear to even have a lining to it. Trista, on the other hand was dressed in a turtleneck with Under Armor underneath, and her favorite LLBean lined three- season jacket. As usual she was wearing her silly red wig and the more he looked at her and saw her in it, the more he was curious to know what color her hair was. He didn't know why, he thought now as he smiled; and got out of his truck, but with her coloring, he'd bet his bar that she was a natural blonde.

"Well good morning, Trista," he said jovially, taking a quick mental inventory of his surroundings. She'd done a lot of work on the place since they'd taken old Mrs. Carver out of it on a gurney six months prior. He surveyed the new fencing around the barn and chicken coop, the repairs that had been made to both the barn siding and roof, and the very high-end security lights that glistened in the early morning sunlight. With the camp being nearly 100 years old and showing every bit of its centennial age, the brand new motion sensors stuck out like a sore thumb, even to an untrained eye, which his was not. She approached his truck, took one of the Styrofoam containers from his arms, lifted it to her nose to take in the amazing aroma coming from it, and letting her guard down just briefly, she genuinely smiled.

"Wow, this smells amazing. Good idea," she said as she turned to walk inside. He started to follow her, and out of the corner of his eye, in that one brief second, saw what he thought was a quick flash of light reflecting off something metallic in the woods. He tried to hone in on what the source was, but as quickly as he saw it, it was gone. His cop instincts kicked in and he knew that at this point he didn't want to get the local authorities, even though they were all his friends and excellent cops, involved. He needed to dig into Trista's past and didn't need someone else snooping into it as well. But if his hunch was right, Trista did in fact have someone out there to be concerned about. And he wasn't about to let someone hurt another one of his employees.

They entered her cabin, and she motioned for him to hang his jacket on the peg next to the other coats. She already had the table set for their breakfast, and he smelled the coffee in the percolator as soon as he entered. No sooner had they sat down, when her tea pot started whistling and they both jumped up to get it. She chuckled and motioned for him to sit back down as she poured him a cup of coffee, black, the way she'd observed that he always drank it at work. She'd noticed that even late at night when he was bartending, Sal sipped on coffee, and occasionally from the bottle of water close by. She then got her cup of tea, which he noticed wasn't some dainty flower infused tea but a robust smelling Earl Grey. He had never thought for one minute that the woman he'd hired, with Laverne's coaxing, had been any kind of wallflower. Looking around her cabin only confirmed what he'd already known.

They enjoyed their meal from Walt's with Trista making a mental note to stop by the diner more often for breakfast. They'd talked about how Laverne had come to work for him, with Sal enjoying telling part of the circumstances, knowing that Laverne would have her own spin that she'd want to share. Trista had already deduced that they'd been lovers at one time, though she didn't think that they still were, and that he still had a very soft spot in his heart for her. He'd told of literally running into her one dark night as she was traveling north toward Lake Placid to meet up with her band for a gig. After plowing her beat up car into his brand new truck, she never made it to Lake Placid, nor ever left Old Forge. He'd given her grief for driving in a blizzard on bald tires, not suited for winter driving. She'd broken down sobbing and being strapped for cash, he offered her a room for the night. He laughed when he said that he'd opened his door for the night, and she'd never left; which was only partially true. They might have been lovers years ago, but that part of their story was over. But the part about her staying was true. She'd taken the job he'd offered her, and was not only his waitress, but also his business partner. He knew that she was the heart and soul of the ADK Bar & Grill, along with being the one who still held his heart. She listened intently as he spoke of Laverne, and she thought to herself that he didn't even realize that he was still in love with the woman whom he'd befriended nearly two decades before. She noticed that he spoke about everyone who worked for him, and told bits of their life stories but never really talked much about himself. She knew that they were both dancing around what they really both wanted to know. So she'd make the first move.

"So what made you leave the force and become a restaurateur?" she asked, never breaking eye contact. She saw the surprised look of recognition flash, ever so briefly in his eyes, and then it was gone. Knowing that she'd been right about her hunch, she waited for him to answer, curious as to whether or not he'd tell her the truth.

He said nothing. Instead he slowly pushed his chair back from the table, careful to avoid scratching her wood floor. He lifted up his jeans leg, revealing a scar that started above his shin, ran across and around his kneecap, and continued up his leg. He simply said, "That," and nothing else, until he'd pulled his jeans back into place, collected the memories rushing through his head, and picked up his half-full coffee cup again. Now it was his turn.

"Why'd you leave the military," he asked, more on a hunch than any real information that he'd had time to dig up yet. She'd known that he'd have checked her out, and up until this point had honestly been curious as to how much he'd be able to unearth. She looked into the eyes of someone who probably had a bullshit radar as well-honed as hers was, and said nothing. She pushed her chair out as he had done moments before, unbuttoned her cotton flannel shirt, allowing it to fall partially off her shoulders, and revealed a nasty looking keloid scar across her shoulder and halfway down her arm.

"That. They said I could stay in, pushing pencils at a desk job. I told them thanks but no thanks and got my honorable discharge and a ranking of 80% disabled. Uncle Sam sends me my check every month, and all's good," she said with more enthusiasm than she was hoping to convey.

"I see. So when were you in and what branch; if you don't mind me asking?" he asked softly.

"It was a long time ago," she said as softly as he had asked. "I was a Marine," and offered no more.

"Semper Fi. And I believe, once a Marine, always a Marine."

She looked up at the man sitting across the table from her. She saw the look of understanding in his eyes and knew from his look, that he too had been in. "I went in right out of high school. I was a mechanic. But it seems like light years ago," she added, glancing away as if lost in her own thoughts.

"What'd you do after the Marines?"

"I finished my nursing degree, why? I had attended BOCES while in high school and was an LPN upon graduation. I always loved tinkering on cars and engines though, so didn't pursue nursing until I was forced to leave the military."

"So you're a nurse?"

"Technically yes; but I haven't worked as a nurse in quite some time. It never was for me. I like bartending much better," she kidded. Attempting to steer the conversation away from herself, she started asking Sal personal questions as openly as he had questioned her.

"What about you Sal? How do you go from being big-time cop to bartender/restaurateur?"

"Well, I did my time and realized that while I enjoyed the structure of the military, I was not cut out to be a lifer; so I got my discharge and I went almost immediately into the academy. Since I was an MP while active duty, it was easy to transition to the police department. I loved being a cop, even more than serving our country. I expected to retire after I did my twenty but barely made it ten before a punk ruined my career when he decided to blow out my knee. And as you said, it was light years ago."

Sitting up, he looked her straight in the eyes. "It's not that I don't love your company, but what's the real reason that you asked me to join you for breakfast this morning Trista? And," he figured there was no time like the present, "Trista certainly is a beautiful name, but the funny thing about it, is that it is as if you don't exist. There's no record of you anywhere. And yes, before you go and get your panties in a wad, I check out everybody who joins the payroll; call it a safety precaution. And when I ran your info, it tells me about a little girl who existed up until age 12 who then disappears." He looked at her, waiting to hear how she'd respond.

"Wow," she chuckled, "we're back on the topic of me again? There's nothing to tell, and your sources are incorrect. I'm sitting in front of you, in flesh and blood, and my life's an open book," she winked. "But to answer your question about why I asked you over for such a delightful breakfast, it's simple; I was wondering if you could point me in the direction of where I could buy some trail cams? I am pretty remote out here and would feel more comfortable if I had a better understanding of what is in these woods." She shifted her position in her seat, knowing that she'd come to a pivotal point in her friendship with her boss. She could either lie, which she was extremely proficient, or she could trust him with the truth or at least part of the truth. "I was born Trista Carpenter, and you are correct, it was my name up until I was placed in foster care at age 12. When I was adopted, my new family felt that I'd assimilate better if I had their name. They asked me if I'd like to change my first name, and I did. They were the best thing that ever happened to me, and still to this day, I thank God every night in my prayers for bringing us together. I reverted back to my original birth name because," she squirmed a little in her seat, "after my divorce from a very cruel, controlling man, I wanted to make a clean break. In the few years that I was married to him, he'd never known that I had been raised with a different name; so I thought if I became that person again, odds were in my favor that he, nor anyone for that matter, wouldn't be able to find me easily. And no," she said before he could say a word, "my moving here and being employed in your bar does not put the townsfolk or my co-workers in danger. He's currently in prison, and when I left the area, I was extremely efficient in severing all ties and contacts from my previous life. I just want to live here in the woods, and write books. I'm almost done with my first one, and would love to have you critique it sometime. I know you love to read; I've seen the books you hide behind the bar, on your truck bench and above your visor."

He listened to her and from research and brick walls that he'd hit, knew that she was not only very intelligent, but correct in her assessment. She had not only covered her tracks in making whoever she was prior to arriving in Old Forge disappear, she'd been very methodical and left absolutely no paper trail.

"I know that you would never intentionally bring trouble to my bar and I know what you did for Tabitha and yes, don't even say a word about it, Laverne and I will be contributing to the funeral expenses. When you care about someone, you are very caring and giving; and no matter what has happened in your past Trista, I will always believe that you have a loving, generous heart. But I also see a lot of me in you. You don't take anything at face value; you need to decipher and evaluate everything to your satisfaction. I'm the same way so I know that you've got many secrets that you want to keep buried. Even though it's very hard for me to ignore that fact, I want you to know. I won't dig any further. Whatever your past holds, it can remain buried as far as I'm concerned," he said with a smile. "That is as long as you're not some serial killer who's hiding bodies out here in the woods," he chuckled, squeezing her hand.

"Then I guess we're both safe," she laughed. "Thank you Sal," she said with more sincerity than she'd expressed in a long time. "There are no bodies out here, except for the breathing kind, and they're in their respective pens," she assured him. "Yet," she silently replied, all the while smiling.

Changing the topic to the real reason she'd asked him out to her home on a very chilly Sunday morning, she told him about how she thought that maybe someone had been snooping around her cabin. She didn't tell him that she knew for a fact that they'd been inside and rifled through her belongings. She told him that she'd like to purchase some trail cams and asked if he knew of any store between Old Forge and Blue Mountain that might carry them. He told her where the best places to look for them were and when she said that she was planning on shopping for them that morning, he told her, (didn't ask her), that he and Laverne would bring a late lunch and they'd be back by 2 to help her install them. She knew it was useless to argue, so she thanked him. She also asked if he'd possibly walk her boundaries with her when he returned, to which he gladly agreed. He wanted to get back to the area where he'd seen something reflective in the woods anyway. As he got up to leave her, she thanked him again for the fantastic breakfast. Putting his coat on, he turned back to her and mentioned casually that Charlie's dog happened to have a litter of puppies a few months back and he'd sold or given away all but two puppies. If she was really planning on putting down roots in their little community, maybe she should consider getting a dog to keep her company. She dismissed the idea but told Sal as he was heading out her door that she'd at least consider it. Just as he was about to get into his truck, her curiosity got the better of her.

"Hey Sal, what kind of dog?" hoping it was some kind of toy something or other so she could eliminate the idea altogether.

"Shepherd-Lab mix," he shouted back. "They sure are cute, and I sure would feel better about you being out here all alone if I knew you had a dog" he added as he shut his truck door and headed down her dirt drive.

"Shit," she thought, as she envisioned what the puppies looked like, knowing that they'd be adorable, especially since German Shepherd and Labs were her two favorite breeds.

She watched his truck disappear as it headed down the drive and out of sight and thought about becoming a dog owner. She'd always wanted a dog but up until that point in her life, had never had one that she could call her own. She sat back down and evaluated the pros and cons of owning a dog, and a large dog at that. When she got up to make herself another cup of tea, she glanced outside to see if the predicted rain had started to fall. She caught movement out of the corner of her eye, and immediately reacted. It took her 8 seconds to retrieve her shotgun, fling open the front door, and fire off a shot. She allowed the echo of the shot to disappear and screamed at the unknown entity she knew was lurking in the woods, her woods.

"You want me? Then fucking come and get me, you coward!" She found herself hyperventilating and furious that someone was toying with her. She just wanted to be left alone, and quite honestly, had no idea who would be snooping around her property. She kept a low profile and knew that she'd covered her tracks when she'd left the Utica area. She was truly stumped about who could be stalking her. She waited in silence but knew that no one would answer her. She saw no further movement in the woods and, though she was mad enough to become the stalker, she was wise enough not to follow her knee jerk reaction and go off chasing shadows. She stood her ground a few more seconds holding the shotgun at her side, but the woods remained silent. She surveyed the area one last time and, satisfied that whoever was out there was no longer within striking distance, she went back inside.

It took her awhile, but she was finally able to settle in to her favorite chair and return to her computer, rereading the last few pages that she'd typed. She had started her novel back when her life started falling apart. Back then, putting words on paper had been a cathartic process, one that allowed her to escape the realities of what her life had become. She had always had a passion for fantasy, as evidenced by the imaginary black unicorn that had been her salvation since childhood; so it was easy to guess what genre it would be when she decided to write her book. As the words flowed and characters within the pages started to develop personalities, it became almost immediately apparent that she had been destined to become a writer all along. Trista couldn't believe how much joy she felt when she sat with her laptop building her storyline. Her black unicorn took on a life of its own and, gearing her book towards adolescents, she enjoyed the adventures and mishaps that the characters encountered along the way. When she doubted herself and her ability to write about subject matter that she herself had no exposure to, or experience with, (having never had a teenager of her own), she quickly thought of Tabitha and Charlie and knew that she could use them as examples and for guidance. She took a few more swigs of her tea and kept on typing.

Before she realized it, she heard the tell-tale sound of Sal's truck once again making its way down her drive. Glancing at her watch, she was shocked to realize that she'd been typing for almost four hours straight. Once she stood to allow her guests entrance, her extremely full bladder informed her that she had, in fact, sat far too long. She opened the front door and retreated to her bathroom, shutting the door behind her. Laverne and Sal could be heard entering her tiny cabin with Laverne chuckling almost the entire time.

"Honey," she shouted out, "you just take your time in there but where am I gonna find a bottle opener?" she inquired. "Oh, and Trista I sure do hope that you're hungry cause we brought enough for an army. Sal said we are going hiking before we chow down," she continued as if she was talking directly to her. She didn't hear Sal yet, but figured that Laverne was doing enough talking for the two of them. She shouted out which drawer to open for the bottle opener; finished up in the bathroom and made her way back into her living room. She was greeted by Laverne, Sal and the cutest little fur ball that she'd ever seen. As if on cue, the puppy ran up to her side. Trista immediately crouched down to greet the little black and tan puppy who climbed into her lap, yipping excitedly. She looked up at Laverne and Sal who remained silent as they watched her interact with the puppy, with Sal finally speaking up.

"Charlie said that this little guy was the runt and no one seemed to like his coloring, so he's the only one left in the litter. He was thinking that if anyone would take him off his hands, he'd be very appreciative since he'd decided to take him to the pound. I told him that maybe I should bring him out here for you to at least take a look at. You said that you were thinking about a dog, and I thought that maybe before this little guy was shipped off to his imminent death, we should bring him out here to you. He's got the makings of being a good guard dog, and with paws the size that he has, I'm sure that he won't stay a runt for too long." Watching her hold the puppy, without even realizing that she'd cradled the pup in her arms and was standing back up as if holding an infant, he continued. "I sure know I'd sleep better at night if I knew you had some kind of protection out here, other than that flimsy spotlight," he winked.

"You two steamrolled me, didn't you?" she said, all the while smiling and rocking the puppy who'd nearly fallen asleep in her arms already. "You knew damn well that I'd pick this little guy up and bam, it'd be all over!"

Laverne was the first to speak. "Well, actually no; but I was hoping. It seems our Charlie has gotten himself an instant family. He's stepped right up to help Tabitha and her little girl, whom you might have already figured out, is his little girl; and well, he's moving them into his house, lock, stock and barrel. She's insistent that they're only friends and it's completely platonic, but if I know Charlie, he'll be trying to put a wedding ring on her finger before too long. He certainly doesn't need any more mouths to feed of the four-legged sort, when he's going to have two ladies to take care of."

"He is so cute, but it wouldn't be fair to this little guy to be crated when I'm at work. He deserves better than being locked in a cage for hours on end."

Sal spoke up. "I couldn't agree with you more." Seeing her immediate expression, he continued. "You'll bring him with you to the bar when you're working. I have an extra crate in the back office and he can have the run of the place."

"You sure?" she asked, knowing that she was already half in love with the little guy but refusing to give in so easily. She pushed the puppy back out toward Laverne, putting on a pout for their benefit. "I really don't think that it's a good idea," she insisted.

"Sure you do. You've already picked out a name for him, and we both know it."

"Well he does sort of look like a Remmy, like in Remington. What do you think?" she said as she held the puppy in her arms. He yipped as if in agreement.

Seizing the opportunity, Sal clapped his hands together in celebration. "Well it's settled then. Remmy it is; welcome to the neighborhood. I'm so glad that you're going to give this puppy such a great home. Just don't introduce him to your chickens quite yet, not sure if they'd get along."

Realizing that she'd definitely been conned, Trista smiled and didn't object. She put the puppy down just long enough to give them both a hug. Knowing that they'd come to her house to walk her property lines, she immediately started searching for something to use as a leash for her new friend. Even before she said anything, Laverne was pulling a new leash from her purse and handing it over to her. "Should have known," she thought to herself, smiling. "Yup, she'd definitely been conned."

The three of them walked the perimeter of her property with Remmy in tow. They spooked a few quail, and pheasants, and many deer but found no signs of intruders, until they were heading back toward her cabin. She saw it, even before his trained eye did. She thought at first that it was a dent or divot in the tree, but as they honed in on the tree catching her attention, everyone quickly realized that it certainly wasn't a naturally-occurring phenomenon. Though it was partially camouflaged, there fastened to the tree, directly facing Trista's cabin in the woods was a trail cam. It was still recording. The three stood surrounding the tree and its' unwelcome equipment with Trista doing everything she could to control her temper. She wanted nothing more than to shoot the damn thing, but Sal instantly redirected her anger to something more proactive and helpful in determining who was behind the invasion into her life.

"Stop. I know what you're thinking and want to do; but stop! What good would it do to blow the thing apart? You won't find out who put it there if you blow it up. Instead, remember that turnabout is fair play, so why not monitor whoever is monitoring you?" Pulling out the newly- acquired trail cam that he'd brought with him, Sal pointed to a tree directly in line with not only her home, but the tree currently holding the intruder's surveillance equipment. As she listened to Sal speak, she knew that he was right. It didn't make her less furious that someone had the balls to not only be on her property, but on her property and spying on her. She'd racked her brain on more than one occasion trying to figure out who and why someone was spying on her and what they could possibly want. She knew that she'd completely covered her tracks and knew that there was no way anyone could tie her to Mandi's unfortunate demise. That she was sure of. She also knew that if her ex-husband's entire team of attorneys couldn't steer the investigation toward anyone other than her beloved Nathaniel, there would be no reason that anyone would be monitoring her because of the murder. She truly didn't understand who or why she was being stalked or by whom, but knew that once her camera picked up who it was, that person would be taken care of; and cease to be of any concern to her.

"You're right Sal. Let's put it up on the tree that you think is best. And you'll keep an eye out for any strangers that seem to stay around longer than the typical tourist? And," she asked innocently, "I know that you're not technically on the force here in town, but do you have enough connections that one of your friends could possibly run a tag?"

"Possibly, why do you ask?"

"No particular reason; except that when I first came here I thought I might have been followed. I haven't seen that particular SUV since. But I have the plate numbers if you would be interested."

"Sure. You wrote down the plate number of someone two months ago and still have it somewhere?"

"Nah, I didn't write it down; it's here," she said, tapping her head. "Numbers are my thing, and they're easy to remember," she smiled.

Surprised, he kept his thoughts to himself, and responded casually. "Yeah, why don't you give it to me. I suppose it wouldn't hurt to find out who owns it and where they're from."

"See, I told ya she was a smart one," Laverne added. Up to this point, she had remained silent, still holding the leash controlling an overly-zealous puppy. Both Sal and Trista seemed to snap back to the moment after each allowing their minds to wander. They acknowledged her, with Sal speaking up.

"Okay, then. How about we attach the camera right here and, unless you were looking for it, whoever's snooping around your woods will have no clue it's out here. I'd say give it a week Trista, and we'll know who your intruder is."

Though Trista knew in her mind that her "unwanted guest" would be out of the way long before the week was up, she nodded in agreement and helped Sal position the trail cam precisely at the right angle to get the job done. When they had it secured, they partially camouflaged it and started heading back toward her cabin. The puppy had been so well behaved, despite his unwavering energy, that Trista bent down and freed him from the confines of his leash, allowing him to take off running, sniffing, and marking as many trees as he could. They walked in relative silence as they made their way back, with the puppy not far behind. She figured that no animal should have to be restrained on their own land so she might as well get the puppy used to freedom, though limited, and also to following commands. Once inside, Laverne asked for direction about how to warm the food they'd brought with them. They warmed up the food in Trista's antiquated but very dependable microwave, had a few beers and enjoyed each other's company for another hour or so before Trista politely shooed her company away, feigning a headache. Her real motivation for sending her friends away was to allow herself a few hours of daylight to finalize the plan that she'd already started formulating in her mind. Once they left, she immediately put her old work boots back on, opened the door for her new companion and headed back outside. While walking her property earlier, they'd discovered several interesting things about her newly acquired property that she hadn't been aware of, including the presence of two old dug wells no longer in use, and the remnants of an old hunting cabin in the far back corner of her land. She took Remmy back to the shack first, making sure they steered clear of the camera that she now knew was watching her cabin. She poked around the building, absorbing every detail.

Realizing that the structure was actually much more stable than she'd first thought, she surmised that it might come in handy, should she figure out who her unwanted guest was. She then made her way back, slowing on occasion for Remmy to catch up. When she came to the first of the two abandoned wells, the solution came to her. She pushed off the heavy wooden lid that had served to protect anyone from falling down the long shaft. Not quite sure how deep the well was or if it still held any water, she leaned over the opening, dropped a rock down the shaft and waited. "One Mississippi, two Mississippi, three Mississippi, four" she counted, waiting to hear a splash or thud. It took eight seconds before she heard the thud. Although saddened that the old well no longer held any water, she realized that maybe that would work to her advantage. She actually laughed out loud as her plan came together. She peered into the darkness of what would become someone's permanent resting place; she hoped it would happen sooner, rather than later.

"You want to mess with me?" she said out loud, talking to her new best friend, as Remmy stared at her as if he understood her every word. "Be forewarned sucker, you have absolutely no idea who you're messing with, but you will when I figure out who you are..."

~~~ Chapter 23 ~~~

Within a week, everything had returned to normal at the restaurant. Trista was back behind the bar where she was much more comfortable, Tabby was back, despite the objections of her parents when she refused to move with them down south, and Charlie was in heaven, being able to drive Tabitha to and from work every day and spending just about each waking moment with her. He was madly in love with the girl, and yet Tabitha had no clue. Her daughter idolized the man that she knew as her mommy's friend. While Charlie was already planning for their future, Tabitha was just trying to come to terms with the fact that she no longer had to live each and every day in fear. After Charlie and Tabby had left for the evening, and while Laverne, Sal and Trista were cleaning and closing up for the night, Sal casually brought up the findings from the investigation into Todd's accident.

"Funny thing about how that kid, though he was a punk, died. Seems that his brake line was faulty, that is kinda weird, wouldn't you think, for someone who worked on cars for a living?" he stated more than asked.

Trista didn't show any kind of surprise or reaction whatsoever. She thought about his statement for not even a second and simply responded, her voice and expression void of any emotion.

"Not really Sal; you know the old expression, the carpenter's house is always the one falling down, the painter's house is the one unpainted etc., etc. I would think it's the same for a mechanic; their vehicles are the ones always in need of a tune-up or maintenance. I'm sure that whatever the investigation revealed showed that it was just a tragic accident, and nothing more. And while it's sad that a young life was cut short, there's nothing that can be done about it right? So I for one think the topic should be left alone and stay dead and buried, just like the police report will be and Todd already is. Don't you agree?" she added, making direct contact with her employer and friend.

For a split second he could have sworn that he'd seen something flicker in her eyes but as quickly as he thought he saw it, it was gone.

"You're probably right. Lord knows that's true for my brother and his house. The man's a plumber, and it's always one thing or another that's not working in his house. Go to visit the fool and I'm sometimes afraid to even flush the damn toilet."

He smiled and saw what he thought was a look of relaxation come over her face, he knew that the subject was no longer a topic for discussion. He didn't really know what to think of it, but knew that nothing good could come out of continuing to poke at the subject, so he let it drop.

They said their good nights and left in their respective vehicles, with Sal and Laverne heading south on 28, Trista turning north. She didn't go a half mile before she saw the lights behind her vehicle. She was always cognizant of who was near her vehicle, and when she felt the hair rise on her neck, she just knew. She waited until they were on a straightaway and started to slow down. Knowing that whoever was following her was in plain view, she put on her blinker and immediately pulled over, forcing the vehicle to go by her or make it very clear that he or she was in fact following her. The driver accelerated as they flew by her, but even with their increased speed, she could easily see that it was the Honda CRV with the license plate matching the one that she'd seen on the day she'd entered town. Her initial instinct was to chase them down, run them off the road or simply kick their ass when she forced them to stop the vehicle. Since she didn't know whom she was dealing with, however she decided to find out who was being a thorn in her side in a less confrontational way. She knew she could ask Sal but wanted to keep some things separate from her new life. She forced herself to turn her truck around and head back into town, where she stayed parked out of sight for a few hours before finally venturing home. She drove the last few turns to her cabin slowly, scanning every turnoff and driveway for signs of the CRV. When she finally pulled into her drive, she was mentally and physically exhausted.

Switchblade ready in her purse, she walked into her tiny abode to total darkness. She flicked her light switch and got nothing. Using her cell's flashlight, she scanned the room, and allowed Remmy to enter. The dog didn't react as if something was amiss so she didn't overreact. Knowing the age of the cabin and the substandard panel box that she had, she just assumed that she'd blown a fuse again and made her way to the basement. The stench hit her first. She quickly retreated back upstairs to the kitchen to retrieve a better lighting and once she grabbed her heavy duty flashlight, she headed back down to the basement. And that's when she found him. She had no clue who he was, or how he'd gotten there, but lying dead in her basement was a man; a man who from the looks of him had not only been dead for quite some time, but had met a very nasty death. She felt ill looking at his face and what the insects had already started to do. She knew normal people would immediately call the police, but also she knew that she was not normal and did not want the police invading her place, asking a million questions or digging up her past. No, that wouldn't do she decided. Even though she didn't know who the poor man was or how he'd come to be in her basement, she knew one thing, and that was that she needed to get rid of the body and any and all traces that he'd ever been in her house to begin with. And she set out to do just that.

It took her almost an hour to wrap John Doe up in a tarp that she found in the barn that she had not touched since moving in. She wore a double layer of gloves while working. Always one to error on the safe side, she also put on one of the wigs that she'd never worn. Even though she hated to depart with it after wearing it only once, she thought it best to make sure that there was no possible way that something containing her DNA could ever be associated with the body found on her land. Once she had him completely wrapped up, she tried to figure out what she would do with the body. In this day and age with cameras and drones everywhere, it wasn't as if she couldn't just drive to the police station and deposit a corpse on their doorstep. Nor did she dare bring him to the only medical clinic in the village. She couldn't just leave him on the side of the road not only because was it morally wrong, but there was also a possibility that even though she'd been meticulous, she could have somehow transferred some minute fiber, hair strand or piece of fingernail onto his clothing. After all, it had been pitch black when she had first gone into her basement and thinking back, she couldn't say with absolute certainty whether she'd brushed up against him. She knew that she needed to dispose of the body but where? And then it hit her. Still donning her disguise and attire, she ran up the stairs and into the spare bedroom where she kept all of her hunting gear. Within a few moments, she found what she'd been looking for. Once she had the night vision goggles in place, she set about finding the easiest way to get the body up the stairs. Although she wasn't in the same shape she'd been in while in the Marines, she still was extremely physically fit and able to bench press much more than most women her age. She looked at the tarp containing the poor man and knew there was only one way to get him up and outside. Even though the thought made her feel slightly queasy, she set about doing what needed to be done. On the silent count of three, she lifted the corpse, heaved him over her shoulder and carried him up the stairs and outside. She was sweating by the time she got him up and outside, even though the temperature had dropped down into the 40's. She laid him across her lap as she started up the four-wheeler that had come with the property, and set out toward the side yard where the deeper of her two wells was located. She knew that it was a gamble, but in her mind it was the only option she had. Someone was trying to frame her for the murder of the man currently riding across her lap, and she'd be damned if anyone would tie her to the poor man's demise. She didn't know who was out to get her, or what their game was, but she wasn't going down for something that she hadn't done. Maybe her dumbass husband wasn't smart enough to get out of jail, but she knew for a fact that she wouldn't have to worry about being accused of anything if there wasn't a body to be found.   She shut off the motor once she reached the well, and spent a few minutes listening in the silence for any sign of company. Her night vision goggles illuminated the blackened sky, and there was no sign of life other than an occasional deer. When she was satisfied that she was truly alone in the night, she set about lifting the wooden cover from the well. It was heavier than hell but at least it had held up for probably decades, she thought as she completely removed it from the well opening. Once it was out of the way, she again lifted John Doe up. Before dropping him in as gently as she could, she said a quick prayer and allowed him to slip from her arms. Not overly religious, she still found herself saddened that someone's final resting spot had to be at the bottom of her well.   She knew that she'd never know his name or the circumstances of how he came to be in her basement. She also knew that if she ever found out who'd put him there or ordered him put there, that person would join Mr. Doe at the bottom of her well, and she'd put him there herself. She waited until she heard the tell-tale thud and only then did she replace the lid to her well. She drove back the way she'd come out and put the 4-wheeler away, again checking the night for any evidence of company. Satisfied that she was still alone she went inside, poured herself a very stiff drink and after stoking the stove, and allowing Remmy to go outside one last time, she attempted to retire for the night. Lying in bed, her mind went crazy trying to figure out who was behind the dead body in her house. Whoever it was not only knew who she was and where she lived, but they obviously had a very big issue with her, big enough to want to try and frame her for murder.

As she lay tossing and turning, a home in Utica remained lighted while the owner waited for a call; a call that didn't come until nearly 8am the following morning.

"What do you mean the police never showed up? Did you or did you not tell me that you put a decaying god damn corpse in her house?" the voice screamed into the phone.

Getting tired of having to repeat himself more than once, he answered sarcastically back.

"Unless I'm stupid or you're deaf, that is exactly what I have already told you. I put the damn body right where you instructed me to. She would have to practically stumble over him to get to her panel box to reset her lights, so yes, I know that she had to have discovered it. And besides, even if she hadn't seen the old man, she sure as hell would have smelled a week old corpse; he smelled to high heaven and back."

"Don't get sarcastic or have an attitude with me you asshole," the voice screamed once more. "You could easily end up like our poor Benny did. He was easily disposable and so are you so don't fucking forget it! Have I made myself clear?"

"Crystal clear," he responded in a monotone voice, seething through his bearded face with clenched teeth.

"Good.   So can you please tell me how, if our dear Jasmine found a smelly body in her home, the police have yet to arrive? While I realize that she's not living in a large city anymore, I do assume that the police do work 24/7, even in Old Forge?" the voice asked sarcastically.

"One would assume so; but maybe even the police department rolls up the streets and calls it a night when the sun goes down.   How the hell do I know?" he responded, once again irritated by the inquisition.   All I know is that I spent the night in my damn car, half frozen to death and saw nothing.   No one came into or left from her place the entire freaking night.   So I don't know what to tell ya," he added for good measure.

"Maybe you should call the local authorities and advise them of suspicious activity around her place and just get them out there to snoop around.   I mean it's not like she could be hiding the body in plain sight."

~~~ Chapter 24 ~~~

Trista had left her new home before seven and was in and out of Lowe's in New Hartford, Home Depot in

South Utica, and Lowe's in Riverside Center and back on the road north before 8:30AM. She'd purchased the supplies that she had been looking for, along with several other items that were more for distraction purposes; paying cash for all of her purchases. One nice thing about working in a restaurant, whether it was bartending or waitressing, was that most of one's income was in the form of cash. For obvious reasons that was the payment of choice for her. She'd picked up framing material to use to shape the patio that she wanted to make, along with several flowers and bushes that she wanted to plant before the frost came, to add to the drab exterior of her new home. She didn't need to buy a mixing trough for the concrete since she had several wheel barrows in the pole barn that were essentially brand new. Once back home, she took a walk out to where she'd set up the trail cam, and once Remmy finished running off some of his energy, she called him to her side and returned to the house and her computer to view what the camera had recorded. Satisfied after viewing only creatures with four legs not two, she felt comfortable that she could start the task at hand and be able to complete it unobserved. She used the four-wheeler to bring the concrete, and water out to the well; having already wheeled the wheelbarrow, shovel and trough out when she went for her initial reconnaissance. It was still early on a weekday and the woods remained as quiet as the streets had been in town.

With the kids back in school and the leaves not quite at their peak yet, the town was quiet for a change. From what everyone had told her, it was just a matter of time before the stores and streets would again be bustling with the sound of tourists, up to take in the gorgeous fall foliage and to attend events such as Brewfest and the Old Forge Marathon. She knew that lack of tourists meant lack of income for people in the retail industry and restaurant business such as herself, but she wasn't concerned about having less pocket change, she needed very little to sustain the self-imposed low maintenance life style that she'd incorporated. She thought of what Nathaniel and his bitch of a mother would say if only they could see her now, living in squander as she would call it, working as a bar keep no less, and wearing generic clothing purchased off a rack from a chain store, not a boutique. In a way, the thought appealed to her, as she finished up mixing water to the concrete powder and stirring it to the desired consistency; she almost wished that they could see her, actually see her living life the way she wanted to, without pretenses or fake friends, without having to have her nails, hair and makeup perfect at a moment's notice, and most importantly, without having to be someone that she wasn't. Nathaniel had never asked or wanted her to change, or at least in the beginning he hadn't; but then somehow, sometime over the course of their marriage, it became apparent that it was expected that she conform to their way of life and she slowly was forced into the mold of a pseudo Stepford Wife. From the country clubs, theatre and endless charity functions that were more about who was wearing what and writing their check for what; than about the charity or organization that they were supposed to be helping. Sure their monetary donation mattered, but to Jasmine, it was just as important in her opinion that people donate more than just their money; she thought that they should donate their time as well. Once she had mentioned that she'd like to volunteer at the hospital, rocking the babies in the nursery or on the pediatric unit; but when her mother-in-law had heard about it, she squashed the idea immediately and permanently, stating that "people of their status couldn't be seen coddling someone else's bastard child." Not one to rock the boat, she didn't pursue the topic any further, but secretly substantially increased her quarterly donation to the pediatric unit.

Once the concrete was starting to set she pushed the wheelbarrow as close to the well as she could, attached the trough that she'd fashioned to get the concrete from the wheelbarrow to its final destination with the least amount of energy exerted, and set about pouring the concrete into the well. She repeated the process over and over again until she was satisfied that she had filled the well with at least five or six feet of concrete. She knew that the well was substantially deeper than she'd originally thought; that worked in her favor in case anyone ever came snooping. She cleaned up the area and made sure that the well cover head was placed exactly the way it was prior to her lifting it off the first time. By the time she returned to the cabin, the area looked completely undisturbed and as if no one had walked around the well since Mrs. Carver had navigated the woods herself.

She showered and freshened up and, although it was only noon, she was exhausted and famished. She inhaled a quick lunch, and even though she could kill for a nap, finished getting ready for work, packed up her puppy and left the house. She and Remmy walked into the ADK Bar & Grill eight minutes before her shift started. Laverne took one look at her and knew that something was either wrong or she'd been up screwing all night; the latter was not something in which she thought Trista was interested. She went to her friend's side after being greeted by Remmy. Even Sal noticed the dark circles under her eyes, in spite of the makeup that she had applied. She tried to dismiss Laverne's concern but couldn't blow Sal off when he asked her two in words.

"What happened?"

How could he see through her so easily, she wondered? She smiled her best bullshit smile, looked him square in the eyes and lied through her teeth.

"Nothing boss. Why do you ask? I'm here as always, ready for action."

"Don't give me a line Trista. You look like crap, no offense and like you didn't sleep all night. So either tell us who jumped your bones all night or tell us what's going on. Any trouble at your place last night? If you had an issue, I would have expected a call."

Laverne picked up on the tone he used and immediately became very concerned. "What do you mean trouble? What does he mean trouble, Trista? What's going on that I don't know about?" she demanded.

Both Trista and Sal answered at the same time, "nothing."

Not satisfied, Laverne addressed both of them. "Salvatore Anthony, so help me God if there's something wrong and you know what it is and you're not telling me, I'll kick your ass from here to the curb; and I mean that both literally and figuratively!"

Before Trista could defend her boss, he spoke for himself, not in the hot-headed fashion that she would have expected, but in a soft, loving tone.

"Laverne, my love, you know that I'd never withhold information from you. Trista asked me to come over to her house the other day to help her install motion sensors and trail cams because she thought that the critters that roam our woods were getting a little too close for comfort, that's all. And when I saw how she looks this afternoon," he turned to Trista, "no offense Trista; well, I was worried that maybe the bear that's been lurking around her place bothered her or her livestock during the night," he said, all the while lying through his teeth. He gently put his hands on her shoulders and leaned in, not to kiss her, but to bring his forehead to hers. "You know I'd tell you if our favorite bartender needed our help."

Not sure whether she was satisfied with his answer or not, she directed her attention to Trista, who remained silent. "Honey, I don't know what your past life consisted of, and I know that you're either on the run or simply hiding from someone or something, I can tell by that silly red wig you wear all the time. But I want you to understand one thing Trista, if you've got any kind of trouble on your heels, you can trust old Sal, and me because we're your friends. Though I might not look it, there's more to this adorable package," she said as she waved her hands from head to toe, "than meets the eye. I can be just as lethal as Salvatore over there; and if ever you need someone, I've got your back just as easily as he does, right Sal?"

"Oh yeah. Trista, what Laverne's trying to say simply is, trust us. If and when you need help, trust and confide in us. I'm no longer a cop, remember that; I'm simply your friend. As a friend, if you need us; we'll be there, no questions asked and no judgement handed out."

Feeling as if they already knew her secrets, she almost blurted out about the body she'd discovered in her basement. Instead she kept it to herself. She had listened to the words spoken and the sincerity with which they were delivered, but she'd learned back in basic training to never trust anyone except herself. She looked at her two friends who were obviously waiting for some type of response, and she simply said "Thank You," offering nothing more.

They finished getting everything in order just as their first patrons walked in. A nice-looking couple, they surveyed the room making note of the large copper bar. They decided instead to take a small table off to the side of the room.   Before they sat, the husband sauntered up to the bar as if he was walking on air. He truly was drop-dead gorgeous but obviously knew that people noticed his looks; and his cocky attitude was apparent in the way he moved. Sal was in the back room so Trista was forced to smile and put on an air of friendliness to the obvious jerk in front of her.

"Good afternoon, what can I get you?" Not sure what she was expecting, she was shocked when he opened his mouth. His tone was pleasant enough, but his words chilled her and his eyes looked like they had demonic qualities.

"The little lady insisted that we come to this dive so let's cut to the chase. I want a Tanqueray and tonic, and I don't expect it watered down. She wants Malibu Rum & Diet Coke. And make sure the glasses are clean," he demanded as he turned around to walk back to his seat, putting on a fake smile for his company.

Immediately furious, and not interested in taking the jerk's bull shit, Trista politely shouted back to him as he walked away. "Coming right up sir; I'll be sure to spit shine the glasses for you before pouring your drinks."

He turned to see her smiling from ear to ear.

Sal entered the bar at the tail end of the conversation, asking Trista what that was all about. She shrugged his question off and, after making the requested drinks, personally delivered them to their table. She noted that the lady in his presence seemed very nervous. She was reluctant to make eye contact with Trista when she addressed her, making small talk about what a gorgeous day it was. Deciding that she wanted to spare Laverne the hassle of dealing with him, and also wanting to delve a little more into the couple's dynamics, she picked up a pad and proceeded to ask them if they were ready to place their orders. She couldn't help but think that the man truly was striking, with his designer jeans, sweater and blazer, jet black hair styled to perfection, piercing blue eyes and high cheekbones. It was a shame he appeared to be such an ass hole. While he ignored her a moment later, as if showing his superiority, she noted that his hands were well-groomed and appeared to never have done a bit of manual labor. He didn't wear a wedding band, just a large fraternity style ring on his right hand. He finally acknowledged her, he placed the order for both he and his guest, which totally pissed her off. She deliberately turned her body to face the young woman accompanying him and asked her what type of dressing she'd like on her salad, even though her entrée didn't technically come with one. The poor thing remained silent, and didn't lift her head up to make eye contact with Trista. Not giving her even a second to respond, the dark- haired man spoke up. "She'll have the house dressing, thank you; now if you would excuse us, we'd appreciate it if you'd do your job and put in our order pronto."

"Yes sir," she sarcastically responded, turning to walk away. Once she'd placed the order, she returned to the bar to Sal's knowing eyes.

"What was that all about?"

"Not sure. But I do know that something's not quite right there. I'm not sure what it is, but something is definitely wrong with that couple."

"Trista," he said, gently touching her left hand, "not everyone is on the run or in trouble. Sometimes things are as simple as they seem. Maybe she likes him ordering for her and taking care of everything. Not all women are as kick-ass independent as you and Laverne. Take our Tabby for example, she's been in heaven since moving in with Charlie and allowing him to take care of her. She loves having someone catering to her every need."

"It's not that Sal," she said defensively. "I've seen her type before. I used to volunteer in a battered woman's shelter, and I know that look. She's not only controlled by him, she's afraid of him, you mark my words."

Surprised, but learning more and more about his bartender every day, he carefully worded his response. "Were you physically abused by your husband Trista? Is that how you know the look you think you see on that woman's face?" he asked, looking over at the couple sitting not twelve feet from them.

She looked at her boss and answered as honestly as she could. "Not physically, no. I was in better shape than he was or is, for that matter; and I would have killed him if he tried to hurt me physically. His abuse was all emotional; I wasn't pretty enough, sexy enough, from the right side of the tracks etc. And while he didn't want to divorce me, he wanted me to sit back idly while he screwed his business associate senseless. She wanted him permanently, and he wanted to have his cake and eat it too. I I helped him make his decision."

"I see."

Realizing that he actually didn't see at all, she just allowed him to speculate and theorize without confirming nor denying anything. She offered no more and kept her hands busy washing dishes in between mixing drinks and pouring beer for the afternoon crowd that was slowly filling the bar. She continued to observe the couple at table 7. Only once did she see the eyes of the woman practically inhaling her salad and sandwich; and they were the saddest brown eyes that she'd ever seen. When the young woman made eye contact with her, she stared just long enough to convey what was unspoken and Trista already knew that she needed help. Before she could figure out what to do to help the obviously frightened woman, he stood, grabbed her arm, threw a couple of twenties on the table and escorted her quickly out of the restaurant. She immediately walked to the window and as they sped off caught just enough of a glimpse of their Crossfire to see his license plate. She closed her eyes, as she always did to allow her brain to process the information and, with that, his tag was permanently ingrained in her memory. She went back to the bar, still concerned for the young woman's welfare. Charlie went to the table to clean up and, when finished, came back to the bar where she was standing to hand her a folded up piece of paper. Not sure what it was, she turned her back so she could read privately whatever was printed on the paper.

"If you are so interested in my lady friend, come and get her, if you dare. PS: I like threesomes, how about you, Trista?"

She read it again, and disgusted, ripped up the piece of paper, but not before Sal was at her side. "Love letter I see? Mind telling me what it said?"

"Actually, yes I mind. It was nothing," she said as she stormed outside to get a breath of fresh air. Sal was relentless, and followed her outside.

"It was something if it's got you this hot under the collar. Talk to me Trista."

"That scumbag hit on me. Or at the very least, was toying with me, and I don't like being toyed with. He's abusing that poor girl that was with him, I just know it. There's not a damn thing that I can do to prove it or do about it, and that pisses me off more than the fool hitting on me," she finished, fuming.

"Go home Trista. Go home with Remmy, have a good stiff drink and forget about it. And if you really think that the girl is being abused or is in any kind of danger, we'll give the authorities a call in the morning and see if he's staying here in town. You've got his tag number, right" he asked, already knowing the answer.

She tapped her forehead, grabbed her coat, whistled for her dog and walked out the door. But when she pulled out onto 28, it wasn't to head north toward her home, but south toward Old Forge and the cluster of hotels and motels scattered along the strip. She was curious about whether they were staying in town; or at least that was what she kept telling herself as she drove from parking lot to parking lot, until she came to the one she sought. There, parked out of the direct light, was a pearl white Crossfire exhibiting the tags that she had memorized. She thought that maybe it was time to give the visitor a taste of his own medicine. She donned gloves, pulled a piece of newsprint from the Adirondack Express, and in the area without type print, wrote a simple cryptic message. "Got your message; might be interested. Hope to see you tomorrow. You know where to find me." Satisfied that it would be enough to lure him back to the restaurant, she stuck the note under his wiper, confident that the security cameras didn't scan that far back in the older motel's lot.

She wanted them to return to the restaurant in hopes of being able to speak with the woman accompanying him. She knew the look of someone in distress when she saw it, and she wanted to be able to reach out to her if she needed it. She just needed the asshole that was controlling her to fall for her dare, so to speak. As she got back into her truck, she knew that he'd go for the bait. Then she'd have to see what she could do to remedy the situation.

He waited until they were inside the cheap motel room before he started beating her. He was always so careful when teaching her who was boss, and tonight was no exception. He pummeled her with his open hand, his fists and his belt, but was always careful to strike only from the neck down. His little Lauren had learned early on that it was her fault that she needed to be punished and therefore it her responsibility to make sure that whatever articles of clothing she wore out in public covered any evidence of the lessons she'd been taught the night before. As with most nights, she truly had no idea what she'd done to deserve such a fierce beating. She was also smart enough to keep her mouth shut until it was over. Just when she thought she couldn't take it anymore, he stopped just as quickly as he started. He left her bleeding on the bed as he turned his back to her and walked into the bathroom. When he finished washing up, he told her to clean herself up and get ready for bed. She did so immediately and silently; returned to his side knowing what he'd want. She was used to the routine by now. After it was over, she'd roll over to her side of the bed, crying silently, praying that someone, somewhere would hear her pleas and help her get back home. All she wanted was to go home and see her parents again.

~~~ Chapter 25 ~~~

Trista tossed and turned all night. She dreamt all night, remembered of the dreams that had plagued her sleep and awakened feeling barely rested. Knowing that she needed to rid herself of the negative energy, she grabbed Remmy's leash and took her pup for a quick run, thinking they'd only do a mile or so. After mile 2 she felt the endorphins release and with another burst of energy, ended up running almost five miles before she returned to her cabin. Both she and her dog drank heartedly once they were back inside, with each sitting down to rest afterward. Within minutes Remmy was asleep, next to the hearth, but Trista decided that she had better wash up in case she had unexpected company. Still somewhat paranoid about the dead body in her basement, she wanted to keep a low profile while also being ready in case someone came along with questions. As if clairvoyant, Sal pulled in not ten minutes after she finished drying her hair.

She met him at the door, without her wig. He took one look at the blonde holding the door open for him and smiled, "much better Trista." He didn't question, judge or interrogate, he simply told her that she looked much better as a natural blonde and to ditch the wig when she felt comfortable doing so." His bluntness made her laugh. She handed him a cup of coffee, though all she had was instant; but he accepted it happily, removed his coat and got down to business.

"I had my buddy run his tags Trista. He's trouble, and I need you to promise me that you'll stay clear of him."

Sitting there without make up and that ridiculous wig, she looked so young and innocent. He knew that she must be pushing 30, if not already there but there, in her faded cotton flannel shirt and ripped blue jeans, dog at her side, she looked like a kid. He still didn't know her real story but knew that she had many dark, sad secrets; and that she didn't trust him or Laverne, for that matter, enough to open up and let them in. He truly cared about her, almost like a daughter he thought now. Having never had children though, he didn't really know what love for a child felt like, he figured that since he was losing sleep worrying about her, that this feeling must be pretty close to the real thing. He wanted to shake her and tell her that he'd help her fix whatever was wrong, but didn't want to scare her away. He knew that if he pushed too hard or dug too deep, she'd run, and disappear from their lives; so he sat there just looking at her as he gulped down his third cup of coffee that morning.

"What do you mean trouble Sal? Who is he and where is he from?" she asked casually. She'd known the instant that he'd walked into the restaurant that he had a familiar face and that he was in fact big trouble; but she still couldn't place who he was. Besides, she was more concerned with helping the woman who was with him, than about whatever his agenda might be.

"His name's David Antoni and according to his rap sheet, which reads like a long boring book, he's been in and out since he was barely a teenager. Started out in juvy for petty larceny, pick- pocketing, and being involved in too many brawls, then worked his way up the ladder to assault and battery, rape though the charge was dismissed, and attempted murder. He's done time, but not nearly enough if you ask me. He must have himself an excellent attorney because the majority of the charges were either dismissed for insufficient evidence or the trials ended in hung juries. He's definitely bad news, and if he shows up in my place again, you find me and he'll be escorted out immediately. I know that look Trista and I'm telling you, stay away from him. And what the hell did the note that Charlie gave you say," he added, just to keep her attention and to remind her that he was still the eyes and ears of the bar. Not much escaped him.

"Basically told me to mind my own business, but if I wanted a threesome with he and his date, he'd be happy to oblige."

"That scumbag, I'll kill him myself if he gets near you!"

"Sal," she said softly, gently touching his arm, "Do you really think that I need you to protect me? Do I honestly look that meek and mild to you?"

"No Trista. We both know that you can be lethal when push comes to shove; but I won't have some two-bit punk harassing someone that I care about. He comes near you, he's mine. Promise me Trista."

"Please don't worry Sal, I promise. Nothing bad will happen to me. Just out of curiosity, how did you find out who he was so quickly? He paid in cash so you didn't have his name and you were in the back room when he left, so how did you discover who our guest was?" she asked.

He laughed, genuinely laughed. "You think that you're the only one who memorized the tag on that cute sports car of his?"

She smiled back at the man who'd become like a father to her.

He pushed back his chair to leave and gave her one last piece of advice. "Trista, I know a loner when I see one; hell I've been one all my life, despite Laverne hanging around all these years. I just wanted you to know, that while you're living in the area and working under my roof, you're not alone. You never have to feel alone again; and know, that no matter what you need to say, I am here for you and I will help you. No questions asked, no judgements, and no interference by me. I am no longer a cop; remember that..." He walked toward the door and turned to face her one last time. "You do know how to use that shotgun correct? And the 9?" he asked.

"Yes. I'm very comfortable with both." She deliberately chose not to offer anything more, at least not at this time or during this conversation.

"Okay. Trista, when you need someone to trust with your secrets, trust me." He said nothing more and walked out, closing the door gently behind him.

~~~ Chapter 26 ~~~

The second Sal pulled out of the drive, Trista was on her throwaway phone with her sister, who happened to be off duty. She asked Rebecca to do some digging of her own to make sure that her beloved husband was still securely behind bars and to find out anything she could about David Antoni. She refused to give her sister any more information, promising her that she was fine, not in trouble or danger, and just wanted to know that everything was status quo regarding her past life. She reassured her that she'd drive down to visit in the very near future and promised her that maybe they could go on a trip to the islands or someplace warm. Her sister didn't believe her for a minute but went along with the conversation anyway because it was the longest that Trista had stayed on the phone with her since starting her new life in the mountains. She worried constantly about Trista's mental and physical state and knew how much losing her child and husband had cost her. She had always known that ever since their childhood, her big sister kept too much inside, and she couldn't help but worry that one of these days, Trista might simply snap. She'd had it all and now, had nothing and Rebecca had to wonder what made Trista get out of bed and continue living day in and day out. She knew that her sister had once been an excellent nurse, then a perfect housewife, expectant mother and then bam, it was all gone in an instant. She had no idea what her sister was now. She claimed that she was enjoying her time writing a children's science fiction novel, up in the mountains in the middle of nowhere. To Rebecca, her sister might as well be in Alaska or Antarctica because it was all so foreign to her. Her sister left a home that to Rebecca had looked like a mansion, a pampered lifestyle that included membership to the country club and pretty much anything that she wanted, to move to something no bigger than a shack in the middle of nowhere in the Adirondack Mountains. Rebecca knew that her sister had suffered terribly when learning of her husband's affair, then the scandal when he was arrested, tried and convicted of murdering his lover. The biggest insult was when she lost the child that she was carrying. She knew how much that child had meant to Jasmine and when she miscarried, Rebecca felt as if she'd lost her sister along with her unborn niece or nephew. Sure Jasmine reassured her continuously that she was fine; but before she knew it, her sister had reverted to the childhood name she hadn't used since they'd left the hellhole that had been their home, she'd sold everything that she could including her home, designer wheels and wardrobe, and had become essentially a hermit, cutting herself off from civilization as she had known it. None3. of it made sense to Rebecca, but she knew that her sister had more layers than an onion and more secrets than the pyramids, and that she'd probably go to her grave never really knowing who or what her sister was. One thing she knew for certain though was that if it weren't for her big sister, Jasmine or Trista, whatever she wanted to call herself these days. Rebecca knew that she wouldn't have lived to adulthood. She knew that her sister had protected her as best she could and was still doing so to this day. Even though she was four years younger than Jasmine, she had been old enough to understand what had gone on in their childhood home at the hands of their uncle and knew that it had been her big sister who prevented him from hurting her. For that, she'd be forever grateful and would do anything she could to help her, even if it meant breaking the law. Rebecca hung up the phone after talking with her and knew that it was time to repay the favor. Regardless of what it cost her, she would do anything and everything to protect her older sister now and in the future. She'd have to wait until she was at the station in the morning but she'd get the answers that her sister requested. And when she went in, she'd request a week or so off so that she could drive up and surprise her sister and see for herself in what kind of conditions she was living.

<center>~~~ Chapter 27 ~~~</center>

"Get up!" he screamed at her, pushing her roughly as she lay in bed, feigning sleep. She had hoped to avoid him just a little longer but to no avail. She'd dreamt of her home, her parents and her dog, and wanted nothing more than to see them and the one horse town that she'd run away from. If she could ever break free from the demon who'd essentially held her prisoner for the past month, she swore silently to herself that she'd never again be unappreciative of what she had. Sure to some she might be just a farm girl from a hick town who loved her horses and reading romance novels; but she now understood that it was okay to simply be who you are. She'd met him on the Internet posing as a sophisticated college student studying premed when in fact she was a high school student who was supposed to be finishing her senior year. God what she wouldn't give to be sitting in a classroom right now, instead of stuck with the monster standing above her. She knew that he'd been drugging her since the time they'd met for what was supposed to be a fun lunch at a trendy coffee house. Instead, that luncheon had turned into her worst nightmare. He was gorgeous to look at, but pure evil inside. He terrified her and had threatened to hurt her family if she ever left him or said anything. He had shown her pictures of her home, friends and siblings proving that he knew who she really was and how to find them. So instead of endangering anyone because of her stupidity, she'd remained silent. The sex had gotten rougher and rougher with each passing week, and the beatings had gotten worse and more frequent. She knew that it was just a matter of time before he killed her. When he did allow her out in public, it was as if she was invisible. No one appeared to even notice her presence, no one except that waitress yesterday. She had actually seen her and acknowledged her, she thought now; and when she looked at her, it was as if she had understood what was going on. Maybe, just maybe, if she could convince David to bring her back there for lunch or dinner today, that waitress would be on and she could somehow get a message to her.

Knowing that she couldn't prolong the inevitable much longer, she opened her eyes, rolled over and purposely let her nightgown fall to expose her breast.

"Good morning," she smiled coyly. "I was just dreaming about you," she said in the most seductive tone she could force from her lips. Catching him somewhat off guard, but definitely catching his attention, she rolled completely onto her back, and put her arms out as if reaching for him.

"Oh yeah?" he asked, looking down at the hot little number lying there begging for it. He'd seen her type so many times over the years. Young things thinking that they were all grown up, but when it came time to prove they were; they wanted to race back to their mommies. He'd taught several of the little bitches over the years that they can't flaunt it and not expect to give it; and he'd taken great satisfaction in teaching that lesson to more than he could count. She'd been no different. Now, a month later, just when he thought that she'd used up all of her usefulness and he'd have to dispose of her, it appeared that she was finally coming around. He didn't think she'd been a virgin when he'd first picked her out, but she'd been close to it. It hadn't taken long for her to understand though that if she wanted to live and wanted her family to live, then she'd do as he told her; and he meant do "everything" as he told her. In his mind, what he said at any given time was never a request but a rather a command and after a few beatings, she'd come to realize that too. Looking down at her now, he decided that maybe he'd allow her to live another week or so, providing she made good on what she was offering him at the moment. And it was. She took him inside her, but not before bringing him to the edge numerous other ways. Whether she'd wanted to be or not, she'd become very proficient with her tongue and knew just what to do to keep his attention but not tip him over the edge. He'd forced her to do things in the beginning that she never would have thought she'd do. Even though she hated the thought of him sticking it in places that should be left for their intended purpose, she knew how much it turned him on, so today, she was the one initiating it, despite the pain the actual penetration cost her. In her mind, she thought that if she gave and gave then he'd be in a really good mood for once and then maybe, just maybe, he'd reward her with lunch at the ADK Bar and Grill.

Two hours later, they both lay exhausted on the bed. She'd done anything and everything that she knew he liked and that he'd asked for; and it was apparent by the look on his face that he was pleased with her. He actually lay there holding her like he cared about her, which she knew was a crock. The bastard didn't care about anyone but himself, and she knew that he was incapable of love, only capable of trying to control. Well, she thought to herself, let's see who's really in control now. She went back to the spot in her mind where she wasn't the person saying the things that were being said, nor was she the person doing these things. This was all just a really bad school play and soon it would be over. She used what energy she had left, rolled onto her side and cuddled with the man lying beside her. "Hey baby," she said gently. "Do you think we could maybe do a little more sightseeing or shopping or something before we head to Florida? I sort of like the whole outdoorsy woodsman-type feel of this place. That is if it's okay with you," she said, strategically placing her hand on a very tired part of his anatomy.

"Yeah sure, anything you want," he said, half asleep, but holding on tight to her breast. Smiling to herself, she allowed him to drift off to sleep. "Phase one completed," she said silently; and prayed that maybe, just maybe, she'd somehow have her freedom by nightfall.

The rest of the morning went quickly for Trista. As she had promised her sister, she had gone into town and used the library's computer to do a little research on Caribbean Islands and all-inclusive resorts. She'd been able to finally get her passport changed to her new name and knew that she had enough money tucked aside to easily afford a vacation. She didn't know if she'd want to travel that far, now that she had a puppy to take care of. She knew that she could ask Sal to watch her animals but didn't want to impose on him. But maybe she needed time with her sister and time away from her life both the old one and her current one. She caught herself thinking about that poor girl from the restaurant last night. The guy she had been with not only creeped her out; but Trista knew that he was big trouble and not at all what he appeared to be, which was a rich boyfriend to the terrified girl. She'd have to wait until her sister got back to her before she could do anything about it or go to the police with her suspicions, and that irritated her whenever she thought about it.

By the time she got back home after grocery shopping, doing her vacation research at the library, walking the dog and feeding the chickens and pigs; it was almost time for her to get ready for work. She had driven by the motel where she'd seen the jerk's Crossfire while she was in town. She knew that she shouldn't have but did anyway. It was still parked in the same location which surprised her. As she didn't want to have the misfortune of being seen, she slowed down without actually stopping. Just seeing the car made her blood pressure rise and for a split second just because she could, she wanted to go pound on the bastard's door and kick the shit out of him. But one thing she'd learned from the military was how to control her reactions and for the most part, her temper. She'd mastered that art while a certain officer had raped her repeatedly while she was under his charge. She hadn't retaliated right away, but planned and waited until just the right moment. And just when she'd finally had enough, her opportunity presented itself. She'd heard that he was going to be going on leave the following morning and both he and another officer would be leaving by 0600; and it just so happened that she was working the evening before. It was unfortunate that whoever the accompanying officer was with him, would probably have the misfortune of dying as well; she knew that it couldn't be helped. In war it was considered collateral damage. In Trista's mind, that's exactly what she was in, war with the officer. It was survival of the fittest, and she intended to win. It had been quite easy when she'd thought about it. It took only a few adjustments. When she watched them leave the compound the following morning, she knew she'd never have to deal with him again. She'd been right. News of the crash arrived back on base within the hour. She had heard that his passenger had died on impact, and for that she was extremely grateful. What she was more grateful for, was the fact that she heard that the man who'd tormented her, brutalized her and raped her too many times to recall, was very much alive when they'd crashed and was seen trapped inside, burning alive. She smiled when she'd heard the news and never felt one ounce of guilt. Pushing those long forgotten memories out of her mind, she started getting ready for another shift at the Bar. She'd come to really enjoy the comradery among her fellow co-workers at the restaurant and continued to work for Sal, not for the money but for the friendships that she'd made with each and every one of the other employees. She thought the world of Sal and Laverne, and was very happy for Charlie and Tabitha who had finally rediscovered each other. Trista appreciated their two short-order cooks' expertise and even the dishwasher had welcomed her as part of their family from the day that she signed on. She'd never forget how much their acceptance of her had mattered when she'd needed it most. She didn't know why, but she'd decided that today was the day to finally be who she really was. When she got ready for work, she did so without donning the wig that she'd been wearing for weeks.

She took a deep breath, and walked into the restaurant, head held high and with her blonde hair sparkling in the bright sun light. Tabitha saw her first and whispered "Holy Shit" under her breathe; while Charlie came out from the kitchen and gave her a once over, smiled and whistled seductively. "Wow Trista, if I was 10 years older and not so in love with Tabby, I'd scoop you up in a minute baby!" he joked as she saw him wink, just to irritate Tabitha. Tabby laughed and told Trista that she could have him, even though she knew it was all in jest. Before the joking and kidding got too intense, Tabitha walked up to Trista, pulling her aside.

"I know it was you who helped me, and I just wanted to say Thank You." Not quite sure what the young, expectant mother meant by her statement, Trista remained silent while Tabitha continued on. "I know that you're the one who tucked all that money into the pockets of the clothes you gave me. I don't know where the money came from Trista because I know you make as crappy a wage here as I do, but I know that I'll pay you back someday. That I promise. Charlie and I have been talking about it, and we'll find a way."

"You want to pay me back Tabby? Be happy; that's payback enough. Smile often; take time for your daughter and for Charlie and for the one growing inside you. Don't dwell on the small stuff, forget about anger and hurt, always remember the good in everyone; that will be the best way for you to pay me back. Live the life that I had always hoped for and dreamt about Tabitha. It's too late for happily ever after for me, but it's not for you. Make the most of every day and live your life to the fullest. If you do that, you'll have more wealth than the richest men, and you'll have repaid me back tenfold. Deal?" She said, smiling at the young woman standing beside her.

"I love you Trista, and I know I owe you my life," she said, throwing herself into her co-worker's arms.

Sal watched the exchange and had been standing close enough to hear the entire conversation. It not only gave him more insight into his bartender, it confirmed what he'd already suspected about Trista. She was a woman on the run, not simply from a man but from the pain of her past. He still didn't know exactly who she was, but he was beginning to realize more and more that she was not only smart, and obviously beautiful, but had lived a previous life that afforded her monetarily important things. He also knew that what Trista had desired was not something that can be bought. He assumed that the money she was always so freely giving away was hers to give and not stolen. He knew that she had secrets and that some of them could land her in jail if discovered; but he knew in his heart that she was not a thief and would never give something to someone if it wasn't hers to give. And while he didn't know how much Trista had tucked into the articles of clothing that she'd given Tabitha, he knew it must have been enough to make a huge impact on her life and the life of her children.

It was finally Laverne that broke the silence. "Hey honey, got any more clothes you're giving away? Cause the only thing that ever came with my sweaters and jeans was the credit card bill," she chuckled. "Come one ladies, let's break this up and get ready for our customers."

"Yes sir, boss sir," Trista responded back sarcastically.

"Hey blondie," Laverne shouted back to Trista as she walked into the kitchen to grab supplies, "love the hair; definitely better than that red shit."

Trista and Tabby burst out laughing, while Charlie walked over to Sal, allowing the women to do their thing. Charlie waited until they were out of earshot and looked at Sal. Seeing his serious face, Sal asked what was wrong.

"Nothing," Charlie answered, "Just the opposite; everything is perfect and the way it's supposed to be. I've got Tabby and my family back, that asshole is out of our lives, thanks to Trista we've not only paid off all of our credit card bills, but were able to put a nice stash in the bank that we'll need when the baby comes. That's what kinda scares me Sal; it's as if Trista is Tabby's guardian angel. Ever since she came to town, good things have been happening to people who deserve to have good things happen. I'm afraid that if she leaves us, cause I might be a kid still but even I know she's running from something, and I'm worried that when she leaves, we'll go back to having bad things always happening. You know I love Tabby and want to marry her someday, and thanks to Trista, we're now together. Well thanks to Trista, and the fact that Todd died, that is. It's almost as if Trista's our good luck charm and I hope that she stays around for a long time.

Sal thought about his young worker's words, knowing that he was dead on with his observation. Sal chose his words very carefully when he responded. "Charlie, I agree with you that good things have been happening since Trista entered our lives, but I think that while she opened some doors of opportunity for us, it was up to you and Tabby to walk through them. Does that make sense son?"

"Yeah, I guess it does. I just hope that she stays around long enough for me to marry Tabby."

"I'd say there's a good chance of that Charlie. So you two lovebirds set a date and I'll take it from there. I know the idea of marriage and a ready-made family is rather new to you, but if you'd like, I'd like nothing better than to host your wedding reception. Whether you have it here at the restaurant or rent out the town hall or bowling alley; as my present to you both, I'd like to take care of the catering and beverages. Think about it, talk to Tabby about it, and whenever you set a date, I'll be available."

Charlie couldn't believe his ears and didn't know what to say so instead of speaking, he simply gave his boss a big bear hug and twirled him around, right there in the bar. The girls exited the kitchen in time to see Sal practically flying through the air and waited until the commotion was over before asking what was going on. Charlie, now embarrassed by his outpouring of emotion, went to his girlfriend's side.

"Tabby, you know how one good thing after another has been happening to us recently? Well, I know that we've talked about marriage and you said that you'd marry me someday when we could afford it. Sal has offered us the restaurant for our reception and as his gift to us, he's going to cater the entire event. So baby, if you want to get married before the baby comes, we can. Wouldn't that be awesome?" he asked, grabbing both of Tabitha's hands and kissing them. Tabby heard what he was saying but wasn't quite as enthusiastic as he was. Seeing her reaction, he looked at her, asking what was wrong, terrified that maybe she'd changed her mind about marrying him. Quickly she spoke up and reassured him that she absolutely wanted to marry him and couldn't wait until the day when she was Mrs. Brown. She tried to quietly explain that even though they now could afford the reception, they still couldn't afford the flowers, or his tux or her dress; and yes, she would have loved to have been married before the baby came, it just wasn't meant to be.

Overhearing the entire conversation, Laverne and Trista practically tripped over one another trying to reach her first. Trista insisted on providing the flower arrangements for the wedding and reception, and along with paying for her bridal floral arrangement. Laverne told Tabitha that her wedding gift to the young bride would be in the form of paying for her dress and veil and she would not take no for an answer. Overwhelmed, Tabitha burst into tears and nodded yes; she'd accept their generous gifts and yes, she'd love to marry Charlie before the month was over if they could pull it off. Charlie felt the salty taste of his own tears as he realized that all of his prayers, dreams and wishes were coming true. He looked over at Trista and mouthed "Thank You," knowing now for sure that she was in fact the best thing that had ever entered his life.

~~~ Chapter 28 ~~~

The restaurant was full when with he parked his Crossfire and escorted Lauren in. She'd been forced to perform one more time before they'd left the motel, but she truly hadn't minded when he'd promised her that they could go back to the ADK Bar & Grill for lunch. Little did he know that she was just as excited about seeing the red-headed bartender as he was. She had no idea if Trista, she'd said her name was, would know what the symbol meant, but she had to take the chance and try. She'd taken her eyeliner and placed a round black dot on the palm of her left hand representing someone in trouble or danger. She prayed that the opportunity to not only make eye contact with the waitress/bartender but also to show her that she desperately needed her help would present itself over lunch. Lauren refused to think about the remote possibility that her hell could end soon and she could be reunited with her family.

The restaurant was bustling as they made their way back to a secluded corner booth, separated from the large groups of families all enjoying their meals. He quickly surveyed the crowd and when satisfied with what he saw, loosened his grip on her. And then he spotted her with her back to the bar. Still conservative and not flaunting her assets, she was wearing a simple solid colored sweater, jeans and boots. The sweater looked generic enough until he realized that it was cashmere, and the boots, though they were a little scuffed up were definitely not off the shelf at some chain store. When she turned and he watched her hair spin in the light, it dawned on him that she'd changed the color from red to golden blonde and it suited her perfectly. She definitely looked hot as a blonde and, with her big blue eyes and that low cut plum sweater, she looked amazing and incredibly sexy, despite the minimal amount of makeup she wore. He felt something pulse in his jeans as he continued to stare at her. She turned almost as if knowing that she was being watched, made direct eye contact with him and gave him a look that he knew meant "Come and get me." Being very self-confident and knowing that most women found him irresistible, he took it as a sign. He told Lauren to stay put, not doubt in for a second that she'd attempt to run away while he walked toward the bar. Trista watched him approach and although she'd hadn't had time to rehearse what she was going to say when their paths crossed again, she knew his type well enough and was prepared.

"Hey gorgeous; blonde is definitely a better choice for you. You get all hot and sexy cause you knew I'd be back in?"

"Yeah, that's it" she said, feigning boredom. "I've been pining away all morning in hopes that you'd come back just to see me." Knowing exactly what she was doing, she deliberately leaned over the bar, as if leaning in toward him to have a private conversation. By doing so, she knew that his vantage point had just changed significantly and that he'd enjoy the view. And he did exactly what she'd predicted he'd do. No longer focusing on her eyes, he blatantly stared at her partially exposed chest, and she could practically feel the hormones ragging through his system.

"See anything you'd like," she asked, knowing full well why she'd worded the question that way. "Would you like Bourbon, maybe a little Jack, or more Tanqueray this afternoon?" she said, never taking her eyes off his, even though his eyes still weren't focused on hers. When he finally looked up at her face, he smiled and responded under his breathe just loud enough for her to hear. "What I would like is definitely behind this bar, is not on one of those shelves." Knowing that he was playing right into her hand, she smiled back; the most seductive smile she was capable of while inside, he made her want to vomit.

"Well then, how about I pour a drink, on the house, for you and your friend? Then we can figure out how to get you what you're really looking for."

Satisfied, he turned and walked back to his table. Lauren was waiting exactly where he'd instructed her to stay; studying the menu as if her life depended on it. He realized that tonight might actually turn out to be one to remember, and if everything worked in his favor, he might be getting two for the price of one. Looking at her sashaying around behind that bar in her skin-tight jeans made him realize that she'd probably give him the ride of his life. He'd just have to convince Lauren to cooperate and go along with the threesome. He knew how to be very convincing and knew that she would never go against his wishes, if she wanted to continue living. He sat down and perused the menu, but didn't actually care what he ordered at that moment. His only thoughts were how he was going to get that hot little blonde to join them in their motel room. As Trista finished mixing their drinks, Lauren looked up and saw that she was about to deliver them. She practically jumped out of her chair in order to get them from Trista, smiling at him, saying she'd be right back. He turned to watch her approach the bar and knew that there wasn't an exit so he wasn't at all concerned. He saw the two women feet from one another and couldn't help but envision them naked, together, in his bed. As he fantasized, what he didn't see was Lauren deliberately putting her hands up to retrieve the waiting drinks. As she did so, she completely exposed both of her palms to Trista with the distinct black dot visible and catching her attention. The flash of recognition in her eyes didn't go unnoticed by Lauren, and she made direct eye contact with the bar tender. Knowing that he would be watching their every move, Trista handed her the drinks and simply said "Here you go young lady. And it will be over with soon and you'll be safe; please trust me." Lauren heard the words but refused to believe they could actually be true, she felt the tears in her eyes anyway but willed them away and turned to return to their table and his watchful gaze. She deliberately handed him his drink and leaned in to whisper to him, with Trista scared for a split second that she might actually have told him what she'd said. When they ordered their lunch moments later she relaxed, knowing that the girl must have just leaned in to say something to reassure him.

As they enjoyed their lunch, Trista stood behind the bar watching their every move, trying to figure out how she was going to get the creep alone. She knew that she could simply snap his neck or blow his head off for that matter, lord knew she still could shoot; but she didn't want the young lady he was holding captive to be a witness. She also wanted to protect her from being exposed to anything that might scar her any worse than she already was. Trista blocked out every childhood memory that attempted to creep back into the forefront of her brain. She would not allow her father or her uncle to invade her life here in the mountains. They were dead and buried and that's where their memories needed to stay. For the first time in a long time, she was happy again, and around people who genuinely cared about her. While the scumbag enjoying his pulled pork sandwich needed to die, she wasn't going to do anything that could be linked to her or anything that might cause her to end up where her ex-husband was currently residing for 20 to life. Trista remained so focused on watching the couple at table nine that she didn't see the Honda CRV drive slowly by the restaurant and pull into the lot.

Sal too was watching the couple seated in Tabitha's section. He didn't know what their deal was, but he hadn't been retired from the force so long ago that he didn't recognize when something looked amiss. There was something about the body language of the young girl that looked reserved, hesitant and nervous; while the man accompanying her looked much older and thoroughly in control. He noticed that she made eye contact with no one except her lunch date and while she picked at her food, she looked very preoccupied and uninterested in eating. He'd seen her interact for just a second with Trista and, while he wondered what her deal was, he knew that his barkeep would only divulge what she wanted him to know.

He'd done a little more digging into Trista's past, against Laverne's advice, and had found that she and her younger sister had nearly perished in a house fire that killed their father. There was no mention of a mother in the picture, and Sal theorized that was why the two children had landed in foster care all those years ago. The information that he'd been able to unearth stated that they'd been placed together in the same family and remained there through high school. Trista had enlisted in the Marines as she had stated, while her younger sister entered the police academy upon graduation. Everything that Trista had divulged to him had been accurate and the truthful; but it was what she was keeping from him that was of concern. He knew that his bartender had a heart of gold, but he also knew that even gold can be hard and unbending. He would bet his restaurant that there was much more just under the surface. What scared him the most was that he knew that she had some very tough breaks as a kid, and knew that she still had many dark secrets locked inside her soul. He just prayed that someday the time bomb that her upbringing had created didn't explode around them.

When Trista finally figured out a way to get to him, she nearly burst with excitement. She poured them each another drink, adding a little something to her young friend's drink and brought their drinks to their table personally. He looked at her suspiciously but, when he saw her genuine smile and she told him that this round was on the house, he relaxed and graciously accepted what was being offered. What he didn't know was that his dinner date was about to ruin the afternoon for him.

It didn't take long for the meds to kick in, and by the panicked look on Lauren's face, Trista knew that the meds were working. After the third time she excused herself to practically run to the bathroom, she could tell that he was getting agitated. It was then that she made her move.

"Say, it looks like your little friend can't handle her booze. What do you say I follow you back to wherever you're staying and help tuck her into bed?" she asked slyly. "My shift is practically over with here anyway, and I could give her a hand or something," she added, deliberately using the innuendo. "You head out when she comes back from the john, tell me where you're staying and leave the door open. I'll be there shortly behind you. Oh," she added, reaching into her snug pants pocket, "Give your little friend one of these once in the car and another when you get to wherever it is you're staying. They're antacids and will help perk her up for tonight's festivities," she winked. Feeling his jeans getting very tight around a certain part of his anatomy, he quickly gave her the name of their motel and room number, and headed out with Lauren in tow. Trista felt badly that she'd drugged Lauren's drink with syrup of ipecac but knew that she had to do something to incapacitate the girl. She didn't want Lauren awake when she arrived at the motel to take care of Slick once and for all. She didn't know what his real name was, nor did she care to find out; it was much easier eliminating someone if it wasn't personal. She didn't want to know his name or where he was from. To Trista, he was just a threat to the child he had kidnapped and he was a wasting air as far as she was concerned. The world would be better off without him in it. She knew that the Benadryl capsules that she'd given him, telling him that they were antacids, would knock Lauren out for at least a few hours and she'd be none the wiser; and if anyone ran a toxicology screen on her, neither drug would show up. It would look like the poor child simply got sick on her lunch and slept it off. Which was good for everyone involved; everyone that is except for Slick who was about to meet his Maker.

She waited another half hour, said her farewells to Sal and Laverne, punched out and headed for her truck. She drove back to Old Forge and as she approached town, pulled down Cosby Boulevard toward the Moose River Bridge, past the old airport. She knew that there were neither cameras nor homes by the bridge, so it was a perfect place to change into something more appropriate for her meeting with Slick. She was careful as she changed into her jumpsuit and wig, all the while wearing latex gloves. She had what she was looking for tucked in her back pocket should she need it, but thought a scumbag like Slick shouldn't be a challenge what so ever.

And she'd been right. She waited outside the door just long enough to hear the distinctive sound of snoring coming from the other side. She tapped ever so lightly on the door before opening it. He'd left it unlocked as he'd been instructed and was standing over the bed with a look of disgust at the completely incoherent girl in his bed. His look of contempt changed to a look of pure lust the second he saw her enter in the skin-tight neoprene body suit that she was wearing. Even though it was black, he could tell immediately that she wasn't wearing anything underneath it. Seeing her in a black wig, enhanced darkened makeup and an outfit that looked like it was painted on, excited him beyond description. She could see the bulge poking out from underneath the half open bathrobe he was donning at the moment, and upon seeing Lauren passed out in the bed, made her move.

"You look like you were about to take a shower," she purred. "Your little friend looks like she needs a nap, so what do you say you help me out of my clothes and we take this party into the shower to freshen up a little?"

He didn't say a word, simply smiled, turned, and walked toward the shower. The second he turned his back to her, she was on him with the garrote around his neck before he'd even stepped one foot into the bath. His immediate response was to attempt to swing at her. She'd anticipated and was ready for this, pushing him face first into the doorjamb, as she tightened the wire with all her might. She really had thought that he'd put up more of a fight than he did and was disappointed when his swinging and thrashing was over almost before it started. The man who'd come across as Mr. Tough Guy and bully to the poor child sleeping just feet away, had actually been a wimp and died far more quickly and easily than she had hoped. When the twitching stopped, she guided his still warm body to the ground and removed her garrote, tucking it back into her pocket for safe keeping. She checked her watch and noted that from start to finish, she'd been in the room less than four minutes. She quickly turned on the fan, shut the bathroom door, and exited the unit. She knew that the unit next to theirs was vacant, and jimmied the lock to gain entrance. She put a huge wad of chewing tobacco into her mouth and when it was moist and thick, placed the call to the front desk, demanding that they do something about all the noise coming from room 202. She hung up the phone and exited the room unseen. She didn't need to wait around to see if they'd come; she knew they would. Trista was inside Kinney's Drugs when she heard the tell-tale sound of police cars speeding. She had told Sal that she needed to run into town after work and made a point of calling him from the store to see if he or Laverne needed anything. She kept him on the phone long enough that people saw and heard her in the store, then hung up and checked out.

She sat in her truck momentarily and while she felt bad that Lauren could have been exposed to what she'd done; she felt no remorse in snuffing out the life of someone as despicable as Slick. She knew that he was keeping the young girl against her will; and it hadn't taken Lauren being daring enough to put the black dot on her hand for Trista to know that the man lying dead on the cold tile of the motel's bathroom floor had deserved everything and more than what she'd dished out. Her only regret was that he hadn't suffered longer. She waited another minute or two before starting her truck and heading north on 28 from Old Forge. Tired, but feeling exhilarated, she found herself singing along with the classic rock songs being emitted from her Sirius radio station.

When she finally got home, it was dark but still relatively warm for Fall in the mountains. She thought about the poor girl who was probably on her way to one of Utica's hospitals by now. She silently prayed that the child's physical injuries weren't as severe as what her emotional ones. Trista tried not to think about what the poor thing must have gone through, and had no idea how long she had been held against her will, being mentally, physically and emotionally abused by her captor. She hoped that whoever was assigned to her case helped expedite returning Lauren to her family. She thought the girl couldn't have been more than seventeen or eighteen and, after what she'd probably been through at the hands of that monster, would probably never be a fun-loving teen again. But it was over for her now, and hopefully soon the child could start healing. Trista only wished that there was something more that she could have done for her and knew that she'd never see her again or know if hers' would be a happy ending. Trista took a deep breath as she exited her truck, and washed the event and Lauren from her mind. Greeted inside by the adorable puppy she'd left at her cabin while she'd worked, Trista immediately sat down to relax with a glass of wine and tried to forget about the nasty events that had transpired earlier in the evening.

He watched her leave the restaurant and head back toward Old Forge, but then somehow managed to lose her. He never saw her turn off the main road leading into town, but somehow she'd managed to ditch him again. Pissed, he drove up and down every street in town, but it wasn't until he turned on a side street on the outskirts of the hamlet that he caught a glimpse of her truck. He passed it, turned around and by the time he went past the area again, it was gone. He saw the taillights pulling away and within seconds turning onto Route 28 and heading out of Old Forge. He stayed several car lengths behind and as a precaution, had rented a generic-looking Prius. From what he'd been told when he had agreed to the job, Trista was not only extremely smart but very paranoid, so he wasn't sure if she was on the lookout for his CRV, hence the Prius. Sure, she'd find out about him soon enough, but not until they were ready for her to know. She'd been so smug sitting in that courtroom all those months ago looking innocent and like the poor victim, while they threw the book at her husband. The jury had convicted Nathaniel based not on any facts but rather on her testimony of the emotional and physical abuse she had suffered during their marriage. Thinking back now, it still burnt his ass to think about how those pathetic saps had listened to her and believed every word, even though there wasn't an ounce of proof that Nathaniel had hurt her in any way, other than getting caught dipping his wick where it didn't belong.

"Dumb bitch," he thought now, "If she'd just kept her mouth shut and left well enough alone, he wouldn't be stuck out in the middle of nowhere, tailing her around in some hick town full of tourists."

While he'd never officially met the woman who now went by the name Trista, he despised her just the same; and a job was a job and he was being compensated very well, so he'd stay as long as it took to get what he needed for his employer.

~~~ Chapter 29 ~~~

She awakened in a hospital room, confused by her surroundings. Terrified, she tried to sit up but immediately felt the room spin around her. Her movement triggered some kind of alarms and within minutes, two women entered the room with serious looks on their faces.

Seeing the child awake and obviously scared, the nurse smiled at her patient, trying to calm her.

"Well hello," she said pleasantly, "Glad to see you're back with us. My name is Jen and this is Veronica," she said softly, nodding her head toward the care attendant who'd accompanied her into the room.

"Let's see if we can't shut off those ridiculous machines, shall we?" she said rhetorically. "You've been asleep for a long time young lady, and I'm betting you're absolutely famished by now. And," she added, with a wink, "I'm betting your bladder feels like it's about to burst. Would you like Ronnie and I to help you up to the bathroom?"

Still very confused, and a little scared, she looked around the room, worried that he'd get mad that she was talking to strangers. She answered in a whisper, "Yes please."

When they tried to help her to a sitting position, the room started spinning again and she felt herself going under.

"Breathe Lauren, breathe. Don't you pass out on me young lady," the older woman sternly commanded, snapping Lauren out from entering the dark tunnel that was calling her. Jen spoke up, reassuringly,

"Come on honey, nice slow deep breaths, in through your nose, and blow it out slowly through your mouth. That's right Lauren, good job. In through your nose and out through your mouth. There you go," she said as she saw the girl's color improve. "Now open your eyes for me Lauren. Good girl. Okay, now let's try it again, but slower this time. When you stand, take another couple of those nice deep breathes, in through your nose and out through your mouth; and before you know it we'll have you in that bathroom so you can pee."

Lauren did as they'd instructed her, opened her eyes and scanned the room once again before starting to walk, with their assistance, to the bathroom. Her legs felt like lead and her head was still spinning but she was determined to make it. Just before entering the bathroom, she stopped and once again searched the room; looking for any signs of him. The fear in her eyes didn't go unnoticed by the older woman, who knew the look of an abuse victim when she saw it. She didn't need to see the bruises, cigarette burns or fresh scars on the child's torso to identify someone who was being abused; she just needed to see their eyes. The poor child's revealed far more than any words could express. She leaned in and reassured her softly, "He's not here baby; he'll never hurt you again. You're safe now."

"Are you sure?" she asked, still not believing that it could actually be over.

"Yes Lauren, he's out of your life for good, I promise." Knowing that she shouldn't ask but unable to help herself, the aide prodded gently. "Were you with him willingly Lauren or against your will?"

Seeing the teen burst into tears was all the answer she needed. They helped her into the bathroom and then back to bed. Just walking to the bathroom and back exhausted her, she couldn't figure out why she was so tired and her head felt so fuzzy. They had no sooner gotten her back into bed when a stern looking man in a white lab coat entered her room, accompanied by two police officers, one male and one female. They all gave her a once over and then made their introductions. Jen and Ronnie stayed in the room to act as referees or allies for the immediately distraught girl in their care. They started out sounding very sincere and caring, asking her how she felt and if she was comfortable. The female took the lead after the physician checked her out and told her that she could be released in the morning. Once he was out of the room, the officer sat down at her bedside and started with very benign, generic questions such as her full name, age, address and parents' names; all of which she reluctantly provided. The older, male officer remained silent for the first few minutes, but then interjected swiftly and rudely.

"So why did you kill your lover?"

"What?"

"Look sweetie, we know you know what we're talking about. We just haven't figured out how you did it and why. Wasn't your sugar daddy providing you with enough? Did you kill him or have your boyfriend do it?"

Watching her expression, both seasoned officers knew immediately that she had not witnessed the murder, nor did she even appear to have any knowledge of it. The doctor had explained to them that she'd been so heavily drugged when brought in, that even after the one-hour ambulance ride from Old Forge to Utica, her levels were still through the roof and that she could have slept through anything, including a struggle in the very room where she was sleeping. They knew that she was in no way associated with the guy's murder but since she had been in his company, she could somehow be connected somehow. Regardless they needed to go through with their routine questioning regardless.

She looked from one officer to the other, and then softly responded "I don't know who you are, where I am, or what you're talking about; but if you're telling me that Adam is dead, then I'm not only happy, I'm ecstatic. That bastard held me hostage, threatened to kill my parents and little brother and sister and chop them up into little pieces and hurt me over the last two months in more ways than I'd thought possible."   She lifted her hospital gown exposing herself from the neck down, revealing new and old bruises, black & blue marks, burns and scars from where he had cut her. She allowed them enough time to absorb the extent of her injuries, or at least see the visible ones, before covering herself back up.

"So in answer to your questions, no I don't know what you're talking about. No I didn't kill the bastard, though I wish I could have, and Lord knows I dreamt about it time and time again. And no, I don't have a boyfriend; or at least not one around here."

"Where ya from Lauren, where's home?" The female officer asked gently.

Lauren remained silent. It was only when Jen prompted her to answer, that she responded.

"I'm from Ohio."

"Okay, where in Ohio Lauren? You must have family worried sick about you right about now. Would you like to phone anyone and let them know you're alright?" the female officer asked.

"Yeah, I guess so," she responded, unenthusiastically.

"Answer some questions for us Lauren, and then we'll let you use our phones to call anyone you'd like," the male officer offered.

Knowing that they were trying to play her, Jen stepped in on behalf of the child.

"Guys, you've got five minutes to ask all the questions you need to ask our patient here. And then as promised, you're going to give her your phone and let her call her family. The five minutes is non-negotiable, and won't drift into ten or fifteen. You're in my house now, and around here you don't make the rules. If that's not acceptable, then bring her down to the station after she's discharged. If you're thinking about doing that though, let me know and I'll call my brother and he'll be present for any questioning of this young lady. You might know him, Jonathan Perelli, of Perelli, Brown and Smithstein. And lastly, Ronnie and I will be right here with our patient while you question her. If she looks tired or is getting stressed by your line of questioning, your interview will be cut short. If we all understand each other, then ask away," she said as she sat down on the edge of Lauren's bed and reached for her hand.

Pissed at the nurse's brass balls and bluntness, the female cop reigned in her temper and started first. "Lauren, how did you meet the man, Adam Cremship, and how long have you been in his company?"

She thought for just a minute to compose herself and then started answering. "I was mad at my boyfriend so I started playing around online, came across a website and responded to a post. He, Adam, said that he was a freshman premed and played hockey at the University of Pittsburgh. He'd posted pictures of himself and he was gorgeous so I thought it'd be fun just to flirt back and forth with him a little, ya know, to make my boyfriend jealous. We emailed and then started texting and after a week of it, then we started talking on the phone and skyping back and forth. It all was fun and innocent, so we kept talking and one thing led to another, and well, when we were skyping, it sort of made us both want to be experiencing it in person instead of via computer."

Wincing when she revealed what they were doing via skype, Lauren continued on even though her face was completely flushed from embarrassment.

"Anyways, I had told him that I was 18 and he had said that he was nineteen almost twenty, and we decided to meet in Cleveland Ohio for a night. That was two months ago," she whispered. "We met, and he was so nice at first. He was kind and romantic and gave me gifts when we went out to dinner. Then we went back to the hotel where he'd booked a room and the second the door was shut and locked, he turned into a monster. I wasn't a virgin and had experimented with, well, different positions; but he was a freak and wanted me to do things that I'd never done before and certainly didn't want to do ever and when I said no, he went nuts. Beat the crap out of me and just as quickly as he snapped, went back to normal, right afterwards. Said he was sorry, and poured me a glass of wine. I drank it, and woke up the next afternoon, hardly able to move and in another state. He'd drugged me with something he'd put in the wine and must have had sex with me multiple times because I had blood stains around orifices that should never have been touched and was raw down there," she said, glancing down at her waist.

"He told me he knew who I really was and started naming off my personal information that I hadn't shared on the website, and said that I was his possession now and that he owned me and that if I didn't do exactly what he said and wanted, that he'd go to my parents' home in Columbus and kill my little sister and brother, and then my parents. And I believed him. He was crazy," she ended with.

"So you willingly left your house in Columbus and drove to Cleveland to hook up, as you said, with a thirty-year-old man?"

"I told you," she said, glaring at the male officer, "He said that he was 19 and yes, I went to meet him, but I took the bus. It was supposed to be for one night, now two months!"

"And you told him that you were eighteen, which is of legal age to give consent, is that correct Miss Jeffers?" he continued, not giving an inch.

Now both irritated and pissed off, she responded. "Look asshole, think what you want. Yes, I lied about my age, shoot me. And yes I went to meet him willingly; but meeting someone for a one-night stand is not the same as being held captive for over 60 days. That fucker held me against my will for 63 days! So judge me for meeting him, but don't you dare judge me for being stuck with him for over two months! Before you even ask, yes I wanted him dead, but no, I did not kill him and I don't know who did. I don't even remember anything from the afternoon on."

Trying to keep her talking and knowing that nurse ratchet would be shutting them down in the very near future, the female officer asked her what she remembered of the day in question. Lauren explained that he'd gotten mad at her again, and had beaten her severely and the beating had been so intense that she'd sworn he'd broken some of her ribs. She'd dealt with it, ignored the pain, and gave him everything he'd wanted. By doing so he'd promised her that they could go out to lunch and she took the opportunity and asked him if they could return to the ADK Bar and Grill, which they did. She told the officers of the bartender who had kind eyes, and whom she'd shown her palm to, and explained to them what she'd done. Impressed by her tenacity, they kept writing down names and notations as she spoke, so that it was possible for them to follow up when they were done interviewing her. Lauren told the officers that she only had two drinks at the bar, and started feeling really sick half way through her lunch. She said that she threw up in the bathroom at the restaurant and multiple times once back in the motel room and next thing she knew, the room started spinning and then the blackness came and when she woke up, she was in the hospital bed that she was currently lying in.

The officers asked a few more questions and then thanked her for her time, reassured the nurse, who had never left her side during questioning that they had everything that they needed from her and when they spoke to her outside Lauren's room, informed her that while it wasn't up to them, they felt confident that she would be free to return to Ohio once she was discharged and shouldn't need to be questioned anymore. They left the hospital, knowing that their next stop would be a tiny bar in the mountains.

Lauren felt mentally exhausted after the interrogation was done and closed her eyes to rest. She had a million thoughts rushing through her mind; and after hearing her mother's voice on the phone, had finally broken down, realizing that it was finally over. Her parents had promised to be on the road within the hour to come and get her. As she lay there in her hospital bed, she thought about what, if anything, she would tell them about the hell she'd lived through during the last two months. She made sure to tell them that she loved them and just wanted to come home. Through her mother's sobbing, she'd heard the relief in her voice and knew that even though things would never be the same again in her family, she was going home and getting a second chance.

She had been undecided up until that point, about whether she'd ever attend college, and if she did, she hadn't decided on a major. She thought about the hell she had just lived through and how alone and vulnerable she'd felt being controlled by a monster while stuck in an unknown city with no way to communicate, no money, and no way to escape. She knew at that moment that she would go to college and in what she'd major. She had been helpless and in a horrible situation with no way out; and if she had her way, no other woman would have to feel the way she had. She knew now that she'd go to school to help other women in abusive situations. She'd study business and finance in order to help every city, big and small, have some type of safe haven for abused and battered women. Someone had killed her captor and given her a second chance, and she was not going to waste it. She suddenly felt more alive than she had since her nightmare began. Thanks to whomever that person was, she was going to give back to others and make a huge difference in abused women's lives. She smiled to herself, feeling finally happy for the first time in months. While she knew that the events of the past months would come back to haunt her, she felt that focusing on helping other women would help her heal as well. She was just drifting off to sleep when she heard Ronnie enter her room quietly. She walked over to Lauren, who appeared to be asleep, left an envelope on the table and silently walked back out. When she knew that she'd left, Lauren opened her eyes to see what she'd gotten. On her table was a Fed Ex envelope, addressed to Lauren in Pediatrics. She wasn't sure who would have sent her something as she didn't know anyone here and virtually no one knew where she was. Curiosity got the better of her and she ripped open the envelope in lightning speed. She peered inside the envelope, shocked to see a wad of perfectly aligned $100 bills, all appearing to be practically brand new and facing the same way. Tucked underneath them, was a small typed note.

Dear Lauren:

I hope that this note finds you well. If you're reading this right now, know that I'm smiling because you're finally safe. Take this money and find your way home again. If you haven't done so, call your family; regardless of the words that were said or the things that happened before you left them, know that hearing from you will be like a gift from God. Return home my friend, and remember that you've been given a second chance on life, use it wisely. Promise me that you'll get counseling; you are going to need it with all that you've been through and only a survivor understands the battle that you faced, and won....

You are a very beautiful, smart and courageous woman Lauren; never forget that. You were saved so that you could make a difference in other women's lives.

Be well my friend...

Lauren read the letter three times before putting it down and looking at the untouched pile of bills, neatly stacked and clipped together. With shaking hands, she gently unclipped the money and started counting off $100, $200, $300 until she came to $2500. She sat there in disbelief, staring at the largest amount of money that she'd ever seen or held in her hands in her life.

Who would have sent her over $2000, not knowing whether she'd even receive the envelope or not? And who had even known, other than the ambulance crew and the cops that she was even in the hospital? she thought to herself, completely baffled. And then it hit her. She knew who her guardian angel was, but wondered how in hell she would have known that she was here, and how could a bartender afford to give away that kind of money. As she lay there, in disbelief, she knew that it had to be Trista who gave her the money, but why she wondered. The woman had been the only person in the last two months that saw her, really saw her. So it had to have been her who gave her what was probably her entire life savings. Tears started to flow down her face when she thought about how a total stranger had saved her. Lauren would never forget Trista's act of kindness.

~~~ Chapter 30 ~~~

Trista slept well, woke refreshed and, after feeding the chickens and her two potbellied pigs, took her puppy, whom she'd finally decided to name Remmy, though she still liked the name Remmy, for a run. The pup loved the act of running, though he hated being restrained on a leash. She got back from their run and decided to take advantage of the unseasonably warm fall weather, and set about splitting some of the wood that Charlie had delivered to her earlier in the week. Still not sure how long she'd stay in the area, but knowing that winter in the Dacks could blow in at any time, she wanted an ample supply of dry wood inside just to be safe. She had the weirdest sensation of being watched but after checking her trail cam again yesterday and capturing nothing except for the same pesky bear that seemed to love her corner of the woods, she dismissed it as paranoia and continued splitting her wood.

He'd positioned himself in a tree on the north side of her home, where he could see not only her cabin but also her drive. He'd watched her leave with her new mutt and come back again, enjoying the view in both directions. He still had contempt for her and the job that he'd been forced to take on because of her; but he could honestly say that he didn't mind seeing her, especially when she pranced around her cabin in next to nothing. She might be a psycho bitch, but she was a psycho bitch with one hell of a body. And sweet Jesus, watching her swing an ax while wearing a skimpy tank top, that had been covered with a flannel shirt until she worked up a sweat, holey jeans and work boots was enough to make his mind go into overload. Certain parts of his anatomy began to dance in his pants. He waited until she had finished what she was going to split for the day, and went inside to shower. With his binoculars, he had a bird's eye view of her bedroom and when he saw her drop the towel after showering, he nearly fell off his branch. He knew it was against all rules, but for a brief moment he wondered if once, just once, he could enjoy a piece of her before he had to kill her. He knew that it was wrong, and sleeping with one's sister-in-law was technically not cool; but hell, it was only his half-brother's ex-wife, and since his brother was rotting away in jail because of her, he figured she was fair game. Of course, he'd never let his mother find out if he did, in fact, sack her. Mommy dearest was a force to be reckoned with he'd discovered, since reconciling with her six months earlier.

He'd found it odd that after thirty years, his long lost mother, who'd given him up for adoption, suddenly appeared out of nowhere and wanted to reconcile and get to know him. He had tried for years to find her, paying the website's fees, filling out their forms and joining their registries, all to no avail. Then out of nowhere, he's working at the garage and in walks his mother, all smiles and hugs. He'd have known her anywhere; they had the same exact piercing blue eyes, the same nose and jawline, and the same sly look about them. They made small talk and became acquainted with one another, while both holding back personal information. It hadn't taken long for him to learn her real reason for searching out and finding her forgotten son. She wanted something from him, and although he didn't give a damn about the fact that she claimed her baby boy was innocent and wrongly jailed, he started caring when he heard about how she would compensate him if he'd take on the job that she wanted done. He played hardball, and when he got her to add another "0" to the fee that she'd initially offered him, he knew that there was no way that he could refuse. She'd given him a $20,000 retainer and he'd packed his bags, such as they were, and headed towards the mountains. He had been living out of his CRV, and now a camping cabin at the local campsite since the nights had turned too cold to sleep without some form of heat.

It wasn't until he saw her leaving in her truck that he descended from his tree branch and headed out of the woods. He got momentarily turned around and walked in a slightly different direction than he'd come in and, unbeknownst to him, walked directly in front of Trista's trail cam. It captured not only his profile but his entire face.

<p style="text-align: center;">~~~ Chapter 31 ~~~</p>

Trista arrived at work early as usual, with Remmy in tow. Most days she brought him with her, and he slept in the office after filling his belly with treats, compliments of both Sal and Laverne. Today was no exception. Sal looked off, she noted as soon as she entered. Even the always loquacious and jovial Laverne appeared reserved compared to every other day. She quickly scanned the room and, seeing nothing out of order or out of place, put on a smile and greeted them like she always did. It wasn't until they were restocking the glasses that Sal finally brought up what was bothering him.

"We had some company here this afternoon before you came in. They were asking a lot of questions about you."

Not looking up from the task at hand, she replied. "Huh, me; why would anyone be interested in me?" she asked innocently.

Playing along with her, Sal responded in the soft tone for which he was known. "That's what I was wondering. It seems that they want to ask you if you knew anything about some customers who were in here the other day. Some couple; sat at table nine and came in two days in a row. Seems the man got himself murdered the other night, while staying in Old Forge. Told them that I couldn't recall anything unusual about any of our customers, but they interacted more with you than me. They went on to ask what your story was and if you were here all evening of the night in question."

"Okay, what did you tell them?"

"Told them that yes, you were here with Laverne and me all evening, and helped us close the joint down."

She looked at him, staring into his soul. "I didn't help you close Sal, and we both know it."

"We know it; they don't. And if that fucker did what they said he did to that child, then whoever took him out deserves a metal," he said, watching her for any reaction.

She didn't play his game but responded sincerely. "Anytime a life is taken is sad Sal. I saw way too much death when I was in the military, as I'm sure you did working the beat."

Laverne watched the interaction between her lover and her friend with scrutiny. It was as if they were in a dance to see who would lead. She didn't believe for one minute that her friend and co-worker had had anything to do with that jerk's death. The officers had come in to speak with Sal since it was established that his restaurant was the last place the couple was seen together before returning to the motel where he met his death. They'd been polite enough, never insinuating or implying anything directly, but they had ruffled her feathers when they started asking way too many questions about Trista. She was one of the kindest, gentlest people that Laverne had ever met. She'd seen firsthand what kind of person she was when Trista who came to Tabitha's aide, both emotionally and financially, when she'd needed it the most; and for those two cops to waltz into the restaurant and start challenging Sal as to what type of employees he had working there was bullshit in her eyes.

"I agree with you Trista, but that man held that poor girl hostage and kept her away from her family for over two months. The trauma he must have inflicted on her, both physically and mentally, will take a very long time to go away. For that reason alone, I'm glad he's dead. They said that the girl doesn't recall anything at all from the time she left the restaurant until the time that she woke up in the hospital, so she wasn't able to provide them with any details. They said that it looked like a professional hit and that there was absolutely no sign of a struggle, so whoever got to him must have overpowered him. Right now they have no witnesses, no motive, other than the fact that he was a scumbag, and they don't have any suspects. They were hoping that we could provide them some information about the guy, but I told them that we had nothing to offer them."

"Are they coming back here to question me, Sal?" she asked point blank.

"I don't think so; but if they do, you tell them the same thing that I told them. You were here with us, closing up. And don't tell them anything different, Trista. Nobody would benefit from telling them anything different, nor would it change the outcome for that scumbag now. Would it?"

Trista looked directly into the eyes of the man who'd become her mentor at the bar, not only her employer but her friend, and also into the all-knowing eyes of a cop. When their eyes locked, both could see the truth in the other with neither wavering. At that moment, she knew that if he chose to uphold the law, he'd have every right to call in the authorities, regardless of whether or not the person who had died deserved it. Their stare-down lasted a few more seconds and then she simply smiled.

"Whatever you say boss," she said warmly. "I WAS right here with you until we closed. I don't understand why we're even having this conversation, especially when I've got work to do before we open."

He smiled, and knew that, at last, they understood one another. He wasn't sure what had transpired in the motel room that had resulted in the death of a man; but he knew that somehow Trista was involved, or at the very least, knew more about what had happened than she was letting on. But, like the young girl who'd been held against her will, Trista also needed someone to protect and save her. "Alright then, let's get to work." And he turned to start refilling the beer refrigerator.

The crowd was steady and downright overwhelming at times once the doors opened for business. Tabby and Laverne had all they could do to keep up with the steady flow of customers flowing in and out of the restaurant. Charlie was at near panic level trying to bus and reset the tables, so Trista give him a hand whenever possible. The crowd was comprised of tourists, with a few locals intermingled here and there who had broken away from the arduous task of raking leaves on the beautiful fall afternoon. Tourists flocked to the mountains in the fall to not only enjoy the magnificent foliage that the Adirondacks provided every October, but they also came to hike the numerous fire towers and high peaks that were sprinkled throughout the 3125 miles that comprised the nation's largest state park. The Dacks were known as not only a hiking and camping mecca, but also a fisherman's paradise with bass, trout, salmon, northern pike, yellow perch, brown bullhead, tiger muskie, and panfish found throughout the Fulton Chain of Lakes. Trista, Tabby and Laverne tried their best to be cordial and polite as they hustled from one table to another. Couples, a few singles, and several families filled the tables as quickly as they became open. While it was a close to hectic pace, no one seemed to be impatient or irritated if they had to wait briefly until the next available table was bused and ready. When the bar finally hit a well needed lull, Trista grabbed her water bottle and dog and stepped outside just long enough to allow Remmy to relieve his over distended puppy bladder. The sky was overcast as the sun finally started to descent behind Rondaxe Mountain, commonly known to the tourists as Bald Mountain and Trista made her way back inside. As soon as she entered, she knew that something was different inside the bar. She could feel the electricity within the confines of the restaurant, and her initial thought was that the cops were back and looking for her. She felt her heart start to race as she scanned the room for the inevitable, and instead of finding them, she locked eyes with Lauren, standing in the presence of two older, very tired looking people, presumably her parents. The moment she saw Trista, she smiled, and without saying a word to her parents, started walking slowly in her direction. She tried to remain calm, but once she was close enough, literally threw herself into Trista's arms. Unsure of what to do, but so very happy to see her young friend safe and healthy again, she did what felt natural to her, she hugged her back; then pulled away long enough to look into Lauren's eyes.

"It's good to see you again, my friend. Are you okay?" Trista asked gently.

Even though she had promised herself not to, Lauren's eyes filled as she nodded yes.

"Thank you. Thank you for everything you've done for me," she whispered, afraid that if she spoke any louder, the dam would break and she'd be sobbing. She again pulled Trista into a hug and only then, when she knew that no one could hear, did she whisper into the bartender's ear.

"I know that it was you who put all of that money into the envelope for me and," she said in barely a whisper, "I know it was you who took care of Adam. I don't know how I'll ever repay you for either, but someday I will. I promise."

Trista stepped back from the teen and, leaning into her ear, spoke softly.

"Just be happy and someday when someone enters your life needs your help, do the best that you can to help them out. You're going to make such a difference in peoples' lives someday Lauren, I just know it. And by returning home with your parents," she said, looking up at the two people holding hands just a few feet away, "You've already started helping people. You've answered your parent's prayers, and they will never forget your gift to them."

Confused, Lauren looked at Trista. "What gift did I give my parents?" she asked, somewhat confused.

"You gave them back their reason for living, Lauren. Now go home and make a difference in this world. I'm counting on you."

Lauren hugged her savior one last time and ran back to her parent's side. Her mother started crying for the fourth time that day, while her father made direct eye contact with Trista, and mouthed just two words. "Thank You." With that, Trista watched Lauren walk out of her life to reclaim her own back in Ohio. As she exited, Lauren turned back one last time and shouted, "I'll never forget you Trista, I love you!"

He'd watched the interaction between the young girl and bartender from the confines of his corner table. He knew that it was risky walking into the restaurant and getting so close to her but she had no clue who he was, or any reason to believe that someone was watching her, so he wasn't worried about it. Maybe he was getting a little too comfortable or a little too cocky, but either way, he felt invisible but invincible. He certainly wasn't worried about some broad taking him down. He'd watched her making small talk with the people sitting at the bar, and watched her hips as she cleared tables to help the kid out. The way she moved swiftly and precisely indicated to him that she was not only in excellent shape but very rigid and disciplined in everything that she did. As he watched the way her jeans swayed as she juggled the plates currently balancing precariously on her forearm, he couldn't help but think it a shame that before the month was out, she'd either be dead or in jail.

She'd seen him as he sat at a secluded corner table. He was dressed generically enough, purposely blending in with all of the other leaf lookers, but the second she'd spotted him sitting alone staring at the menu as if he needed to memorize it, she'd known that he wasn't just there for the pulled pork sandwich. She'd never seen him before, but her gut instinct told her that he was something other than a tourist. He had a familiar look to him, but in the split second that she'd studied his face, she couldn't pinpoint where'd she'd seen it before. It wasn't until she was busing a table that had held a very rowdy family of eight that it dawned on her who he reminded her of. The second that she realized that the lone man with the hat and pouty face looked remarkably like her ex-husband, she looked over in his direction and saw nothing but an empty chair. She quickly walked to the window, in time to see a Prius pulling out of the lot and heading south toward Old Forge. She only caught the last numbers of his license plate, but that glimpse was enough to trigger something in the recesses of her brain.

She remained unsettled the rest of her shift. She'd been so elated to see Lauren not only alive but well, or at least as well as she was going to be until she got back home and hopefully into counseling. Even though they'd been swamped at work, she had enjoyed her shift until whoever that man was in the back corner had dampened her mood. It pissed her off to no end that just the reminder of her husband could still upset her so much, but she tried to compartmentalize her feelings, just as she done so many times before. She made a mental note to take a little trip into town in the morning and see if she happened to run into a certain male driving a certain Prius.

He'd purposely taken a roundabout way to get back to Old Forge and his hotel. He'd turned onto Route 28 upon leaving the restaurant and then almost immediately turned onto South Shore Road which brought him back to his destination. It just took a few more twists and turns to get there. On the way, being paranoid, he pulled over on a long straightaway and waited a good five minutes before continuing on, just to make certain that he wasn't being followed. He might not be a licensed PI, but he knew enough to not go directly from point A to point B without making sure he wasn't being watched; after all, he'd spent most of his life watching cop shows. Besides, the broad had been on the clock so it wasn't as if she could just walk out on a whim. The old man on the other hand, might pose a problem. He had the look of a cop. Walked like one, talked like one, and had a way of canvassing the area, albeit inconspicuously. He decided, as he took another swallow of the half empty beer that he was currently enjoying, that the old man might need to be taught a lesson also, if he got too close or in his business. After all, he was just another tourist enjoying the mountains. "Yup," he thought to himself, looking down at the rifle lying across his bed, "Just another tourist."

He drank another beer before checking in with Mommy dearest, as he called her just to piss her off. He knew that he'd never be considered her child, her first born son, the one she'd thrown to the curb just like she did his father; but what the hell, she had contacted him after all these years, not the other way around, so he'd ride the gravy train for as long as it was mutually beneficial. He knew that she didn't honestly give a damn about him, and that the only reason she had paid a PI to illegally open his sealed adoption records and track him down was so that she could use him. He knew it, she knew it and they both seemed to understand what the other wanted.

He'd agreed to meet her, initially stringing her along for a bit just so that he could feel that he had the upper hand; but when he finally agreed to reunite with the one who'd given him away, he had wondered how he would feel upon seeing her for the first time. He was relieved to feel nothing, she was simply a paycheck to him and he was her solution to a problem, nothing more. They both understood one another perfectly, but before he agreed to take on the task she wanted completed, he made her answer some of his lingering questions about how he came to be. He forced her to reveal the name of his father, and whatever information she had about him, including the school he attended, along with his parents and sibling's names, his last known address and what he had studied at college. She reluctantly explained that he'd joined the service right after she'd given their child up and broke up with him; and had only offered the fact that she knew he'd been overseas during Desert Storm. She claimed that she'd lost contact with him after that and, although he didn't believe her for one second, he'd let it go. She was currently paying him handsomely to do a job, so do it he would. When it was over, he'd never have to see her again. She rejected him once, and he'd do it right back to her when this was over with.

"Yes, yes I saw her. Yes, she's working up here as a bartender. Yes, I'm positive she had no clue who I am and hasn't even noticed me," he replied to her onslaught of questions.

"Are you all set to do what needs to be done? I want that bitch to pay for imprisoning my son!" she demanded.

"But momma," he teased, "She only framed one of your son's. I'm your son too."

"Yes, yes, of course you are. When this is all over with, I'll not only pay you," she said, knowing how to manipulate him, just as she'd done all the men all of her life, all her life, "but we'll really get to know one another, son" she added for good measure.

Knowing that she was lying through her teeth and he was nothing more than a means to an end to her, he smiled at the phone in his hand before he responded.

"I'd like that so much, mother." He gave her the rest of the information that he'd obtained and then ended the call. He popped open another beer and drank it, but not until he'd turned his computer to one of the many private adult sites he tended to enjoy far more often than he should. Maybe he'd have to see what was inside those jeans of Trista, Jasmine or whatever she called herself now, before she died. He knew that his employer, his mother, had just said that he was to set her up, like his mother suspected Trista had done to her beloved son Nate. He also knew however it would be so much easier to eliminate her altogether. Setting her up would require exact precision and a whole lot of planning and luck. He didn't want to be stuck in this bum fuck town for any longer than necessary and that either way, dead or alive, as long as she was out of the picture once and for all, it didn't matter how he did it.

He finished his beer, movie, and jerking off before falling to asleep. He dreamt of Trista and her cabin, waking up tired, and horny. Conversely, Trista slept just fine. She'd dreamt about Lauren and how happy the child must be now that she was safe and back home with her friends and family. She would never know how well the child was doing, since she didn't even know what her last name was or where she was from. All Trista knew was that wherever she'd returned to, she was in a much better place than she'd been just a few days before. She prayed quickly to her maker, asking him to watch over the child that she knew only as Lauren, and that everything would work out okay for her. Trista had overcome some horrible obstacles and hoped that her new friend could do the same. She grabbed Remmy's leash, and set out to on her routine run. She did her usual four miles and upon her return, walked toward the barn to feed her pigs and check on the chickens. She wasn't sure why, but something kept telling her that she should check on her webcams again. In the past they'd been void of anything except the expected deer, a couple coyotes and a very pesky black bear and she wasn't sure what compelled her to think today's tape would reveal anything. When she had completed what needed to be done with her ornery chickens and always-hungry pigs, and was just about to get on her four-wheeler to go for a ride in the woods, she saw Charlie pulling in with his antique-looking pickup truck, towing a wood chipper behind him. As soon as he saw her, his arm was out the open driver's side window, waving feverishly. She had momentarily forgotten that he'd promised to drop it off and pick up the wood splitter than his father had loaned her. Looking at the number of tree branches that she had piled up in a huge mound, reminded her just how much she really still needed the splitter. She promised Charlie that she'd return it to his father before the week was over, and he reassured her that they didn't need it for another few weeks or so. She invited him in to have breakfast with her, but he politely declined stating that Tabby and their daughter were waiting for him at home. His voice was so full of love when he spoke of her that it warmed Trista's heart just to hear him mention her name. They were young, and parents prematurely, but Trista knew in her heart that they'd make it now that they'd been given another chance.

He didn't know why he did it but he blurted it out to her just before he got back into his truck to return home.

"We're getting married Trista! She said yes. I asked her, and she said yes; and I have you to thank for that. If you hadn't come into our lives, she'd still be with that asshole. I wouldn't be with the love of my life and my daughter, and we wouldn't have the financial security that we currently have. You've given us another chance to make it, and I can't speak for Tabby, but I know that I'll never forget your kindness."

She had a lump swell in her throat as the lanky kid walked back to her, threw his arms around her and gave her a bear hug. She hadn't been touched by a man since her husband's last embrace months ago. For that brief moment as Charlie held her tight, she felt the warmth of someone who cared about her and realized how much she'd missed it.

"I don't know if I'll always be here for you Charlie, and I'm not the great individual that you think I am. I do know though that you and Tabby are meant to be together and if I helped you both realize that, well then I've done my job. And lastly, the clothes that I gave Tabitha are no longer of any use to me, so I'm very happy that she can use them, and the money that might have found its way into the pockets."

He loosened his embrace and looked down into the blue eyes of his friend. "I don't know what your past is, or what your future is Trista; but you being here now, in the present, has been nothing but a blessing to those of us with whom you've become friends. And while you might not put permanent roots put down in our little neck of the woods, we'll cherish and enjoy every day that we have you in our lives. And now that I sound absolutely ridiculous and have embarrassed both of us, I'll just get in my truck and head home before I say anything else to make both of us uncomfortable," he said as he turned toward his truck for the second time in five minutes. She watched him get in and drive away; to return to his waiting woman.

After he was out of sight, Trista decided to take a walk in the woods to retrieve the memory card out of her trail camera. She wanted to see if she'd caught that darn black bear again. There was still a chill in the air and while she kept her flannel buttoned all the way up as she walked through the dense forest, she wished that she'd had the foresight to grab a pair of mittens. She'd always loved hiking or simply walking in the woods. Having grown up in a very rural setting, she had used the woods surrounding her childhood home as her escape. Remmy ran back and forth as they made their way toward the tree holding her camera, while she enjoyed the silence that her woods afforded. Once she grabbed the memory card out of the camera mounted discreetly on a majestic looking red maple, she walked briskly back toward her tiny cabin. Once inside, she threw another log into her wood stove and put more water into the pot sitting atop the stove. She'd never known that a pot of water could work as well, if not better than a humidifier, but it was quite evident since taking possession of the miniature-sized camp that one-quart sized pot could provide all the humidity she needed. She made herself another cup of tea and then sat down to view the pictures on the card. She was sipping her second cup when she saw something she'd never expected, anticipated or thought possible. There, frozen for eternity on her computer screen was a face not of a bear but of the homo sapiens variety. As she studied the face looking back at her from the screen, she felt her blood start to boil. This time she made no effort whatsoever to curb the intense rage she felt coming on. Staring back at her was the man from the restaurant, she thought as she continued to stare at the series of pictures that her trail cam had captured. Then it hit her that not only was he the guy from the restaurant to whom she'd actually spoken, but he was the mystery man who drove the Honda CRV.

"Why you son of a bitch!" she nearly screamed, startling her sleeping mutt. "You wanna play games with me you fucker?" she nearly spit the words out. "You want to get to know me asshole? Well you've got it. You and me are about to become very well acquainted, and before I'm through with you, you'll wish that you were never born," she said calmly, pacing. A plan to remedy the situation started forming in her mind.

By the time she'd fed the do, and finished her now cold cup of tea, she knew exactly how to take care of her unwanted company. She knew that it needed to be taken care of during the upcoming week. Though her blood pressure was still elevated and her anger was still not under complete control, she'd been able to keep her faculties together long enough to plan every last detail of how she was going to handle this particular nuisance. She knew that she had to start by finding out who her admirer was, if he was a local or not, which she doubted, and, most importantly, where he lived. She knew that once she knew where he lived, the rest would be easy to take care of. He didn't look like he'd pose any real challenge to her, and if he truly were comfortable in the woods, he would have seen her trail cam and certainly wouldn't be front and center on her computer screen. She resented the fact that not only had he been brazen enough to come onto her property, but he had also had balls enough to stroll in and invade her place of work knowing full well that she would be there and could have identified him from the memory card had she viewed it earlier. "Oh yes, he will pay," she thought as a smile came across her face and she leaned back in her chair and closed her eyes, with the smile still firmly planted on her lips.

~~~ Chapter 32 ~~~

It took three days before she finally saw him again. She'd combed practically every mile of every road from Thendara to Inlet trying to find his CRV. It wasn't until she came upon the Prius with the tags matching the one from the restaurant that she put two and two together, realizing that sometime during the past week he must have traded in his Honda for a rental. She now realized that John Doe had to be somehow linked to her past, but for the life of her, she couldn't figure out who he was or what he wanted with her. She'd already made up her mind though that she'd find out before she killed him.

His rental was parked at one of the more obscure, smaller motels on the outskirts of town. The car was in plain sight which lead Trista to believe that whoever he was and whatever his agenda, he was either confident or stupid enough to not be hiding in plain sight, and unconcerned with about being spotted. He'd strolled into her restaurant as if he hadn't a care in the world, and had talked directly to her as he'd sat not two feet away. It dawned on her that he was probably the person who'd invaded the sanctity of her little cabin and who'd gone through her things, and that thought alone made her want to go bash his face in or rip his throat out. Even though she knew where he was staying, she still didn't know who he was, so it wasn't like she could walk into the lobby and ask to speak to him or get a key to his room. She'd have to come up with a way to lure him to her turf and end the nonsense once and for all. Little did she know that the opportunity would present itself that very day.

He knew that he shouldn't return to the restaurant, but there was something about this woman now known as Trista. He'd never known his half-brother and other than hearing about how wonderful Nathaniel was per Mommy Dearest, Blane had no idea what type of woman he'd been attracted to. One thing was certain, he thought to himself as he finished getting ready to head out the door, his little brother's taste was exquisite with regard to at least his ex-wife. Whether or not she set him up for the murder of his lover was irrelevant to Blane; he just knew that Trista had a body that most men would die for or at least drool over and he intended to see what lay under the layers of clothing that she wore to discreetly downplay her figure. It was as if she were a Siren luring him to her. As he jumped into his rental and headed north on 28 toward the ADK Bar & Grill, he still hadn't figured out quite how he was going to get her to come back to his motel room. Always one to work best under pressure, he wasn't worried about it and knew that before the night was over, they'd have a night neither would ever forget. As he drove out of town, his mind wandered back to the vagrant that he'd planted in her basement and briefly wondered how she had gotten rid of the body. How had she done it on her own, and without the assistance of a man? He knew how heavy the guy was from hauling him into her basement. The stench alone from the decaying corpse had been enough to make him nauseous, and he wondered just what this Trista chick was comprised of. Not only had she obviously easily dealt with his surprise head on but had done so independently and without missing a beat in her daily routine. He'd seen her the same day after she would have had to take care of her unexpected guest, and she appeared totally unfazed by what had to have been a strenuous workout. He still wondered how she disposed of the body. In hopes of seeing her again, he put his car in park and glanced one last time in the mirror and headed inside the tiny restaurant.

Trista stood next to the bar bullshitting with Sal as a few families made their way inside for what appeared to be the start of a busy early dinner shift. She'd come in early to give Laverne a hand since Tabitha wasn't feeling well and was starting to retain fluid now that the she was nearing her due date. Worried about the expectant mother, Trista insisted on stopping in town to see her before coming in to wait tables in her place. She'd offered to not only work Tabby's shift but stay until closing. Sal insisted though that he'd be fine working solo later in the evening. She still despised waitressing and felt that she was so inadequate at it compared to Laverne and Tabitha, but knew that she could fake her way through a shift or two to help the young mother out. With her back to the entrance, she hadn't seen him enter and head toward the same table that he'd sat at previously. With a tray full of beverages, she turned from the bar and headed toward the table full of five very rambunctious kids and two very exhausted-looking grandparents. It wasn't until she'd handed out the last root beer that she saw him. It only took one nanosecond for her to realize who he was. She stared at him until he looked up from the menu and their eyes locked. In that moment, she knew that one way or another, she would get her answers tonight and then he'd be out of her life forever. As she sauntered over toward his table their eyes never wavered from one another and she greeted him with a smile that revealed nothing but warmth and kindness.

"Welcome to ADK Bar & Grill. I'm Trista, and I'll be your server this afternoon. What can I start you out with?" she all but purred.

Looking deep into her crystal clear blue eyes, and seeing no sign of recognition, he visibly relaxed and turned on his boyish charm.

"Well good afternoon to you too," he smiled, just enough to show off his dimples. "Your smile certainly warms a man on a chilly day like today," he added, pretending to be slightly shy.

Two can play this game she thought as she watched his expressions more than listening to the words. And she should know, she thought to herself; she was the queen of being something that she was not. Pretending to blush, she smiled coyly.

"Well, don't you know how to put a smile on a girl's face."

He gave her an all-knowing look and responded more confidently than he intended to sound. "I do know how to, in more ways than one."

She looked into his eyes and although she knew that he was the one spying on her home and invading her personal life, held her temper at bay and responded. "You decide what you'd like, on the menu that is, and maybe we can discuss those other ways, after I get off of work." With that she turned and walked toward the bar, making sure that she walked slowly and deliberately, knowing that he was watching her every move.

Sal hadn't heard the dialog between his bartender and his patron but was wise enough to know that the guy sitting at the corner table had hit on Trista. What was slightly confusing to him was that, from her body language, it appeared she might be flirting back. He'd seen him in the restaurant previously, and even though he couldn't recall which day it was, Sal made it a point remember his patrons, however insignificant his exposure to them. He knew that this was the guy who drove a Prius even though it seemed out of character for a lanky fellow such as the one currently mesmerized by his bartender. Trista had worked for him for a few months now, and not once had she ever shown any interest in or attraction to any of the customers or locals for that matter. If he were a betting type of person, he'd have bet the restaurant that she'd have gone for some rugged, outdoorsy type, not some tall, lanky, geeky looking thing like the guy currently sitting at table number six.

"What can I get ya," he asked nonchalantly as she approached the bar.

"He wants a Saranac Pale Ale," she said, not making eye contact with Sal. He noted that she appeared visibly distracted as she placed the order.

"You sure that's all he wants?" he asked in a tone that caught her attention.

"What?" she said, coming out of the trance-like state that she'd been in.

"I said," he continued, speaking in a soft tone so that their conversation wasn't overheard by anyone else, "are you sure that beer is the only thing he's asking for?"

Surprised by the innuendo and caught off guard, Trista felt herself becoming defensive. "Not quite sure where that question came from boss, but yeah, that's all he's asking for."

"Trista," he responded, continuing to keep his voice low. "I don't care if you're interested in and/or are involved with someone; it's just that I wouldn't have pictured you with someone like the guy sitting back there who can't keep his eyes off your ass. I guess he's not the type of guy I would have expected you to go for."

It was Trista's turn to respond softly, but with a definite attitude. "Sal, I'm no more interested in that guy, than I am in becoming a pole dancer; but if I was, it truly would be no one's business but my own as long as it didn't interfere with my work here, correct?"

Knowing that the topic was closed, he patted her hand and smiled. "Correct." He handed her the requested bottle of beer and, as she turned to bring the patron his drink, heard Sal say just one more sentence. "If you become a pole dancer my friend, let me know cause that I'd love to see!"

Laughing, she flipped her boss off and headed toward the back of the restaurant and the guy who was waiting patiently for her return, watching every move she made.

As she neared his table, he set down the menu that he had all but memorized.

"Sorry to keep you waiting, sweetie. Did you find anything you'd like to eat?" she asked, knowing full well how she'd worded the question.

"Why yes, yes I did." As he leaned back in his chair like he was the coolest guy in not only the restaurant but the county, he couldn't get over his luck in finding the broad standing just feet from him. He had guessed that she'd be some frigid, tightly-wound bitch who wouldn't give him the time of day; someone quite similar to his birth mother. But the cute waitress with the cocky attitude and flirtatious style was not only receptive to his innuendos but was actually coming on to him! If she was as hot as she appeared to be and acted, he had absolutely no idea why his brother would have felt the need to go dogging to find another piece of ass. She might actually just be a tease, but he'd take the chance if it was offered and find out for himself.

"I'd like the pulled pork please, Trista; you said your name was Trista, correct?" he asked innocently.

"Great choice for lunch, and great memory. Um, I'm sorry, but I don't know your name."

"It's Blane," he said as he extended his hand, formally meeting her for the first time. He knew many personal

287

details about the woman whose hand he was currently holding.

"And it's a pleasure to meet you, Trista. I just love your accent," he added, even though he knew that it was all for show. "What part of Ireland are you from, and how long have you been in the States?" he asked, curious about what her response would be.

"Oh, I've been here since I was a wee tike, barely eleven or twelve. The brogue gives me away, now don't it?" she said, purposely trying to sound like a country bumpkin.

"Some days it's so pronounced, I feel like I finished a pint over there at me brother's pub and somehow woke up here!" she said, with a laugh. She didn't mention the name of the county in Ireland but as she leaned in to write his order, she offered him something better. He shamelessly glanced at her cleavage, and she allowed him a good view before straightening back up and pretending to be stretching. She once again made direct eye contact with the man sitting at her table and, even though she wanted nothing more than to rip him limb for limb, maintained her composure and continued on with the charade.

"Now Blane darling, you've had plenty of time to figure out what you want, so tell me and I'll be more than happy to get everything started," she finished with a seductive grin. He still couldn't believe his luck with the broad, but who was he to look a gift horse in the mouth? If she wanted a little romp or one-night stand, who was he to turn her down? He'd just screw her, kill her, collect his money from Mommy Dearest and take a little vacation down in Mexico for the holidays. Yes, he thought, finally something in his life was going the way it was supposed to. He figured that it was now or never as she stood above him, waiting to finish taking his order.

"Trista honey, I'd love another cold beer when you place the order, please. And if you're interested, I'd love to have a few cold ones with you this evening when you get off work."

He didn't ask whether she had plans or even if she had kids to attend to after her shift; she noted by his tone that he just assumed that she'd drop everything to have an opportunity to spend the evening with him. She was never one to simply react and do things on impulse, but the sooner she found out who this guy was, why he'd broken into her home and why he was staking out her property and stalking her, the better.

"Tell you what, I just happen to be free and have a full 12 pack in my cuisneoir, I mean refrigerator; and I do believe I'd love to share it with you. I get off at 4, but you've got to let me go home and, um, freshen up a bit; okay love?" she asked in her most seductive voice. "And I live a tad bit off the main road, so I can meet you wherever it is that you're staying and bring you home with me. I suppose since we'll be drinking, the safe and prudent thing to do would be to extend an invite for you to spend the night; you know, drunk driving laws and all."

He nearly choked on his beer, but recovered quickly. "Yes, you're so right. We wouldn't want to get into trouble with the local authorities, now would we?" he answered in a tone that Trista didn't quite know how to interpret. "But my hotel is such a dive; how about I meet you in the parking lot of Enchanted Forest?"

She didn't want to pick him up at an establishment that she knew had security cameras but figured that she could agree with him and then park on the road when the time came to meet him. He'd actually given her a perfect opportunity, and he didn't even know it. The parking lot of the local water park was always filled to capacity during the day and typically had numerous cars parked overnight, so his rental would blend in with the rest of the vacationer's vehicles and it might be days or weeks before someone noticed that it hadn't moved. By then Blane would be a distant memory.

"That sounds like a great idea. Why don't we plan on you parking your car there and meeting me by the road at 7? That way, I don't have to deal with fighting for a spot, and we can get the party started even quicker. Now I'll go put in your order so I don't get my ass fired," she joked as she turned to walk away.

After she placed the order, she turned and looked into the all-knowing eyes of Sal, her boss and former cop. "Anything you care to tell me about?" he asked, wondering why she was being so nice to the scumbag sitting at her table.

"He's having the pulled pork and another beer; is that what you wanted to know?" she teased.

Gently reaching for her arm, he looked at her with genuine concern.

"I have a bad feeling about that guy, and I really want you to keep your distance from him okay?" Before she could dismiss him, Sal continued. "I don't know what it is about him, but I know that I've seen him before. He's bad news, and you don't want to get tangled up with the likes of him. Promise me Trista."

She hated deceiving the man standing beside her as he was not only her boss, but her friend. Sometimes though, her work, and personal lives needed to remain separate; this was definitely one of those times.

"No worries, Sal. I have no intention of getting involved with him or anyone else who has a Y chromosome. I don't have the time nor inclination to hook up with someone now or in the foreseeable future. I'll let you and Laverne, and Charlie and Tabitha enjoy being lovebirds. I have Remmy and my animals; that's all I need to be very content and happy. So don't worry about me, my friend, okay?" she said as she winked at the man who'd become a second dad to her. "I'm a big girl and promise to take care of myself," she finished as she turned and walked toward the next table where she was greeted by four very energetic children and two frazzled parents.

He ate his pulled pork sandwich in silence as his mind played out different scenarios of how the evening could unfold. He decided that he'd bring his Glock just in case she proved to be a little stronger than she appeared. He could see that she was physically fit but so was he, and if push came to shove, he'd use his strength for pleasure and pain. He finished his third beer and waited until she came back with the check. She gave him the description of her truck and told him where she'd meet him at seven. She made small talk for just a minute before collecting his money and continuing on to the next patrons.

Sal watched their interaction closely, knowing there was more to their conversation than Trista was willing to divulge. Quite frankly that pissed him off, but he'd have to trust her and not challenge her. The stranger on the other hand was fair game, and he'd look into Mr. Prius thoroughly to find out more about him and his game. If

Trista wouldn't protect herself, he'd just have to do it for her he thought to himself as he restocked the bar glasses.

As soon as there was a lull, Sal told Laverne that he was heading up to his office for a few minutes to catch up on some much needed paperwork. Once inside, he made a call to his former partner and best friend from the force. After explaining what he was looking for and giving him the tag numbers from the rented Prius. He then sat back in his chair and closed his eyes, hoping to ward off the headache that he felt coming on. The jerk of course had paid in cash. It would have been so much easier if only he'd used a credit card. Nothing was that easy, Sal chuckled to himself. He still couldn't pinpoint what was off about the guy, but his gut told him that he was absolutely bad news. He didn't want Trista getting hooked up with anyone who gave him the kind of bad vibes that this guy did. He ended the call with his former partner promising to get back to him by the morning. Sal knew that he'd be good to his word.

The rest of the afternoon flew by and as soon as her shift was over, Trista didn't loiter. She said her good byes and cut out as quickly as she could, a move that didn't go unnoticed by her co-workers. After she sped off in her truck, Sal casually approached Laverne asking if she had plans for the evening and also whether she knew what Trista had any plans. Seeing right through his line of questioning, Laverne told him that it was none of his business if she or Trista had plans that didn't involve him. Seeing his hurt expression, she quickly gave him a hug and a quick pat on his rump, reassuring him that after closing, she was in fact available for their usual Friday night date night.

~~~ Chapter 33 ~~~

Rebecca, still concerned about her sister's physical and mental condition, packed a small overnight bag. As she sipped on her glass of Pinot Noir, she still wasn't sure about dropping in on her big sister unannounced. She knew that Trista had always been a very private person. It was a trait that had started in childhood when Trista wouldn't tell her what was wrong all those horrible nights that they lay in bed nursing their injuries. Deep down she knew that her sister had taken the brunt of the terror that had occurred in their childhood home and that she'd probably never truly know how horrible it had been for her. If she had to spend the rest of her life making it up to Trista, she would. She had vowed when she'd first taken her oath as a police officer that she'd protect and serve her community, friends and family. Trista was her number one priority. If she could, she'd make sure that no one hurt her big sister again. Even though she put on a very tough front, Rebecca knew that her sister, like any human, could only take so much. So if her sister wouldn't come down to the city to visit her, then she'd just have to take a road trip north to surprise her. She planned on setting out first thing in the morning so that she could get there before lunch. She smiled as she zipped her Victoria Secret bag, knowing how surprised her sister was going to be.

~~~ Chapter 34 ~~~

Trista made a few quick stops on her way home from the restaurant to pick up a few munchies for her "date". Knowing absolutely nothing about the man except that he had messed with the wrong lady, she started formulating a plan as she turned onto the dirt road leading to her cabin. She certainly hadn't anticipated the events of her evening unfolding the way that they were, but the Military had taught her that sometimes the best plans were those ones that were made and implemented on the spur of the moment. She would take what was being offered and get rid of him once and for all. First she wanted to find out who he was and what his motives were.

Her biggest concern had been how she was going to dispose of the body; it hadn't occurred to her that the easiest way was staring at her as she exited the barn to feed her pigs. Charlie hadn't come to pick up the wood chipper yet and, as she looked over at the huge mass of metal, she knew her worries were over. Both pigs snorted as if they knew what she was thinking, when in reality they were just hungry and knew that she was carrying their dinner. She fed her pot-bellied friends and gave them fresh water, (not that they seemed to care), as they inhaled their dinners while standing in mud up to their knees. She'd never known how true the expression "that pigs will eat anything" was, until she got two of her own. As she stood watching them, with her faithful dog Remmy by her side, she knew that once Blane gave her the answers, her pigs would have a banquet. Then she would take care of whoever had hired him to stalk her. Whoever that person was would also get what they deserved, she thought as she returned the bucket to the barn and went inside to get ready for an evening that neither she nor her guest would ever forget.

Blane waited anxiously for the designated time to arrive. He left his motel room earlier than he needed to but didn't know how busy town would be. He wanted to get to the parking lot and out of his car before meeting up with her. He'd checked and rechecked his supplies to make sure that he had everything he needed to make the evening enjoyable. He picked up a bouquet of flowers and a bottle of wine as a special touch, making it appear that he was a gentleman and that the evening was an official date.

She saw him before he saw her and for just one second she was moved by the fact that the man she was about to kill had bought her flowers and was holding a bag that appeared to contain wine. It warmed her heart to think that he had wanted to make a good impression and had gone to the effort to not only look good, but to present her with gifts. The feeling of pleasure was gone as quickly as it had come on. The woman who brought her truck to a stop, stepped out and greeted him with a fake smile was all business; he would figure that out soon enough.

"Hey darling, you looking for someone special?" she teased as she pushed open the passenger door.

"Why yes ma'am, I sure am. And it appears that I've found her," he said as he slid in beside her. "And she sure does look beautiful this evening," he added, turning on his boyish charm. "Thank you again for taking time out of your busy schedule to spend your evening with me."

"Trust me Blane, the pleasure's all mine," she responded, staring ahead as she pulled away from the curb.

They rode in silence for a moment or two which made Blane suddenly feel very uncomfortable. Trying to make small talk, he asked her how bad the cold and snow got up here in the mountains, knowing full well that she hadn't spent a winter season in the area. She answered on the fly, lying easily as she found several half-truths rolling off her tongue. During the entire drive up Route 28 toward Inlet, they asked each other questions with neither answering truthfully. She started down the road toward her tiny cabin and noticed that not once did her passenger comment about how far out in the boonies she livid. "Interesting" she thought to herself. She knew for certain now that he was guilty of trespassing on her property and entering her home.

"Sorry about the road back in here. It's really easy to mess up your suspension so I need to go rather slow."

"No problem. I'm just enjoying the view. If you don't mind me saying so Trista, you really are gorgeous."

Taking the compliment for what it was, she smiled, but became no less certain of his true nature. "Why thank you Sugar. That sure is a nice thing to say," she purred. "I try to take good care of myself, but who has time you know?" she kidded.

"You look like you take time to work out, my friend. I'm sure that most women must be envious of your looks. As soon as you speak, they must also hate you for being so smart."

"What makes you think I'm so smart?" she asked, sounding almost accusatory.

"Well, okay, maybe smart isn't the correct word. I'd say from this terrain that you're bringing me back in to that you must be not only smart but also fearless and ballsy. You or anyone else who dares to live this deep in the woods must have to be creative and improvise when situations arise. And I simply cannot imagine navigating these roads in the wintertime. The bumps and ruts must raise hell on your suspension."

Not willing to explain that she probably knew more about a vehicle's suspension than he did, she let the comment pass and played the helpless female. "Oh Lord I know! Luckily the owner of the bar keeps my truck under his watchful eye. If I need a tune-up or oil change, I call him, and he calls his brother and next thing I know, my truck is back in working order."

"I see. Is that the owner who bartends?" he asked innocently, even though he knew it was. "He reminds me of an ex-military man or a former cop."

"Why do you say that? He reminds me of my daddy back in Dublin," she said, acting nostalgic and pretending to let slip her supposed hometown.

Letting his guard down momentarily, forgetting that she wasn't in fact some cute little fawn from Ireland, he answered. "Oh I don't know, he just has the stance and stare of someone who seems structured and rigid, sort of like a cop or soldier."

Laughing out loud, Trista continued her charade. "Ha! Sal is about as laid back as they come. He took over the bar from his daddy and his daddy before him. They've had it in their family for over sixty years. Sal tried living in the city for a spell when he was fresh out of high school, but you know, it's the grass is always greener somewhere else kind of thing. I guess he lasted less than two months, returned to the North Country with his tail between his legs, apologized to his pa and never left again. I've been here for years, and while he runs a tight ship, he does it with nothing but love for his staff and patrons. Oh Lordy, he's going to get such a kick out of you thinking that he was a cop!" she exclaimed, slapping her thigh for effect.

He realized that he must have misread the old man during the two times that he'd actually been inside the bar. Maybe he was simply what she said he was. He knew for certain though that Trista or Jasmine, or whatever the hell her real name was, was not the innocent girl from Dublin she professed to be. He smiled warmly at her. "Good grief woman, you live out in the middle of nowhere!" he exclaimed as they made the final turn onto the dirt road that led to her cabin. Of course he knew exactly where her cabin was since he'd been staking it out for weeks but gave a convincing performance.

"You get used to it I guess. And here we are, home sweet home," she said as they pulled up to her cabin. Remmy, who'd been sleeping in the back seat, sat up immediately as soon as the truck came to a halt.

She'd left a few interior lights on and the cozy glow made the tiny cabin look like something out of a Norman Rockwell painting, with smoke billowing out of the chimney. The forest surrounding the cabin and the decorative fall wreath that she'd made herself displayed proudly on the front door gave the cabin a homey feeling. He appeared in awe as he stepped out of the truck and made his way quickly over to her side to open the door for her. She gathered up her purse and a few odds and ends and smiled as she exited the open door. She walked ahead of him and purposely handed him her bag as she lifted her keys to unlock her front door. They entered her cabin and, while he was still had his arms full with her belongings, she whirled around and attacked. He never saw it coming.

He woke, naked and tied to a chair. His wrists were bound behind his back, with some type of electrical cord was wound very tightly around his waist, and his feet were bound to the chair legs. His head was killing him, and he quickly realized that it was very hard to swallow.

He looked around the room trying to acclimate to his surroundings when it slowly came back to him how he'd gotten where he was. He remembered flirting with the woman who called herself Trista, making a play for her and meeting her in town. The memories started becoming clearer as he took in the smell of the wood stove and some type of cinnamon that seemed to warm his sense. The rest of him felt chilled from the cold room and the fact that he was tied to a wooden chair and butt ass naked. As he surveyed the room, the same one that he'd broken into and gone through dragging that old vagrants' body, he recalled the last moment before everything went dark. He'd been carrying her bags for her as they entered her cabin; one second he was making eye contact with her and the next, nothing.

She sensed he was coming to even before he realized that he was. She sipped tea from her spot on the couch, with his back to her, and never made a sound. She was not only proficient in physical torture, but also in creating mental terror. The scumbag currently coming to in her living room would find out just how experienced she was in both soon enough. Right now, he was too busy trying to remember how he'd gotten himself into his current situation to be scared. As she sipped her tea, she decided that it was time to change all that. Without giving it a second thought, she pushed the button next to her and instantaneously heard the wimp yelp like a puppy whose tail had been stepped on. Annoyed that he'd screm like a baby at the one low-voltage shock that she'd given him, she immediately pushed the button again, holding it down longer just for spite. She heard him not only shriek again but curse loudly as he swiveled his head from side to side, trying to figure out where she was in respect to his location. He couldn't see her but called out anyway.

"What the fuck? Hey look, Trista, I'm all for kinky, wild sex, but being naked, tied up and getting the hell shocked out of me does not constitute my version of fun. So honey, why don't you come on over here and untie me? Okay baby?"

She said nothing, allowing him to squirm a little more. He still had no idea how dire his current situation was. He still thought that he was getting laid tonight, a thought that made Trista almost laugh out loud. As she watched him tugging at the restraints on his arms and legs, she set her tea cup down just loud enough so that he'd hear the noise. She smiled as she saw his body flinch as if anticipating another shock, so she gave him one. This time he didn't scream, he just swore loudly. She decided that it was time to get her warped version of a party started, time to get the answers that she wanted and needed, and then time to pick up the mess.

As he strained and tried to turn around farther than his spine would allow, she got up and approached him. Saying nothing, she walked around the front of the chair and stood directly in front of him, never making eye contact. She allowed her eyes to gaze down at a certain part of his anatomy which in its current state looked pathetic and very unattractive. She continued to stare as if showing her disapproval of his size. He looked at her with eyes almost pleading and suddenly became aware of where her eyes were focused.

"Hey, there you are. What the hell Trista? It's fucking freezing in here. And why am I the only one without clothes on? Say baby, why don't you untie me, and I'll show you what my package can really do."

"Shut up! You'll talk when I say you can talk, understand?" she responded in a voice that he'd never heard before. Gone was the sweet, angelic voice of the girl claiming to be from Dublin; in its place was a voice that sounded like it was coming from Satan himself.

He didn't know how to respond as she circled around the front of his chair, still too ignorant to be alarmed. A small part of him thought she was doing some kinky role-playing and when she saw that he was becoming aroused, she took her blade and in one swift movement nearly severed his organ. He screamed in agony as her blade cut off part of his shaft and blood started pouring from the wound. In shock, he started screaming obscenities at her until she lifted the blade of her knife high enough for him to see his own blood still dripping from it. He promptly was silenced. It was only then that he started to grasp the severity of his situation and changed his attitude quickly.

"Hey Trista, I'm not sure what your game is, but I don't think you want to really want to hurt me now, do you honey? So why don't you untie me? There's no need for you to give me a ride, I can walk back to my car, and we'll call it a night okay?" he said, both asking and pleading. "Really, just let me go Trista, and we can forget all about the evening okay? Just let me go honey, please." Her response was a swift backhand to the side of his head and another shock.

"Open your mouth one more time when I've told you to keep it shut unless spoken to, and you'll get more than just a shock. I'll take the coil, wrap it around that sorry excuse of a cock of yours and stick the other end up your ass."

Knowing that she probably meant it, his eyes bulged as he envisioned what she was threatening. She watched his body language and when she saw his shoulders slump slightly, realized that she'd won. She knew that now was the time to get the answers that she wanted and needed.

She gave him some credit. He actually was slightly tougher than she'd thought he'd be. It took nearly an hour for him to break, despite her techniques. By the time it was done, he had a shattered knee cap, broken nose, enough electricity enter his body to light up an entire house, and more slices to his skin, soft tissue and muscle than she could count. She had found out that her ex-mother-in-law was not only behind everything that he'd been up to, but was also trying to get her beloved son a new trial and his guilty verdict thrown out. By the time she was finished with him, Blane had reluctantly given her all the answers that she desired. He hadn't withheld one morsel of information. He thought that he would be spared if he cooperated. By the time she was through though, he realized that death would be a welcome thing and couldn't come soon enough. He knew that she was probably going to kill him and he knew for certain that she was absolutely insane. What he didn't know was what she had in store for him next. She walked out of the room and left him alone in the dark. His eyes were nearly swollen shut and, even if they weren't, he didn't want to look down at what was left of his body. What he really wanted was for her to come back in and shoot him and end his pain and suffering.

She left him alone for another few minutes while retrieving the vial from the locked safe under her bed. It contained one tiny vial and syringe, two throwaway phones, a switchblade, her 9mm, and what was left of her cash. She drew the clear solution into her syringe and. saying nothing, walked up to what had been a nice looking man. She plunged the needle into his bicep and pushed the liquid in, not bothering to cleanse the area with alcohol. Potential infection was the least of his worries now and he wouldn't be alive long enough to develop one. She opened her wood stove and threw the syringe into the flame, closed the door and turned toward him. She saw how pathetic he looked but felt not one ounce of pity for the man who'd been stupid enough to go up against her.

"Blane, listen to me carefully." She walked up to him again, this time gagging him with the filthy handkerchief she'd used for the past week when she was working cutting wood. She knew the stench and taste must have been revolting, but she really didn't care. She knew that if given the opportunity, he'd be very verbal once she told him the last bit of her surprise. Quite frankly she was sick of listening to him whine, plead and beg for her to spare his miserable life.

"Blane, honey," she nearly spit out, "what I just injected into your arm is called succinylcholine. You will start to feel its effect within a few minutes. Maybe you've heard of it before or maybe even had it. It's an agent used in surgery to paralyze the muscles in a person's body. You'll remain completely awake and alert, but within a few minutes, you won't be able to move your arms or your legs. Eventually, you won't be able to breathe because your diaphragm, which is a muscle by the way, wouldn't be able to rise. You would suffocate." Seeing his eyes widen, she laughed. "Don't worry Blane, I won't let you die that way. Once you can't move, I have much bigger and better plans for you. Believe me, I want you fully conscious for them," she added, in a voice that was so sinister that it didn't sound human. "Did you happen to see the wood chipper sitting off to the side of my house love?" she asked, chuckling. When he realized what she was saying, he started thrashing violently with both his arms and legs. He remained unable to move more than an inch or so and although he tried desperately to scream, beg or simply plead with her, his words came out garbled and as twisted as his captor's mind. She let her words sink in completely, burst out laughing and walked away, to change into clothing more suitable for the task at hand. By the time she came back into the room, she could tell that the drug was working. He was close to suffocating so she knew she had to work fast. She wanted him alive when she turned the chipper on and fed him to it. She felt that it was a fitting retribution for the man who'd stalked her, invaded her space and acted superior to her. After she'd taken care of him, she'd go after her beloved ex-mother-in-law. She hadn't figured out yet what she'd do to Mrs. Benedict, but she'd work that out once she'd finished this job.

It took her less than thirty seconds to untie him, throw him over her shoulder in the same fireman's carry that she'd used on the corpse that he'd planted in her basement, and walk outside. When she got close to the side of the house next to the barn where the wood chipper was sitting, she dropped him on the ground like a sack of potatoes. She let him lie facing her as she pulled the wood chipper from its' current location over to the fence next to her pigs and their trough. He realized then what she was going to do to him, finally accepted the fact that he was about to die and there was not a damn thing that he could do to stop her. The woman was insane, and she was about to feed him to her pigs. Not being a religious man, he nevertheless started praying fervently to every God that he could think of as she lifted him and started to feed him feet first into the churning teeth. He felt the pain but somehow accepted it, knowing that it would be over within seconds. He thanked God that she wasn't sadistic enough to stop the feeder midway.

The wood chipper ran until he was threaded through and her two pigs were feeding hungrily. She had already burned his clothes and shoes. Now all that remained of the man who called himself Blane, was currently being devoured by her pigs. She was grateful that she'd had the foresight to wear ear protectors. She could only imagine how noisy it must have been when his bones crunched as the teeth shredded his pathetic body. When she was finished, she quickly hosed down the chipper, pulled it a safe distance from the pigsty, poured several gallons of beach over it and rinsed it with water again. Satisfied that no DNA would ever be found on Charlie's father's chipper, and after stripping out of the clothing that she'd been wearing, she returned to her cabin. She shut the door as her pigs continued chowing away.

The cabin was toasty warm as she made her way inside, opened the wood stove and threw her work clothes inside. Comfortable in her skin, she walked over to her refrigerator and poured herself another glass of wine, as Remmy slept soundly on his oversized dog bed. She finished her glass of wine before heading into the bathroom to shower off any of Blane's remains. As the scalding water hit her, she marveled at the fact that the guy who portrayed himself as so big and tough, had not put up a better fight. She thought back to her days in the military and thought with disgust that a wimp like that wouldn't have even made it through basic training.

Her skin started to burn as she stayed in the tiny shower longer than she should have, thinking about the fact that her mother-in-law had in fact been the bitch who had invaded her life. She felt rage building the more she thought about her next challenge. Facing the woman who started this war would require that Trista return to Utica. Then the bitch would have the hometown advantage, something that she did not want to happen but knew that it was inevitable. She would have to come up with a plan fast and then implement it in one swift move. If the bitch didn't like what she'd done to her conniving, cheating husband, just wait until she saw what Trista had in mind for her. Knowing that if she continued dwelling on the topic, her temper would escalate and she might do something rash, she stepped out of the warm water into the frigid air of her bathroom, and change the subject playing in her head.

Remmy was waiting for her as soon as she opened the bathroom door, and made it very apparent that he wanted a quick bathroom break before retiring for the night. She let him out, and he immediately made a bee line for the pig pen. It took her only a second to realize what he was after, or to be more precise, who he was after. She called him back, but the desire for a free buffet was more tempting than his faithfulness to her command. He squeezed his way between the rails in an attempt to enter the mud enclosure where her two pigs were currently eating to their hearts' content. She managed to grab him by the hindquarters just as he was about to dive into the mud and mess that was what was left of her unwanted guest.

"Okay Remmy, nice try, but he wouldn't taste good to you. My boys will eat anything, and by morning, will have devoured my friend. But you, my baby, should have more refined tastes than that. Let momma bring you inside and I'll give you a nice rawhide bone." She stroked him lovingly like she would a child's hair, and she held her puppy, rocking him gently in her arms. As she sat on the frozen ground, rocking and singing to her puppy, her pigs continued to finish off what had been Blane Johnson.

~~~ Chapter 35 ~~~

Rebecca tossed and turned all night, knowing that she needed to get to her sister as soon as possible. Their bond was such that even though she didn't know what was wrong, she knew that it was imperative to be with Trista and see for herself how she was making out in her new environment. She grabbed a quick bite and was on the road by eight with her overnight bag and service revolver on the seat beside her. Years ago she had tried to separate herself from being a cop when she was off-duty but she quickly realized that she felt naked and exposed if she didn't have her gun with her at all times. Luckily, she'd never been in an off-duty situation where she was forced her to use her weapon, but, she still felt much more comfortable knowing that it was there. Just in case. Besides, her sister had moved to the mountains and Lord knew what types of creatures lurked around her tiny cabin when the sun set.

Trista woke refreshed, having slept just fine. The elimination of one Blane Johnson didn't faze her, and her conscience was clear as she woke to see Remmy staring at her. Knowing that he only partially wanted to go out to pee, and to his dismay, she put him on his runner. She then retreated to her bathroom to relieve herself. She didn't know what it was, but there was something in the air. She could feel it but since she didn't know what "it" was, proceeded with start her morning.

She used the restroom, washed up and threw on her running clothes. She could definitely feel that winter was just around the corner. She checked to see how much wood was already stacked on her porch and tried to visualize how much she'd already tucked into the woodshed attached to her little cabin. Remmy waited anxiously to start their run and pulled on his leash as his patience waned.

"Alright, alright," she said, picking up the leash from the floor and opening the door for her four-legged friend. "Jesus it's cold out here," she snapped, as she quickly pulled gloves on prior to starting down the driveway. Remmy kept pace with her as she started out slowly but increased her pace as she reached the end of her drive and the beginning of the old dirt road. While the town considered the road to be in good shape, the potholes on both sides of the road were large enough to engulf a Mini Cooper. The shoulders were nonexistent in other spot, but Trista didn't complain since it was her idea to live in such a remote, isolated area. Yes, there were definitely adjustments to be made when she'd chosen to live in such a rural area of the mountains, but the benefits certainly outweighed any inconveniences. Having her privacy and the ability to live this chapter of her life the way that she chose to was more important to her than a bumpy ride into work. So as she headed down the road with her overly rambunctious puppy at her side, she knew that she had finally found her home. The possessions that she'd acquired when she'd been with Nathaniel were insignificant to her both then and now. She'd never belonged in their world nor did he in hers, but for over five years she had been very happy. She'd truly loved the man, not what his name and money could buy. She'd fallen in love with his boyish charm, warm smile and kind heart, and not as his mother had always accused, his fat wallet. Yes, financial stability had its' perks but their relationship had worked, even though they were from different sides of the tracks. Their genuine love and respect for one another was what had bond them together. "Life time ago," she said aloud as she increased her pace, much to Remmy's pleasure. She waved at Mr. Taylor as she passed his yard. He was out cutting wood just as he did almost every day, despite turning 84 just a few weeks prior. She made it just a few steps past him before she turned around, thinking his color hadn't looked right. Her intuition had been right. She watched him start to buckle and raced to catch him as he went down, clutching his heart. His color was ashen-gray and his lips looked blue. She lowered him to the ground, feeling for a pulse. She found none. Screaming for Mabel, his 82-year-old wife and commanding her dog to sit and stay, Trista quickly ripped open the old man's Carhartt jacket, revealing a tattered and well-worn flannel shirt. Making sure that her assumption had been correct, and hoping that Mabel had heard her call for help, she gave him two rescue breaths. She had already started compressions when she saw Mabel make her way to the doorway, and a look of surprise come over her face when she saw her husband on the ground and their neighbor hovering over him. Not one to mince words, Trista was loud, and to the point.

"Mabel, I need you to call 911, and tell them we need them out here pronto. Tell them Henry's having a heart attack and we need help out here as soon as possible. You got that, Mabel?" Not waiting for a response, she barked another command. "Go call them NOW Mrs. Taylor! I need help!" And with that, she went back to the task at hand. She completed her cycles of 30 compressions and 2 breaths and refused to think about

315

the fatigue setting in. She'd keep going until the old geezer started breathing on his own or help arrive. Either way, she wasn't abandoning her neighbor and friend. It took less than a minute before she saw Mrs. Taylor make her way outside, as fast as her wobbling legs would carry her. One thing she noted about country folk was that even in a crisis, they didn't panic. Here was her husband of 64 years lying on the frozen ground at her feet, looking half-dead, and the matriarch of the family didn't cry or break down. As she stood there in her dress, with a shawl wrapped around her shoulders, she told her husband just exactly what she thought of him deciding to have a heart attack. She stood looking at her man, and the woman trying to save his life, braced her shoulders and willed him back.

"Henry David Taylor, you stubborn old man, you listen to me! Don't you dare think you're going to die on me! Our Trista here is pumping the hell out of your chest and breathing for you, but damn it, she's getting cold and tired. So you cut this crap out right now and start to breathe on your own, you hear me? Don't you dare leave me, ya hear? Now get that old heart of yours going, you come back to me and you do it right now!" she said, as Trista noted a lone tear running down the old woman's face. Starting to lose feeling in her nearly frozen fingers, she silently prayed that the ambulance would arrive soon. Just went another level of fatigue starting setting in, Trista and Mabel heard the wail of a siren in the distance. Knowing that it was just a matter of time before help arrived, Trista felt a surge of energy and continued, willing him to come back to her, though not quite as gruffly as his bride had.

The ambulance set a time record getting to the home, as Henry and Mabel were lifelong residents of the area, and honorary grandparents to half the town. When the call came over the scanner, more than a dozen men and women stopped what they were doing and raced to the Taylor's homestead in the woods. Mrs. Taylor had done what Trista had instructed her to do, she'd called 911 and told the dispatcher that her husband was having a heart attack, but failed to mention that someone was on scene doing CPR from onset. The ambulance appeared in the driveway with three men jumping out almost before it was in park. Several trucks carrying volunteer firemen and paramedics streamed in behind it with all racing to the front yard to find Trista bent over their patient. Seeing the fatigue written all over her face, Marilyn quickly kneeled down to relieve her. Relieved, Trista gladly accepted her replacement. It wasn't until then, that she saw that Sal was one of the volunteers in attendance. Ignoring him, she rattled off what she had observed, and his down time.

Sal wrapped his jacket around her shoulders and noted how truly freezing the poor girl was. Helping her to a stand, he quickly moved his arms up and down her shoulders and arms, trying to warm her. Knowing that it was probably 80+ inside the Taylors' cabin, but also knowing that she wouldn't leave Henry's side until they took him away, he didn't even suggest it. He'd listened to her excellent triage of their patient, who now had a pulse after being shocked only once. The volunteer paramedics were already loading him onto a gurney and calling the ER in Utica, apprising them of the patient they would be transporting in and their ETA. As Sal had listened to Trista use of expert medical lingo and thoroughness in her assessment, he quickly surmised that his star bartender must have been an excellent nurse when she had worked as one. He also knew that the topic would have to wait and be the subject of discussion for another day. Right now what mattered was that she had been in the right place at the right time and knew what to do to increase old Henry's chances of survival. As the ambulance loaded up both Mr. and Mrs. Taylor, he silently observed Trista and knew that what he saw in her was genuine concern and love for her neighbor, even though she'd known him less than a year.

They shut the doors, tapped on the side of the rig for good luck and sped off towards Utica and the ER team that would be waiting for Henry when they arrived. Once the ambulance was out of sight, he saw her finally relax, and walk over to her dog, kneel down and hold him tightly.

"You did a great job Trista. You saved a man's life this morning and I'm very, very proud of you."

She let the words sink in, lifted her head toward him and smiled. "Thanks."

"Look at me Trista. Look me in the eyes," he commanded more than asked. When he knew he had her full attention, he smiled warmly.

"Not sure how you were able to remain as calm as you were during the whole event, but I just wanted you to know that a seasoned paramedic might not have lasted doing CPR as long as you did, especially in the light attire that you're wearing, and in such frigid weather. All I'm saying is that you are one tough cookie and again, I'm so proud of you. Once Henry is okay and Mabel is back from the hospital, be forewarned, you'll have enough pie, cakes and sweets to last a lifetime. She's an amazing cook and will never forget what you did to save her Henry. So when she comes calling at least once or twice a week, be gracious and accept what she is offering. And if ever she brings you one of her Pecan Pies and you don't want it, I'll gladly take it off of your hands since she makes the best Pecan Pie in town," he added, winking.

She laughed, and stood up to face him. "Well," she teased, "It just so happens that Pecan Pie happens to one of my favorites as well, but I'm willing to share."

She unhooked her dogs leash from the tree branch that one of the volunteers had tied him to when everyone had arrived on scene. Knowing that he was free, Remmy attempted to run over toward Sal, in search of a biscuit. His efforts were not in vain when he was rewarded with a couple biscuits that Sal always kept in his truck. As he gobbled them down in just a few quick bites, Trista waited for him to finish so that they could head back home, so she could park herself by the stove to warm up. She had anticipating going grocery shopping right after her run but now that she'd lost so much of the morning decided that spending her hard earned money on groceries could wait until another day. Right now all she wanted to do was return home and change into something much warmer and curl up with a cup of tea. She prayed that she'd put a log big enough in her Franklin wood stove to keep the cabin warm and cozy while she'd been gone. When Sal realized that she intended to walk or run back home, he opened the passenger side door or his truck and spoke.

"There is no way in hell that I'm going to let you stay out in this temperature one minute longer, especially dressed like that, so don't even bother saying a word. Get in, and I'll drive you home Trista. You don't have to invite me in.

I know that you aren't used to the cold up here yet and you'll end up with pneumonia. I can't afford to have you out sick now that are busy season is just around the corner. So keep quiet and get in. And that means you too Remmy. I'm not going to ask you twice you mutt, so get in before I change my mind," he kidded, seeing both dog and master doing what they were told.

He drove them the half mile down the road to her driveway and bumped his way down her long driveway toward her cabin. She had been so preoccupied with being half frozen that she hadn't given it a thought about Sal offering her a lift, until she stared at the wood chipper sitting right in front of her barn. Parked in the sun it seemed to sparkle, gaining everyone's attention.

He put the truck into park and shut off the engine, even though he'd said he wasn't staying. Trista didn't say anything, just practically jumped out of the truck and called her dog, hoping that they could exit the truck and Sal would leave the premises, which much to her dismay, didn't happen.

"He walked over toward the wood chipper and recognizing it, turned toward Trista. "If I had known that you'd borrowed Charlie's wood chipper, I'd have helped you some afternoon you know. Why are you so damn independent Trista? Sometimes it's okay to ask for help you know!" he exclaimed, somewhat exasperated at her.

He knew that she was physically capable of splitting her own wood and running a wood chipper, but he hated the fact that she didn't trust their friendship enough to ask for help. He walked over toward the splitter, which seemed to glisten in the mid-morning sun. He turned back toward Trista and headed toward her front door, leaving her standing there, not sure what to do.

"Come on, let's go inside. I need another cup of coffee."

Given no choice, she opened the door and invited him inside her cabin. The warmth hit her and was such a welcome relief that she stood still momentarily, absorbing it into her lungs and skin. He made himself at home, walking over to her coffeepot and pouring them both a cup. He then sat down at her tiny kitchen table, with its mismatched chairs and embroidered tablecloth that Sal knew the former owner had hand-stitched months before she'd died and that there were probably another half dozen or more tucked away in the pantry or one of the many closets in the tiny cabin. He thought he saw her hesitate as if in a mental battle with herself, but finally she sat down at the table next to him. He sipped on his coffee casually, never looking directly at her. He took a few more sips and then finally spoke.

"Trista, do you trust me?" he asked softly.

She looked directly at the man who'd become one of her best friends, not just her boss. She wasn't sure where he was going with his line of questioning but answered honestly.

"Of course I trust you Sal. Why do you ask?" she asked innocently.

"Because I know that you don't trust me enough to talk to me. And I know that you're keeping secrets from me Trista, and I just wish that you knew that you could count on me, no matter what" he added for good measure.

He saw her gulp and casually take a deep breath, indicating to him that he'd been correct in his assumption that she was keeping something from him. He gave her credit though for not lying or changing the subject.

"Cut to the chase Sal," she demanded. "What are you talking about?"

"I'm fucking talking about the fact that you cut all of that damn wood, split it, and now obviously just recently must have spent hours chipping all of the leftover branches! You have numerous friends who love you and who would have come over to help you out damn it," he said, exasperated. He got up and paced, not sure if he was frustrated with her independence or her stubbornness.

"I cannot believe that you work full time, take care of your menagerie of animals, and still had time to cut up all of that wood. I need the exercise and I know that the wood splitter belongs to Charlie's dad, so I'm betting that Charlie would have been over here in a heartbeat to give you a hand if you had just asked. Shit, Laverne would have come too! That woman loves to get her hands dirty sometimes and is as strong as an ox, despite her fancy appearance at the restaurant. She would have been right at your side the entire time you know. We are your friends and that what friends do damn it! They help each other out!"

"I know Sal." She looked directly into the piercing blue eyes of her mentor and friend. "You've figured out by now that I'm a very private person, and one who needs to keep her personal life personal. But in answer to your question my friend, yes I trust you and I know that you, Charlie and Laverne would have come to my aid in a heartbeat if I had asked for it. But, the manual labor was something that I needed to do, actually wanted to do, if that makes any sense."

He got up to leave and Trista could tell that he was no longer upset with her.

"Yes it makes sense Trista. Just remember," he said as he headed toward the door, "No matter what, you need to know that you can trust me and count on me. You're in the North Country now and up here we count on our friends, regardless of the circumstances. You'd be smart to remember that okay? Oh," he said as he walked out onto the front porch and just before he shut the door to leave. "You must have had a field mouse or a rabbit's nest stuck in your branches when you put them through the chipper because I noticed something that looked an awful lot like blood on the shaft and a few of the blades. You might want to hose it off some and clean it up before Charlie heads back over to pick it up."

He made direct eye contact with her and in that moment, they both understood each other perfectly.

"It was a rabbit's nest Sal. I felt bad about it but it is what it is, you know. It couldn't be helped and won't happen again. I thought I'd cleaned up all the mess but obviously missed a spot. I'll be more careful next time."

"I'm sure one dead rabbit won't be missed right?"

In that moment she knew that she had an ally. "Right," she responded.

He waved good bye and as he headed toward his truck he shouted back just one last thing.

"Thank you again for knowing what you were doing. You are solely responsible for saving Henry's life. No one will forget what you did for him. And Trista, please be more careful."

He left that particular statement up to her interpretation, got into his truck and left with her standing on her porch, dog at her side.

~~~ Chapter 36 ~~~

She was pissed, absolutely pissed. Her useless son hadn't reported in to her in over 48 hours and that fact, along with the fact that he hadn't been able to set the little bitch up yet, not only pissed her off but quite frankly, infuriated her. She'd given him totally explicit instructions and so far he had screwed up every one of her orders. Nit wit dumbass she thought as she paced. She'd kick his ass herself if she was forced to head up to those god-forsaken mountains to finish the job that he obviously wasn't capable of doing.

Meredith knew that she shouldn't have hired a loser like her son to take care of the bitch who'd set her favorite son up, but he'd been so pliable and had settled for far less money than what a real hit man would have cost her, and besides, he was expendable. Now it seemed that she'd given the fool her money and now he was nowhere to be found and hadn't completed what he'd been sent to do. Even though she was infuriated by his actions, something in the back of her mind told her that something had gone terribly wrong in her plan. Meredith tried to calm herself with a large glass of bourbon, to no avail. She just needed to located her useless son and then find someone who could take care of Jasmine/Trista or whatever the hell she was calling herself these days, once and for all. She poured herself another three fingers of bourbon as she stepped outside to retrieve her mail. Bills, bills and more bills she thought as she grabbed the stack of envelopes out of her mailbox, along with a plain manila envelope. She hadn't ordered anything that she could recall but wasn't really interested in seeing how much she owed this month, nor what was inside the package. She threw the pile on the table in the foyer and proceeded to finish her now nearly empty glass of liquid enjoyment. As the last few sips burned her throat, and she felt no better than she had before she'd started drinking her first glass. When it was empty, she forced herself out of her oversized black leather sofa and proceeded toward the stairwell to head upstairs. She caught a glimpse of the generic looking envelope, and curiosity got the best of her. Opening it as she climbed her stairwell, she ripped the top of the corrugated cardboard open and looked inside. Seeing just bubble wrap, she slid the contents of the envelope out and into her hand, still having no clue what was wrapped up inside. She unrolled the wrap, and opened the plastic bag, allowing its' contents to slide into her hand, and then proceeded to scream and scream and scream as she looked down and realized that she was holding what was left of a human finger. Once she processed what it was, she dropped the severed finger onto her wooden stairwell as if it were on fire and ran up the stairs, never looking back.

She ran into her bedroom, slamming the door shut as quickly as possible, as if the bloodied finger she'd left half way up the staircase could come after her. Her heart was racing and her hand was shaking as she dialed the police. The gruff sounding voice on the other end told her to leave it where she'd dropped it and that he'd send a squad car out to her home. It wasn't until she hung up the phone that she knew, knew who the finger belonged to and started shaking all over again.

~~~ Chapter 37 ~~~

Rebecca made good time as she exited the thruway in North Utica and followed her GPS's directions. Once she found Route 12, she pulled into BJ's gas to fill up and use the rest room before heading north. According to Viola, the female voice on her GPS, she had roughly another 60 plus miles before she reached her destination. Knowing her sister's cabin would probably be void of food, she made a last minute decision to grab a few essentials. Not one to dawdle, she was in and out of the wholesale store within a half an hour and once she had the groceries loaded into the back of her truck, sat her cruise on and headed north for the last leg of her journey.

Of course she hadn't mentioned to her sister that she was making a road trip up to see her, nor did she mention that she was in route when she'd spoken with her a few minutes earlier. All she had casually asked was if she was going into work today or staying at home. Rebecca had a general idea where her restaurant was but from the map that she'd pulled up on Google Earth, still had no real idea how to get to her sister's little cabin in the woods. From what the computer screen had shown her, the cabin was nestled in such thick forest, that it wasn't visible from the satellite images that Google had been able to capture. She just hoped that she'd be able to find it once she got into town. Rebecca had no doubt that wherever her sister was now calling home, it would be remote, isolated and would appear desolate to most people; but then again, Trista was not like most people. Even when she'd been with Nathaniel, Trista had always preferred to beat to her own drum and not rely on him or anyone else for that matter, to come to her aid. She'd always been very proficient in taking care of herself and as Rebecca crossed the Blue Line entering into the Adirondack Park, she knew that her big sister was probably doing just fine up in her mountains. She just needed to see for herself and within the hour, she would.

The police came, interviewed her, took her statement, took the finger and left, leaving Meredith alone with her bourbon. Her life had become such that the only people she really spoke with were business colleagues or clients within the firm. Whether by choice or not, she had no real friends, male or female that she could confide in and wasn't close enough with anyone in what was left of her family to open up to them. All she knew was that she'd given birth to two sons, and if her hunch was right, she'd lost both of them; one to prison and one to a fate worse than incarceration. And as she drank another swig of her drink, she knew that Trista was to blame for the demise of both.

It hadn't taken long at all for forensics to determine that the finger had belonged to a blood relative of Meredith's. She had provided them with a blood sample and allowed them to swab the inside of her cheek to compare DNA. Of course, they'd had plenty of questions for her when she stated that she knew the finger must have belonged to her son. After she'd answered what seemed like endless questions, they'd left her home to run the analysis and submit the formal report. She'd told them about how her son was MIA, and that she hadn't heard from him in days. What she hadn't told them was where she knew he'd gone or why he was up in the North Country to begin with. They'd told her that they'd follow up with the information that she'd provided them and they'd get back to her but she knew that they were full of shit and that the only interest they had at the moment was not nailing her former daughter-in-law, but determining whether or not the finger belonged to her son and where the rest of his body was, that is if there was a body.

Once it had been determined that the severed finger did in fact belong to her son Blane, the police took more interest in the case. She'd told them just enough information to point them in Trista's direction without divulging why he might have been in the Old Forge area for an extended period of time or what his business was there in the first place. She gave them a description of his vehicle, and offered that he had said that he had wanted to spend a few weeks researching the area in hopes of finding a piece of land to purchase. It was a complete fabrication but knew that it would sound plausible to the police. Besides, if her hunch was right, her first born certainly wouldn't be able to collaborate nor deny her statement. As she sipped on the contents in her glass, she felt sorry for Blane and also for herself. She felt sorry that her son was most likely dead, probably killed somehow by that psycho ex-daughter-in-law of hers. And she felt sorry for herself. She especially felt sorry for herself because she didn't, in her self-centered way, think that it was fair that she had to go through the inconvenience of losing another child, even if this one hadn't really been part of her life, until recently. She secretly had known his whereabouts and social status for year; she'd made it a point to know. A woman with the number of assets that she had within her portfolio knew the importance of keeping tabs on any potential players within her social or personal circle. It had taken her a few simple phone calls to actually locate her long lost son once she wanted to. He had been so easy to manipulate, she thought back now. All he'd wanted at first was for her to answer his million questions about how he came to be. She didn't' give two shits about playing mommy to the bastard that had inconvenienced her so long ago and screwed up her freshman year of college. And she certainly hadn't wanted to discuss his father with him. She tried telling him that he'd been the product of a one-night stand but he'd seen through that lie and was relentless until she finally told him what he wanted to hear. He'd told her that he simply wanted to know whom he looked like when he looked into the mirror. She didn't want to tell him that he could have passed for his father's double at that age. The first time she'd agreed to meet with him at a coffee shop, it nearly took her breath away seeing him sitting there in the corner booth. He was Danny's son all right and if she'd had any doubt about whether or not he was legit, she simply needed to look into his eyes and knew that he could be no one else's but Danny's, and looking at him sitting there took her back to a time long ago.

She'd been so in love with her weekend warrior back then. He was the epitome of tall, dark and handsome, her Danny. They'd met on the ski slope her junior year of high school and before summer break, were inseparable. Where she was a studious bookworm, he was a natural born near genius who never needed to open a textbook, yet still maintained a straight A, 3.99 GPA. They spent every possible waking hour together and both went away to college in the Rochester area so that they could still see each other as often as possible, despite attending different universities. And then the unthinkable happened. She'd missed her period and although she wasn't a rocket scientist, she knew what it met and that her life as she knew it was essentially over.

Of course he'd wanted to run away and elope when she'd eventually told him the news. He was ecstatic and wanted to get married as quickly as possible. While Danny was the incessant romantic, Meredith was the realist and she knew that a baby would not only destroy her dreams, but theirs as well. Neither was ready emotionally or financially to bring a life into the world, but Danny wouldn't listen to reason. For the first time in their relationship, they fought, and fought viciously, with the love of her life giving her an ultimatum. He told her that if she gave the child away, that they were through. That one bold proclamation was the beginning of the end for what had been the best three years of her life. She'd made up her mind that she would not keep the child under any circumstances, and with that, Danny walked out of her life before her son was even born.

Had she been right in her decision all those years before, she thought now as she sat alone in her massive house, sipping on the last few drops of the now empty bottle. Because of her decision, she had given the child a chance to grow up with a family that could provide him with the things that she couldn't and hopefully provide not only a stable loving environment but also a financially secure one. Well it was all for moot now she thought angrily, since it appeared that her boy had not only lost a finger but most likely lost his life as well, and she'd just have to wait until they found his body to confirm it. The more she thought about that damn nurse Jasmine sitting pompously in her new life somewhere, mocking her; the more her anger turned into uncontrollable rage. And while the bourbon was destroying the oxygen carrying capacity of her blood, she made up her mind then and there that enough was enough, if the law wouldn't take care of someone like Trista/Jasmine or whatever the hell she called herself these days, then she would. She then sat in her darkened bedroom and began plotting out her revenge.

~~~ Chapter 38 ~~~

Rebecca made her way through Old Forge and started looking for her destination. She felt that it was important to speak with her sister's boss prior to seeing her in person. Knowing that Trista had always been one to keep things close to her chest, Rebecca thought that maybe if she spoke with the people who'd spent the last months with her only sibling, she'd get a better understanding of her current mental state. That way, she'd gain some insight into her present state of mind and her overall well-being before seeing her in person. Rebecca realized as she continued north on Route 28, that she was also subconsciously postponing the inevitable. She was excited to see her sister, but also a bit uneasy. Her sister was not one to like surprises, and her showing up on her doorstep was definitely going to be a surprise. But the visit was long overdue, she thought now as she slowed when Viola announced that their destination was coming up. Rebecca followed the French accent of her GPS and turned into the parking lot of the quaint looking restaurant. Nothing fancy from the outside, Rebecca took a few seconds to fluff her hair, check her teeth for residue of the raisins that she'd been munching on for the last half hour, and after one last check in the mirror, exited her vehicle and walked toward the entrance. She surveyed the parking lot quickly for Trista's SUV but didn't see it as she entered the establishment. As soon as she stepped inside, she realized why Trista had chosen this place in particular to try her luck at waitressing. The interior's knotty pine was accented by red leather booths and enough chrome to put most motorcycles to shame. The floor was a dark mahogany with its wide planks appearing to be decades old. The long bar at the end of the building featured more lights than most people's Christmas trees and appeared very well stocked from her brief observation, and at the moment, came with a middle aged man who was intent on scrutinizing her and she checked out the place. He didn't give her but a few more seconds before he made his way over to her.

Appearing all serious, he put out his hand to introduce himself, or so she thought.

"You have a license to carry that 9?" he asked casually as he took her hand in his, smiling while his eyes were not.

She never broke stride with the shake. "Actually yes," she responded back, matching his smile.

"Are you here for business or pleasure Miss?"

"Pleasure, unless you or the proprietor of this fine establishment has an issue that I need to make my business," she answered in a monotone voice. As the two faced off, eye level to eye level; Laverne came out of the kitchen, and only took two seconds flat to figure out who Sal was currently in a stare down with.

"Well would you looky here! It looks like Trista's sister must be paying her a surprise visit."

Running toward Rebecca in order to break up the showdown, Laverne wedged herself in between Sal and Rebecca, who still hadn't broken their respective stances. It wasn't until Laverne's words finally sunk in, that Sal visibly relaxed. He heard himself repeating what Laverne had already acknowledged.

"You're our Trista's sister?"

"That would be me. And you must be Sal, her boss. Up until my arrival just a few minutes ago, I'd had a wonderful visual of what you looked like and what a great guy you must be for taking my sister in, offering her a job and showing her such acceptance along with kindness. Now," she added curtly, "Not so much."

"Back at ya kid. I'm not used to people strolling in here packing some heavy heat and me not knowing who they are and what their reason for carrying is."

"Last I knew Sal," she answered somewhat sarcastically, "A gun owner didn't have to announce that they were carrying if they have a license to do so. Hence the reason it's called Concealed," she added.

"You are absolutely correct," he said through teeth that were clenched shut and a temper that was close to showing its' ugly head. But when you're in my town, drinking in my bar and eating food in my family oriented restaurant, I'm gonna know who's carrying and why. So deal with it."

Knowing that they were at a stall mate, with neither quite ready to concede, Laverne pulled Rebecca into a big bear hug welcoming her. As she held her near, she whispered into her ear.

"Don't pay any attention to Sal. He's just so used to playing Papa Bear protecting his cubs that he forgets that the world isn't always filled with bad guys ya know."

Rebecca looked into the eyes of the woman holding her, and felt her eyes starting to swell.

"She's okay right?" she asked sincerely. "Trista's been doing okay since she moved up here right? After everything that she's been through, I worry about her," she added as she looked into Laverne's telling stare.

Laverne thought about how she should answer the question and decided that the woman deserved a straightforward answer instead of some sugar coated bull shit. "Your sister hasn't really opened up about her life before she came here so I'm not really sure what you're talking about. The only thing that I can tell you is that meeting your sister and having her enter our lives has been a blessing to not only Sal, Tabby and myself here at the restaurant, but also to so many others in our tiny community. We don't know what her life was like before she came here but we all know that ours has been enriched, thanks to her many kind acts. She is truly an angel and there's not a soul who has met her who doesn't love her."

Sal listened to Laverne giving her accolades about his bartender while he was still deciding if he liked Trista's little sister. As he saw the sincerity to which she'd asked about her big sister, he decided that he would, in fact, at least give her a chance. Or he'd at least give her a chance based on whether she answered one simple question honestly.

"What department and in what capacity?" he asked, breaking up the little love fest between the two.

She knew that they were at a pivotal crossroads and although she usually never spoke of her work life with civilians, she decided that they deserved an honest straightforward answer.

"Downstate, Swat," she answered, offering no more. "And you?"

"UPD, retired."

Rebecca took in what he'd told her and in their exchange, Laverne saw the dynamics of their power struggle change.

"Alright then," he added, and smiled.

"Alright then," Rebecca agreed. "If my sister has kept her past life buried, just be aware that she's no wallflower, and know that my big sister can definitely take care of herself. I might carry the shield but Trista has more training than the academy ever taught me. Even though she appears very introverted, my sister could kick most peoples' asses if she wanted to, included mine," she said laughing. "But I'm glad to see that she has good people like you two looking out for her while she's living up here in your neck of the woods."

"She does, and we'd do anything to protect her. Always remember that," he added.

Not quite sure how to take his statement, Rebecca looked at Sal questioning. He added nothing more so Rebecca changed the topic.

"So she's adjusting to life in the mountains?"

Laverne spoke up. "Adjusted?" Laverne laughed a full hearted laugh, holding her insides.

"Let me tell you something Rebecca, it's as if that girl was born and raised up here in the woods. She's adjusted so well that she fits in as a local and to an outsider, you'd assume that she was born and raised in that little cabin that she now calls home." Still not ready to get off topic, Sal spoke up.

"Rebecca, just tell me one thing. Our Trista isn't in some kind of trouble is she? Or running from a man or anyone who's trying to hurt her?" he asked in a tone that conveyed nothing but concern for a friend.

Almost immediately Rebecca's radar honed in on not so much what he'd asked, but the way he'd asked it. Knowing that her biggest fears were probably about to come true, Rebecca looked directly at the proprietor of the restaurant.

"Tell me why you'd ask that question Sal? Has anything happened while she's been up here? Is she alright?"

Like Laverne, Sal choice not to sugarcoat his response. "She's fine. It's just that she had someone keeping an eye on her place who wasn't invited. But he's gone now so there's nothing to worry about," or at least Sal assumed that Trista's unwanted guest had vacated the premises. Having his suspicions but refusing to think about them or buy into what might have happened to the stranger, he chose to remember that he was no longer a cop and simply a bar tender looking out for his staff. When he'd realized who the scumbag was that was hitting on Trista in his own restaurant, it was too late to do anything about it. He'd disappeared and while Sal didn't know the circumstances of what happened, when Sal looked up and into the eyes of the officers walking into his establishment, he had a sneaky suspicion that he was about to find out. He promptly excused himself, but not before Rebecca had glanced their way and determined that they were cops as well. She might not be in a large city at the moment, but a cops a cop and she knew instantly that the two who'd just entered the ADK Bar & Grill were all business and not simply stopping by for the BBQ pulled pork sandwich.

She couldn't hear much of what they were saying but heard enough to catch the gest that they were investigating the disappearance of one Blane Johnson and that sources had told them that he'd been seen hanging out and getting cozy with Sal's newest bartender. He'd immediately shut down that line of questioning and explained that from the picture they'd shown him of the missing person, that yes he'd eaten in his restaurant one or possibly twice. He went on to inform them, while both Laverne and Rebecca listened on, that in no way, shape or form did he ever see Trista or any other member of his staff reciprocating his passes. And that he appeared to flirt with all of the female staff in his restaurant. He also made it very clear that the man in the picture had come into the restaurant and had left the restaurant, alone. He provided the work schedule of all his staff and when they were satisfied with the answers that he'd provided them, they thanked him for his time, and made their way to a table to grab a couple cups of coffee. He knew that their real reason for staying was to get a feel for the restaurant and to wait for Trista. He was not going to tell them that she wasn't scheduled to come in until the supper hour. It they want to sit on their asses all afternoon waiting for something that wasn't going to happen for a few hours, let them, he thought to himself.

After they moved to the corner table where they were currently talking with Tabby, Sal rejoined Laverne and Rebecca. He hadn't even had an opportunity to take a swig of his now luke-warm coffee before Rebecca nearly pounced. When she saw them speak with the waitress Sal had identified as Tabby, she immediately turned toward Sal.

"Care to tell me what that was all about?" she commanded more than asked.

He knew that he could make something up but opted for the truth instead.

"Seems one of our former patrons has gone missing and they were just following up on all leads. His rental car was found abandoned in a parking lot and his hotel room hasn't been used in a few days according to the maid there. The detectives," he said, nodding over toward where the two burly looking men were finishing up their respective cups of coffee, "found a receipt for our restaurant along with other establishments in his room so they're doing what any seasoned detective would do, they're following up on any and all leads related to the missing person. Right now he is just a missing person and they're just collecting information for their report," he added.

"And how does he connect to my sister?" she asked, not quite sure if she wanted to know the answer.

He saw her hesitancy in asking the question. "It isn't at all connected to your sister except to say that he was flirting pretty hard with her the day that he was in here. But with that said, he came in alone and left alone and your sister worked her entire shift just like she did all her other shifts."

"Then why did I get the distinct impression that those two," she said, nodding her head towards the two plain clothes cops where were now sitting outside in their unmarked car, "were snooping around here asking about my sister or waiting for her to come in so that they can interrogate her"

"They won't interrogate, question or harass your sister without our presence, and legal counsel and I made that very clear to both of them. They know me and they know I am a very straight shooter, literally and figuratively so they know not to fuck with me or mine," he added. "And that is why they opted to leave before finishing their cup of Joe. They knew that they weren't welcome here.

Seeing a quick flash of anger, she looked at her sister's employer.

"You guys really care about her don't you?" she asked quietly, reaching over and gently touching his hand. He looked across the bar to Rebecca and smiled, with Laverne speaking up.

"We know Trista has had some tough breaks in her life, although she's never indicated what they were. And we know that she is fiercely independent and has a temper that matches my Salvatore's. But we also know that she has a soft side, and would do anything for someone that matters to her. She's proven that over and over again, though she has yet to admit that she's the one responsible for providing a few select people with their good fortune," she added, smiling when she glanced over at Tabitha and Charlie.

"She is a very hard worker, but also knows how to have fun. I could go on with my accolades, but suffice it to say that yes, yes we love your sister, and I don't think there is anyone who's met her who doesn't feel the same way. She is someone that once you've met her, you will never forget her. Whether it was a positive or maybe even a negative experience," she said chuckling. "Lord knows she certainly knows how to rub some the wrong way. Remember when she cut old McKenzie off and literately threw him out when he wouldn't leave?" she said more to Sal than to Rebecca. Laverne was on a roll and continued. "Out of curiosity Rebecca, was your sister ever a cop because she certainly knows some interesting moves to get people to do exactly what she wants. McKenzie's a huge bull of a man, but before I couldn't even get Sal to give her a hand, she had him with his arm behind his back and walking right on out the front door without one more bit of fight in him. Never seen anything like it, asked her to teach me that move and she just chuckled. So was she a cop?"

Both Rebecca and Sal answered simultaneously. "Marine."

Surprised that her big sister had revealed that part of her past, Rebecca turned to Sal.

"She told you that?" When he didn't immediately answer, she came to another conclusion and felt her temper once again flare. "Or did you have her investigated?"

Refusing to feel guilty for what anyone would have done to protect the interests of his other employees and himself, he was not going to lie to her nor would he try to defend his actions.

"Of course I ran her name and social security number. Funny thing about that is the fact that Trista doesn't exist for a number of years." He saw her shift, just enough to catch his eye. Still refusing to apologize, he continued, "the funny thing about it is that Trista existed until approximately age 12 and then again, not until recently. It's as if she'd assumed a new identity for more than half her life. You know anything about it Rebecca? Or maybe have anything to add?"

Before she answered, she glanced over at the two men who had once again taken up residence at the back table. They appeared more interested in who was coming in and out than the people positioned at the bar. She thought about her response for just another few seconds before responding.

"If Trista told you that she was in the Marines, then she must trust you completely. Yes, she was a Marine. Our early childhood was horrific to say the least and the best thing that happened to us was being placed in foster care and adopted together into a very loving home. Our adoptive family thought it best that we make a fresh start, in a new town and with new names. So we both were able to choose our new names and move on with life. You know she was a Marine, but did she tell you that she was also a Registered Nurse?

Rebecca shifted her weight from one leg to the other. She hadn't lived with her older sister in over a decade, yet their posture and mannerisms were eerily similar Sal thought as he watched her.

"The Marines taught her how to kill and she felt that by working as a nurse, she could somehow pay her self-imposed penance to society. She never spoke about what exactly she did while she served, but I know that when she came out, she made it her focus to continuously search out the people whom she thought needed her help the most. She was always giving things away, donating her time to too many organizations to count, and talking about starting a family and wanting at least a dozen children."

"And you?"

Caught slightly off guard and in her own thoughts, she snapped back to reality and looked over and Laverne. "And me what?" she asked.

"Did you want children and does our Trista have children and a family?" She asked gently.

Like her sister, she kept her personal life very private but didn't want to be disrespectful to her sister's employers so she gave the shortest answer she could think of. "She had a family but lost it all. "

Sal and Laverne said nothing but exchanged glances. Before they could say anything, Rebecca added one last insight into Trista's mental state.

"When she lost her child, I saw something die inside my sister and she's never been the same since. It's like the person I knew and loved died in the hospital the day her baby did."

<div align="center">~~~ Chapter 39 ~~~</div>

Lost in thought, at first nobody noticed that they were being watched, until her four legged friend made his way toward Sal. When he realized that Remmy was heading in his direction, he looked up and into Trista's eyes. His first impression of the eyes burning into his was that she looked like a stranger, someone he'd have feared if he hadn't known her. As quickly as her demonic look appeared, it was gone. Her eyes lit up when she saw her sister. Rebecca felt her stare and turned to see her only sister and best friend standing not 15 feet away. Her first thought was how wonderful she looked. Up until that moment, she had worried about how she'd find her sister but seeing her standing there, she knew that returning to the country had been the best thing her sister could have done. She looked so natural and happy in her element, and so unlike the stiff pompous looking sister that she'd known not that long ago. Their eyes locked and as everyone watched on, they practically ran to embrace each other in the middle of the restaurant floor. As they hugged, both started talking at once, laughing in unison at their own private joke, and nearly knocking each other over in their theatrics. Rebecca stood a good four inches taller than Trista and her body composure was lanky compared to her sister's more compact, muscular physique but anyone could tell simply by looking at the two women that they were both in excellent physical shape, and definitely sisters. As they embraced, her appearance in the restaurant didn't go unnoticed by dark haired man sitting at the table at the rear of the restaurant. He'd come in shortly after the detectives, wearing dark glasses and an even darker black leather jacket which stood out compared to the cotton flannel and Carhart jackets.

When she and her sister finally separated, she turned back toward Laverne and Sal, asking them if they'd known about their surprise visitor. They both assured her that her sister's appearance had been as much of a surprise to them as she had been to her. Sal then handed her a beer, and the four clanked bottles in unison officially welcoming their guest to The ADK Bar & Grill.

Knowing that Charlie could pitch in at the bar if he needed him to, Sal told Trista that she could have the day off and sent them on their way. Trista thanked him profusely and knowing that the restaurant was closed the following day, she made Sal, Laverne, Charlie and Tabby all promise that they'd all come over for a celebration dinner. They all agreed and with that, Trista left the restaurant with her sister in tow.

He continued to sip on his black coffee, forcing himself to not get up and leave when he saw the women making their departure. He knew by looking at their appearance and by the way they embraced that they were family, most likely sisters at that. He studied them as they hugged, talked and eventually left the restaurant together. He'd have to find out who the other woman was and report back in. He wasn't interested in having this job drag out any longer than a week tops and if the other broad was still lingering around and got caught in the crossfire, so be it he thought as he finished the last of what had been a very good cup of coffee. The woman who'd hired him had made her intentions very clear. Find her, hurt her, and then kill her in any manner of his choosing. She'd made her instructions extremely easy to follow and although he wasn't necessary interested in killing a woman, he wasn't able to pass up the bounty that his current employer had placed on this bartender's head. He didn't know that the story was between the two women, the one who'd hired him and the one he'd eliminate, nor did he necessarily care. A job was a job. He'd have been a fool to say no when it appeared to be a very cut and dry hit. How hard could it be to take her out when she lived alone in a very isolated area of town he thought to himself. He'd only been in the area for less than 24 hours but had already ascertained where she lived and confirmed that she had no other occupants in the home other than the mutt that seemed to follow her everywhere. Ridding himself of the dog was easy, and from what he'd seen of the woman calling herself Trista, this assignment should turn out to be one of the easiest job that he'd had in months. He could tell from looking at her, that the woman who now accompanied his target was a cop. She walked like one and from the sidearm that she was carrying, she must be one. Cop or no cop he thought to himself as he pulled out cash to pay for his bill, if she got in the way, she'd die as well. From the sizable down payment that had been wired into his bank account, he knew that his new employer would expect the job to be completed quickly and professionally, and if she got two for the price of one, so be it.

~~~ Chapter 40 ~~~

Trista spent the remainder of the afternoon and evening just hanging out with her sister, her best friend. She gave her the two second tour of her new home and introduced her to her livestock and new way of life, all the while careful to keep her away from the wood splitter that she hadn't cleaned again, since her conversation with Sal. Rebecca had always been more of a city gal so when

Trista opened the door to the cabin and invited her in, she entered immediately. The fall air had just enough of a bite to it to command one's attention and as Trista stoked the old Ben Franklin stove, she knew that winter in the mountains would be just around the corner. She made a quick mental note to have Charlie or Frank down at the garage take a look at the tires on her truck to make sure they were good enough to make it through the season. Reaching for her sister's overnight bag, with Remmy practically underfoot, she smiled, so happy to have family, her only family with her.

"Wow, this place is great Trista! It's actually more spacious than it appeared from outside," she added.

"It's all I need and is the perfect size for us."

Turning in a 180, Rebecca took in all the minute details that she knew her sister had added, giving the home its unique flair. In her former life, her sister had lived in a mansion four times the size of the little cabin that she now called home, but Rebecca couldn't help but feel that it had never been a home for her sister. Looking around at the antiques intermingled with impressionist art, old mixed with new, this was her sister's style.

Making herself at home, she walked over to the refrigerator, and grabbed two Coronas out of it. Handing one to her sister, she made herself comfortable on the one couch in the room. Remmy was at her side looking for loving in two seconds flat. As she petted the pup's head, she looked over at her sister and began speaking

"So tell me all about your life up here in the mountains Trista? Sal and Laverne seem like decent people to work for. You ever hear anything from asshole or his lawyers, or his dear mother Meredith?"

Looking outside to the densely forested woods, she added, "And isn't it a bit creepy being this far out in the middle of the woods and alone at night? It would creep me out I think," she said, in a half laugh. "And I'm the one who carries a gun for a living," she chuckled.

Sort of under her breath, Trista responded, lost in thought. "You're not the only one who knows how to shoot little sister."

Snapping back to the present, Trista continued on before her sister could comment on her remark about marksmanship. "Nah, I have neighbors just down the road. And we have cell coverage here so help is never more than a quick phone call away."

Not quite certain if her sister was buying her speech or not, she changed the subject away from herself and her new lifestyle and back to something safer.

"So what do I owe this surprise visit? You know I don't like surprises but having my favorite sister drop in is a totally different story!"

"I'm your only sister so I'd better be the favorite one!"

She loved her sister with all her heart but couldn't help but feel that something was off, somehow she'd lost part of her sister when Trista had lost the baby. She looked into the same blue eyes that had always shown so brightly even on their darkest days when they were children, and somehow they just didn't seem to have the same luster anymore. As she looked at her sister sitting not six feet away she couldn't help but think that it was her, but it wasn't. Something had changed within her. She had the same look in her eyes that she had upon her discharge from the service. Her eyes held many secrets, many of which Rebecca knew would probably terrify her if they were revealed. Just like she never spoke of her experiences as an officer of the law, Trista never spoke of what she'd went through, done or seen while serving her country.

"Hey," she couldn't help herself, "Talk to me sis. Tell me that you're okay Trista. Are you happy with this life that you've chosen for yourself? I can't help but think that there's a reason that you chose such a secluded spot and I want you to talk to me, tell me what's really going on."

She knew that she'd lost her sister. The eyes looking back at her confirmed her biggest fears. As she sat in the oversized leather chair, sipping her now half empty beer, the sister that she knew and loved was no longer in the room. The woman sitting on the sofa in her place, in her physical body, was not the one she'd grown up with. Having no idea why the long ago memory came into her head, Rebecca just blurted out the words without even thinking.

"Trista, where are you right now? It's okay to tell me. Are you soaring on our black unicorn honey? Are you riding high in the sky on our beautiful boy? Talk to me baby. Tell me how you're feeling. You know he's our secret if you're with him right now. Please tell me Trista," she begged.

Before her sister could answer or think about answering, both were startled by a knock on the front door. She saw a look of panic flash in her sister's eyes as she practically jumped out of the chair. Rebecca's natural inclination was to reach for her gun upon seeing her sister's reaction. She saw her sister moving toward the shotgun sitting against the wall and practically screamed to get her attention and hopefully reorient her. Upon hearing her name, Trista stopped mid stride, looking back at her little sister. It took her only a few seconds to remember where she was and who was in the room with her. Rebecca noted that her eyes were back to the crystal clear blue eyes of their youth. Trista smiled, genuinely smiled at her little sister, and for that brief moment, it looked like she was back to the sister that Rebecca knew and loved.

"Hold that thought sis," she replied warmly. "Not sure who's coming to visit but let's see and then we'll continue that conversation, okay?"

She turned back to the door, where another rap from outside penetrated the wood. Trista opened the door, with her dog at her side to two very tall, serious looking police officers. They didn't offer to identify themselves, nor ask if she was the person they sought.

"Sorry to bother you mam, but we're here on official business and were wondering if we could have a moment or two of your time."

Seeing the men at her doorstep, Rebecca immediately went on the alert and walked to her sister's side to show solidarity.

"Mind if we come in?" the taller man asked.

"Yes," Rebecca answered for her sister, putting her arm on her sister's back.

"We'll have this conversation right here on the porch. What is the nature of your visit gentleman?" she asked, in an all business tone.

Deliberately putting her hands on her hips, Rebecca's jacket opened just enough for both men to see the badge at her side and the sidearm on the other. Realizing that neither woman was going to be intimidated they immediately changed their tactics.

"We're just following up on a missing person lead. Seems that someone who was in the restaurant where you work has gone missing and we're just talking to everyone who might have seen him."

Pulling out a picture of Meredith's son, they offered it to Trista who reluctantly took it and stared at the man in it. Everyone watched her, looking for any kind of recognition or emotion with Trista not showing any, actually showing no emotion at all. She passed the picture back to the one named Malone, according to his ID, and spoke.

"I recognize him. He came into the restaurant twice that I remember. He came in once, less than a week ago when I was behind the bar and then again the other day when I was waitressing. He ordered the pulled pork, two beers, hit on me, and left a decent tip. He came in alone and left alone," she added for good measure.

"You say he hit on you?" the shorter one named Goggins asked.

Trista looked directly into his eyes and responded. "I'm a bartender. Mix alcohol and testosterone and of course men hit on me, and on Laverne and also Tabby. It's a normal expectation that comes with the job. So in answer to your question and to the question you have yet to ask, he hit on me and I politely declined his invitation, despite how sincere he sounded."

"So you never went to his motel room nor had our missing person come here?"

Now becoming irritated and slightly agitated in their attitude, Rebecca tried to intervene with Trista immediately cutting her off.

"Um, I don't think I stuttered. I told you that he came in alone and left alone and I chose not to pursue his advances."

Rebecca straightened her shoulders and knew that the conversation needed to end soon. She could feel her sister tensing up and knowing how volatile her temper could be when she felt threatened or provoked, so she immediately spoke up.

"I believe my sister has answered your questions gentlemen. So unless you have anything else you'd like to ask, I believe this conversation is over. And I'm sure you know your way home boys," she said deliberately to downgrade their status in her eyes.

Knowing that it was futile to keep pushing, they thanked the women for their time and turned and headed back toward their truck. Trista and Rebecca waited until they were out of sight before they turned their backs to the drive and headed back inside.

Trista went back inside, not giving her visitors another thought. Rebecca on the other hand, wanted answers. She went to the frig, grabbed another couple beers, handed one to her sister and started.

"Okay, spill."

Giving her sister he most innocent look, Trista looked over at Rebecca.

Not falling for it, Rebecca took a huge swig of her beer and pushed the issue.

"I know the look Trist. What happened to their missing person?

Trista smiled but it wasn't a warm genuine smile indicative of someone who was totally sane.

"You sure you really want to know what happened to Blane?" she asked in a voice that sounded like it belonged to someone else. Be careful what you ask sister dear."

Feeling the hair go up on the back of her neck, Trista answered her only sister. "Yes Trista, tell me what happened to Blane? Did you see him after he left your restaurant and if so, what did you do to him?"

Knowing that she really didn't want to know the answer but could tell from the satanic looking smile that her sister was now exhibiting, she needed to know what she was dealing with.

"I killed him."

Nearly spitting out the beer that she'd just ingested, Rebecca looked up at her sister.

"What? Trista tell me you're kidding honey because that's not funny. Please tell me that you had nothing to do with that guy's disappearance."

Looking into Rebecca's eyes, but devoid of emotion, Trista continued. "You want the truth?" she continued. "He was a scumbag and came sniffing around. He thought I didn't know who he was but I did. And I'll be damned if Meredith, Nathaniel or her bastard son is going to take advantage of me. He wanted a piece of me and wanted to destroy me so I took him out, that simple."

"What?"

In a deadly serious tone, Trista continued.

"You heard me. He wanted a piece of me so I killed him and fed him to my pigs. In our respective professions, you know it's kill or potentially be killed." She said the statement as if talking about the weather as she took another swig of her beer.

Feeling the color drain from her face, she looked at the person sitting next to her and once again was looking into the eyes of a stranger. Keeping her cool, she took another swallow of the beer that she was still holding in her now shaking hand. She casually continued the conversation.

"What do you mean you fed him to your pigs?"

"Just what I said. I found out who he was and who'd sent him here to interfere with my life. Hey, I didn't draw first blood, he, his dumb ass brother and bitch mother did. I just ended it" she said, believing every word that she was speaking.

In Trista's fractured mind, she had simply eliminated a threat, not taken the life of another human being. As Rebecca gently pried the details that she couldn't believe she was hearing come out of her sister's mouth, it was then that she realized that her sister was ill, seriously ill, and needed psychiatric help, not a prison cell. Trista told Rebecca about how the man whom she'd murdered and dismembered via the wood chipper still currently sitting in her yard, had tried to set her up by planting a corpse in her basement. Rebecca felt ill as she listened to her sister's tale and blatant paranoia. She silently chastised herself that she hadn't seen some signs or warning of her sister's mental break from reality coming on. Her sister spoke of dead corpse's being placed in her basement, people spying on her from the woods and in the restaurant, people breaking into her home and rifling through her most prized possessions and the same said people trying to kill her. Rebecca listened without comment as her mind raced. She was a police officer and had taken an oath to serve and protect. But she'd also made a promise to her maker when she'd become an officer to protect her sister, the same way that her big sister had sacrificed herself to save her when they were children. Rebecca never forgot what it cost her sister when she time after time endured the advances of their perverted uncle. They had been just children, yet her sister had assumed the role of big sister, mother and protector even at the tender age of twelve. Rebecca knew that her sister was mentally ill, drastically severed from reality but also knew that she had to be accountable for taking a human life, no matter how despicable that person might have been. Whether or not her sister was speaking the truth about the individual and his acts was irrelevant, if her sister took a life, then she had to face the consequences.

When Trista finished speaking, she finished her beer and casually set down the now empty bottle. She stood and looked at her sister with the same eyes of the stranger who now occupied her mind.

"You ready for another one sis?"

Breaking her train of thought, Rebecca looked up at her sister, her one-time hero and forced her head to nod yes.

"Yeah, Tris, that would be great, thanks." Watching her sister smile, then turn her back to her to walk into the kitchen, bought her a minute to regroup and gather her thoughts. Her stomach was literally flipping in knots and the thought of alcohol repulsed her at that moment but until she could figure out how to get her sister into a facility that could help her, she knew she had to stall and act as normal as possible. As if reading her mind, Trista called out to her little sister, as her head was practically inside the refrigerator.

"You know Bec that you can't tell anyone. It's our little secret," she half chuckled. "And if you tell anyone, I'll have to kill you. You know that right? You're my sister and I love you and blood is thicker than water, thicker than water, thicker than water," she repeated over and over.

"So you can't rat on me, okay?" she said in a voice that sounded almost childlike and that no longer had any resemblance to the soft, nearly angelic voice of the sister she'd known all her life.

Forcing her voice to sound calm and casual, Rebecca's heart broke as she looked at the shell of what her sister had been. She smiled. "Of course it's our secret honey. No one needs to know."

"Good."

For the brief second that their eyes locked, she had her sister back. And in that moment, the love that they'd shared for their entire lives couldn't have been more evident. Just when Rebecca thought that there might still be a part of her beloved sister within the monster that she'd become, Trista laughed and struck. The blow came so hard and so fast that Rebecca not only didn't see it coming, she didn't react as the bottle crashed into the side of her head. She felt, for one brief second, pain like she'd never felt before. And then she welcomed the darkness.

~~~ Chapter 41 ~~~

Sal didn't know what was nagging him but knew that something was off. He couldn't pin point what it was but like when he'd walked the beat, his sixth sense had alerted him time and time again to impending doom. For some reason, he couldn't shake that same feeling. While Laverne straightened up his already tidy home, he spoke with majority of his staff, either in person or on the phone. He now only needed to touch base with Trista and then he could relax and dismiss his fears. Putting on his reading glasses to look up her number, he felt Laverne come up behind him and gently put her hand on his shoulder. She saw the frustration and concern on his face when the phone rang and rang, finally going to voicemail. He left a message and something told him to call back, which he did. This time, his call went directly to voice mail as if the phone had now been deliberately shut off.

"Drive out to her place if it's bothering you that much. She and her sister are probably just partying and didn't hear the phone. But I'm serious Sal," she said, rubbing his back reassuringly, "Head over there if you're that worried about her. Hell, I'll even tag alone if you want."

While he appreciated the gesture, something akin to that same sixth sense told him that she shouldn't be with him if he decided to make the trek up to Trista's little cabin in the woods. He tried one last time to call her cell.

She initially heard her phone ring the first time and when she saw who was on the caller ID, disconnected it and shut off its' power. She looked over at her sister who was slumped down in the chair where she'd left her. The welt on the side of her head was done swelling, and had already turned black and blue with a hint of purple surrounding the edges. She wasn't sure why she hit her sister and didn't actually even remember doing it but since she and Rebecca were the only ones in the room, and she wasn't the one unconscious at the moment, she must have done it. The bottle lying at her sister's feet must have been what she had hit her with, but as she rubbed her eyes, trying to will the severe pain between them away, she couldn't remember anything after they entered the cabin and started drinking beer. She'd have to do her best to explain to her sister that it had been a terrible accident, or a simple misunderstanding that had caused her indiscretion. And if Rebecca didn't understand, well then she'd just have to make her understand, she thought as she looked down at her unconscious sister. She reached inside her sister's jacket, and then gently covered her with a wool blanket that was lying close by. Knowing that it was time to feed the livestock, she looked down at her sister again, but forced the thought from her mind. The pigs were her babies but this was her sister and if she were forced to eliminate her, she'd do it in the most humane way possible. Trista pulled on her work boots, barn jackets, hat and gloves and after calling for her dog, headed outside.

He watched from his spot in the woods. He had originally thought that the broad in the cabin had been family or a good friend, but when he'd watched her smash the bottle into the side of the woman's head with such velocity and anger, he realized that he must have been incorrect. He didn't know who the unconscious one was, nor did he care actually, and as long as she stayed incapacitated as she currently was, she was of no concern to him. He watched Trista head outside and into the cold, heading towards her barn with her long legged mutt in tow. Using the scope on his rifle to watch her, he knew that he could eliminate her at any given moment. Knowing the hatred between his employer and his target, he contemplated finishing the job then and there but thought that he'd maybe receive a bonus is he not only completed the job, but made her suffer before ending her life. Up until the point when he had witnessed her attempt to murder her house guest, he'd never have suspected that she actually had a violent streak. When he felt himself wince as he witnessed the attack, he rethought his previous analysis and realized that she should not be demised as weak based on her gender. He'd use the element of surprise and knew that he outweighed her by at least 60 or 70 pounds, so he felt confident that he could overpower her if it came to that.

The air was calm but Trista could feel the negative energy as soon as she stepped off her porch. As she looked into the forest surrounding her home, she could feel the evil. Silently she rubbed her temples and tried to adjust her vision. The pounding between her eyes had shifted to the side of her head and rubbing hard enough to nearly remove her skin did nothing to squelch the stab-like pain. She searched the woods, but seeing nothing, hearing nothing and smelling nothing but the smells of the balsam trees surrounding her home, she entered the barn to start her chores. Once inside, she forgot about her paranoia and started singing to the music as she attended to the animals and their supper.

Sal drove in silence, attempting to reach Trista twice more as he made his way down the narrow roads leading to her home. Cell coverage was marginal at best, and with the low cloud cover, he couldn't get through even where there should have been good service. His anxiety level increased with each passing mile and as he passed her neighbor's home, he prayed that his intuition was wrong and that she and her sister were just piss drunk and having a ball.

Rebecca fought the darkness, trying to fight her way back to consciousness. Her mind told her to rest but her heart told her she must wake, must fight the pain and escape the darkness.

Trista continued singing away as Sal pulled into the drive, shut off his truck and walked toward her cabin. He could see smoke billowing out of the chimney and numerous lights illuminating the interior of her little home, but saw no movement from within, nor did she open the door to welcome him in as she always did. He knocked gently and waited. No answer. Growing impatient, he knocked again and when she still didn't answer, he leaned around the porch post and attempted to peer inside the sheers covering her window. He felt the hair rise on the back of his neck as he saw the body slumped in the oversized chair. He couldn't tell which sister it was, nor did it matter. It took him exactly two strides to enter the cabin, and with gun drawn, he scanned the room. Quickly realizing that the room was secure, he raced over to Rebecca with his hand immediately reaching for her carotid. He felt his heart start beating again once he realized that she was in fact alive, despite the golf ball sized welt on the side of her head. He called Trista's name and upon hearing nothing but his own heartbeat, he went room to room looking for her. Due to the size of her tiny abode, it took him less than a minute to search her cabin. Heading back up from the cellar, he heard a moan. Knowing that it had to be Rebecca, he went back to her side and attempted to help her sit more upright as she started to come around. He practically ran to the kitchen to retrieve a glass of water. Knowing that something terrible must have happened to his friend, he willed Rebecca to wake up and after what seemed like hours, but was actually just a few minutes, she started to regain consciousness.

She had enjoyed the darkness, for in its' blanket she'd felt no pain. But hearing the voice calling her, willing her back, she knew that she had to return to the present. The urge to help her sister was the only reason she pushed her way through the pain, through the darkness and back into the light of the tiny cabin. She slowly tried to open her eyes but the pounding on the side of her head combined with the piercingly bright lighting of the room made it painful to open them. She squinted, trying to adjust to the light. Sal knelt in front of her, trying to steady her and holding out a glass of water. As soon as he knew that she was coming around, he brought the glass to her lips for her to moisten her mouth. Very impatient to find out what had happened not only to Rebecca but also to Trista, he started talking the second he thought she was cognoscente enough to listen and answer.

"Hey there, take a small sip Rebecca. Slow honey, you've got a nasty bump on your head."

Kneeling in front of her, he noted that her sidearm was missing. Seeing the empty holster twisted his gut and put him on alert all over again.

"What happened," she said as she nearly choked on the water. Bringing her hand to the side of her head, she moaned. "Trista, where's Trista?" she asked, still groggy and with a pounding headache. It was coming back to her now. Sitting there laughing with her sister, catching up and bullshitting with her only family member and then seeing her change in front of her eyes. They had been drinking beer and telling stories and then Trista was telling her about murdering a man and feeding him to her pigs.

"Oh my God!" she exclaimed as the memories came rushing back. Forcing herself to sit up, she dealt with the pain and looked directly into the eyes of the man supporting her. His pleading eyes willed her to continue.

"Trista's ill. She needs our help."

"What's wrong with her Rebecca and where is she? Is she hurt? Who did this to you? "

"Trista. Trista hit me. Sal, she was my sister but she wasn't. She looked crazy and her eyes were that of a stranger, a monster. She said that she killed a man. Said that some guy was snooping around the restaurant and around here and when she realized that he was, she killed him. She told me that he was spying on her and trying to frame her, so she killed him and fed him to her pigs. Oh my God that's so sick. I'm a cop and I've seen some deranged shit, but that's disgusting," she said, still rubbing her temples.

Not wanting to believe a word that she was saying but knowing that it was probably true, his need to find his employee, his friend, increased exponentially.

"Where is she Rebecca? Where is our Trista? We need to find her so we can get her help," he added, helping Rebecca sit more upright in her chair.

Looking out into the darkness, she answered.

"After she hit me, everything went black." He helped her stand and when she scanned the room and finally processed that Trista was nowhere to be found, she looked at Sal with a look of panic on her face. When her arm brushed the empty holster at her side, she saw the concern on Salvatore's face.

"My gun's missing Sal," she nearly shrieked. What if Trista has it or someone took Trista and they have it or used it on her?" she said, panicking and starting to hyperventilate. We need to find her!"

Sal quickly went to the tiny bathroom situated in the rear of the cabin to retrieve Rebecca a cold wash cloth. When he did, he caught the glint of light emitting from the barn off in the distance. Racing back to Rebecca who was now upright but still rubbing her temple.

"She's out in the barn. Or at least someone is. You stay here, and lock the door behind me. I'll go check it out," he said heading toward the door, gun already drawn. She cut him off mid stride.

"You go, I go. And you can't hurt her Sal. She's sick, and might be a murderer, though her tale might have just been some delusional outburst. She's still my sister and she needs our help. So don't hurt her Sal, promise me that you won't hurt her!" she pleaded, gently touching his arm.

"I won't hurt her. But if she's as delusional as you say she is, she might be dangerous so I need you to stay here."

"I'm coming with you Sal, like it or not." Knowing that they could be wasting precious time arguing, he conceded and handed her his pistol. She looked into his eyes and when their eyes locked, they understood each other and in that moment they both understood what needed to be done to help the woman they both loved. She accepted the gun and in doing so, accepted her destiny. Sal moved to the tiny dining area and retrieved the rife that Trista always kept leaning up again her china hutch. Confirming that it was in fact loaded, he rejoined Rebecca as she waited by the door. A million thoughts raced through Rebecca's mind and even more scenarios filtered through Sal's as he opened the door and headed outside with Rebecca in tow. As they approached the barn from the side so as to not be in any direct line of vision for whoever was inside, they felt their hearts racing and fearing what they'd find once they got close enough to see. Rebecca has seen it firsthand and Sal had only had a slight hint of

Trista's fractured psyche during their conversations. He worried about her instability as they got to within a few feet of the barn. He wanted to find a vantage point in which to look inside and found one when he moved around the side of the barn. And then he heard it, more specifically, heard her. The voice he heard was that of his bartender, who was not only his employee but one of his closest friends. Up until today, he'd thought that he knew her as well as any of his other employees, but in listening to Rebecca's version of what had transpired earlier that evening, now he wasn't so sure.

Her voice sounded so sweet, innocent and almost angelic. She certainly had a beautiful voice he thought as he listened to her pounding out the lyrics to Zeppelin's Stairway To Heaven. She was mucking out one of the stalls and seemed oblivious to the possibility that she was being watched. For the few seconds that they watched her in silence, she looked no different to them, she was simply Trista. So how could it be possible that she was not only capable of the assault on her own sister, but the brutal murder of a man? Neither had time to ponder very long. Trista had felt the air change around her and in one second went from singing, to whipping around and screaming at the very window that they were peering in.

"Who's there? Whoever you are, come and get me you bastard! I'll kill you mother fucker! I will chew you up and spit you out so come and give it your best shot!" she screamed. Rebecca and Sal were taken back momentarily by the sound that had come out of Trista's body. She looked like the woman they both knew and loved but the sound resonating from her was anything but familiar. The voice was female and demonic at the same time, and sounded nothing like their beloved Trista.

He stayed back far enough to go unnoticed but close enough to see the scenario playing out in front of him. It was becoming apparent that the chick had absolutely lost her marbles. He didn't know how or why but she had absolutely lost it and was delusional, paranoid and potentially lethal from the pistol she had tucked behind her back. But so were the two staring back at her through the window. She was screaming from within the barn, and had yet to see who was threatening her. He left his vantage point and started slowly, silently nudging closer so he could hear what he expected to be a confrontation. With a little luck, either the boss or the chick would eliminate his target and he'd get paid for essentially doing nothing. Yup, he thought to himself as he inched closer, rifle in hand just in case, this job could get wrapped up by nights' end and by the weekend, he could be relaxing somewhere much warmer than the God forsaken mountains that had held him hostage for days now.

Rebecca looked at Sal for guidance as Trista continued her rant inside the barn. Her voice had grown louder and louder and when they hadn't come forward, acknowledging their presence, she become even more angry than she had been when she started her rant.

"You've got ten seconds to show your face or I'll burn this fucking place down, with me in it and you'll never get me." Knowing that her sister never said anything that she didn't mean, Rebecca immediately started moving toward the entrance and stopped short of entering when Sal's arm grabbed her from behind.

"What in the hell do you think you're doing?" he whispered, keeping his voice low enough to only be audible to her.

"She'll do it Sal. Let me go to her," she begged. "I know her better than anyone and she'll listen to me."

"She's not your sister anymore Rebecca. You've heard first-hand what she's capable of."

She glared at him and in that moment he knew that there was no arguing with her. So instead of wasting his breathe, he simply reminded her to be careful and to stay out of his direct line of vision of Trista. Looking down at the gun at his side, she knew exactly what he was implying but would never allow him to harm her sister, no matter what. She was and would always be her sister, her mentor and her best friend, regardless of her mental state. She nodded at Sal and slowly made her way toward the entrance where Trista was last seen inside. As Rebecca made her way into the doorway, she called her sister's name and prayed that her sister was still somewhere within Trista's head and would recognize her own sister. Hearing her voice, Remmy came running up to her, tail wagging. She knelt and greeted her sister's dog with a quick pat on the head. Looking up, she looked into the barrel of her own pistol.

"How did you get out here? You're supposed to be dead?" she said in the same tone as Rebecca had heard earlier. Looking at her only sister, she smiled and even though her heart was breaking at the cruelty of her words, she knew that somewhere deep inside the woman standing several feet away from her, was her sister. And knew that they were at a pivotal moment, and one wrong word might cost her her life. But she'd freely walked into this faceoff and it was do or die, literally.

"Hey sis, it's me, Rebecca. Look into my eyes Trista or do you want to be called Jasmine? Honey, look at me. What happened inside was an accident and I know that you didn't mean to hurt me right?" she said as she lifted her hands slowly to show that she wasn't armed. As she stared at the gun pointed directly at her chest, knowing it was her largest body mass area, she quickly realized that her sister's intent if she chose to shoot was not to incapacitate her but to kill her. Her sister said nothing as she continued to point the gun in her direction but her facial expression revealed what her words did not. She could tell that her sister was having an internal battle within her own mind as she didn't flinch, didn't waver at all, nor did she lower the gun in recognition.

"You should never have come here Rebecca. This is not your battle. Now you've come here and ruined everything. I'm not going to jail sis, and you coming here to arrest me was the wrong thing to do."

Knowing that her sister might still be inside the fragmented shell of a woman standing just feet away, she didn't react but spoke casually as if she hadn't heard her sister at all.

"Trista honey, I came up here to your home to visit you because I love you and I missed my big sister. Remember all the fun we used to have together as kids? I came up to visit so we could spend time together and maybe you'd want to come live with me. I have room for you and your puppy and I was hoping that you'd be sick of living up here in the mountains by now. That's why I came Trista."

Seeing her facial expression change almost immediately and her posturing become very rigid, Rebecca realized that she had made a grave mistake in suggesting that her sister leave the sanctity of what was now her safe haven. Trista's change in behavior did not go unnoticed. Both Sal and the stranger still partially hidden in the woods saw the transformation as well. He watched through the scope of his rifle as the scenario unfolded in front of him. He felt his own heart racing as he watched the ballsy, unarmed cop confronting the lunatic with a gun. He also saw the restaurant owner watching from his vantage point, with what he assumed was a loaded rifle pointed in the women's general direction. He knew that the guy couldn't get a good shot because the cop was intentionally blocking his target. Having no idea what words were being spoken, he just continued to watch from his vantage point.

"I'm not going anywhere with you. You're just like Nathaniel, and the others. You're trying to set me up and send me to jail and I'll die before I'll go to jail and be stuck with Nathaniel again. He never wanted our baby and never wanted me and I was such a good wife and would have been a great mother," she said as the tears rolled down her face. She continued on with her tirade, never wavering in her positioning of the gun. "I gave him everything and he took it all away from me and now you're trying to do the same thing," she screamed, "And I won't have it!"

The warning shot startled both Sal and Rebecca with Rebecca tucking as if to avoid being hit. Trista laughed out loud at her sister's new found fear.

"If I had wanted to shoot you, you'd be dead. You should know that by now.

Rebecca decided to try a different avenue in attempting to reach her sister. "I know that Trista. And I know that you've always been there to protect me, not hurt me. And sis I still need you around to help and protect me, so why don't we go inside and talk okay honey?"

"No! I'm done talking and done protecting you and done picking up the messes. I'm done! I just want to be left alone! Why can't people just leave me alone?" she almost pleaded.

"I know baby, I know," Rebecca reassured.

"You don't know shit," she screamed at her sister. "I had to take care of daddy after what he did to momma. I had to take care of Nate and his slut of a girlfriend. I had to take care of Nate's brother and so many others. I'm tired sissy and I don't want to have to take care of any more people. I'm so tired and just want to be left alone here in my mountains with my animals. I'm a good bartender, aren't I Sal?" she said, looking directly in the direction of where her boss was hiding.

Knowing it was futile to pretend that he wasn't present, he stepped toward the entrance to the barn, maintaining enough room for his gun to remain by his side, ready should he need it.

"You are an excellent bartender, mediocre waitress and one of my best friends Trista," he said sincerely. And Laverne and I love you like a daughter and want nothing but the best for you. And if Laverne, your sister or I can help you in any way, we'll move heaven and earth to help you, and I hope that you know that," he added.

She laughed and in that quick brief second, sounded like the woman that both he and Rebecca loved but then as quickly as she was there, she was gone again.

Rebecca spoke up, but felt ill in asking the question. "How did you take care of daddy, and Nathaniel honey," she asked, in a mere whisper.

The question caused Trista to burst out laughing. "You remember how I told you when we were kids and after our last beating, to go into our room and pack your make-believe runaway bag? Well, I made sure we needed it that night didn't I? Once our beloved father passed out from the booze, I helped myself to one of his cigarettes and lit it for him and put it in his hand. Not my fault he was too drunk and asleep to smoke it!" she chuckled.

Listening in disbelief, Rebecca couldn't help but confront her. "You lit the cigarette? Oh my God, we nearly died in that fire. What the fuck Trista! You could have killed us both!" Rebecca screamed back at her sister, not giving a shit that her sister was still the one holding the gun.

"And what do you mean you took care of Nate and that dumb-ass that he was screwing? Trista, don't tell me you had something to do with what's-her-name's death as well? Oh my God Trista, what did you do to them?" she asked, now feeling completely sick to her stomach for the third time in one day.

"I did what any woman or man for that matter would do. I eliminated the threat. And if it cost by beloved husband his freedom, oh well. He should have thought of that when he was sleeping with her. They both got what they deserved. And I don't have one ounce of regret." Knowing that she'd already admitted to too much, Trista became visibly uncomfortable. "You and Sal need to leave in his truck, and get far away from here. I don't want you here anymore Rebecca. And I quit at the restaurant" she shouted to Sal.

"Give my check to Tabby and tell her it's an early wedding present okay" she said with a voice that sounded surprisingly like her own. She still hadn't lowered the pistol that she'd taken from her sister's holster, a fact that neither Rebecca or Sal hadn't forgotten. Also knowing that her emotional stability remained questionable, Sal hoped to rectify their current standoff as soon as possible. Taking the opportunity to attempt to rationalize with his bartender, he smiled and looked directly at Trista.

"Trista, I don't care what you did to that scumbag who was harassing you, nor do I care what you did to your husband or his friend, the only one I care about is you. And your sister and I can help you, and will help you get away from here if you need to. No one is going to take you away from us Trista. You have to trust us."

"No! You lie. Men lie and tell you what they think we want to hear. I don't believe you! You're just like all of them. Daddy, our uncle, the sergeant, my husband, all of them; they all lied," she screamed. "I'm not going to jail, I'm not getting committed, and I'm not crazy! I know that's what you're thinking but I didn't hurt anyone who didn't deserve what they had coming to them."

Feeling ill, Rebecca looked at her in disbelief. "What have you become Trista?" she asked in disgust. "How many people have you killed? Oh my God Trista, what have you done?"

"Nothing that I am ashamed of. And nothing that I wouldn't do again. Now, since it's obvious that you and Sal don't approve of my methods, I'm sorry sis, I really am." Trista looked at her sister and mouthed, "I love you," and pulled the trigger.

The shot was not a kill shot, though it could have been if she'd chosen it to be. Trista deliberately shot her sister in the right shoulder, just high enough to drop her and make her shooting arm useless. It took both she and Sal a millisecond for it to process the fact that Trista had just shot her only sister. Wanting to rush to Rebecca's aid but afraid of getting shot himself, Sal screamed for her to put down the gun to which he got his response back almost instantaneously in the form of a shot whizzing by the side of his head.

"Back off Sal or the next one will be twenty degrees to the right and through your skull." Leave her be. I need you to unload that gun you're trying so hard to hide, and I need you to do it now. I don't want to kill my sister, nor do I want to shoot you Sal, but you know I'll do both if you don't unload that rifle and back away. I'm not going to be taken anywhere and there's only one of two ways our disagreement is going to be settled. Either you do it my way, or some of us are going to die tonight, and I'm betting it won't be me. So if you want to return home to Laverne shortly, I suggest you do as I say and back off."

"I can't do that my friend. Trista, you need help and I want to help you."

She didn't hesitate, and pulled the trigger. This time her shot gazed her sister's side, causing her to scream out in pain, grabbing her side as the blood immediately started gushing out. The voice that came out of Trista sounded alien, nothing like neither Rebecca or Sal had ever heard before.

"Don't do as I tell you and she'll bleed to death or die with the next bullet. Are you willing to take the chance?" she taunted, smiling.

It was Rebecca who broke the stalemate.

"Take the shot Sal. She needs our help. Take the shot and get her. The doctors can fix whatever you injure and then we can get her help. Down on her side with her half of her body out of view due to the way that she fell, Trista couldn't see the way her sister was moving her uninjured hand. She been shot in her right shoulder but what Trista didn't remember was that she was in fact left handed and also kept a second back up pistol strapped to her calf. As she kept her eye on her sister who was now pacing back and forth as if she were having an internal mental debate, Rebecca screamed once again for Sal to take the shot even though it was killing her inside to think that she was ordering her sister to be injured or possibly killed. But knowing that the situation was coming to a head and needed to be contained sooner rather than later as Trista was appearing to become more and more unstable and volatile, Rebecca knew that it was the only way to possibly save her sister and herself. She trusted Sal to shoot to incapacitate not kill, and once she was subdued, they'd get her whatever help, both physically and mentally that she needed. She'd been there all their childhood for her and it was Rebecca's turn to repay the favor. Starting to feel faint from the significant blood loss, Rebecca tried to rationalize one last time with her sister, to no avail. When she saw Trista's face contort as if in pain, and her facial expression change into something unrecognizable, she knew that she was doomed. Sal saw the change as well and knew that it was now or never to save his friend and spare Rebecca's life. Trista lifted the pistol again, pointing it directly at her only sister as Sal and the stranger watched. Hearing the siren of the police trucks pulling down her drive, Trista's dog broke the silence with his growling. Momentarily distracted, Rebecca attempted to roll for cover but it was too late. Trista saw the move and reacted.

The shot came without warning and not from Trista's gun. After hearing the blast, Trista looked down in disbelief at the gapping whole in her side. She couldn't believe she'd actually been shot. With Trista momentarily distracted, Sal made his move and raced to Rebecca's side to pull her out of Trista's direct line of fire. In that ten second interlude, Trista realized what was happening. Refusing to give up, she grabbed the gas can a few feet away,

387

dumped it in the fresh straw that she laid down not even an hour before, flicked her lighter and threw it in. She was not going to go to jail, and dying here in the home that she'd come to love would be better than rotting in some prison cell. Like father like daughter she thought as she contemplated burning to death.

Once Sal had Rebecca secured, he took a brief second to look at her injuries. She remained nauseous but conscious and assured him that she would be okay. "Did you shoot to kill her Sal or just to injure her? I need to know."

"I didn't take the shot. I thought you did in the commotion."

"I didn't take the shot, I'd die before I could shoot my sister, my own flesh and blood."

"If you didn't take the shot, then who did?" he asked as the first two officers arrived on scene. Black smoke could be seen billowing out of both doors and the two side windows. The air was already filling with the toxic smelling fumes from the straw and century old wood that the barn was comprised of. While the straw smoldered, the wood lit up immediately and the flames spread with the blink of an eye, engulfing the entire structure within seconds. Seeing the inferno in front of him, Sal tried desperately to find a way around the flames to get to

Trista, to no avail. He then ran around to the rear of the structure, along with one of the officers. As they rounded the corner to the rear of the building, they heard the faint hum of a four-wheeler in the distance. Assuming that it was one of the neighbors who'd seen the smoke and was coming to help with the fire, they ignored it and focused on finding a way in. Sal attempted to run into the rear of the barn, despite the flames biting at him but the officer restrained him.

"It's too late Sal; it's too late for her now."

"No, Trista! I've got to try and save her. I promised her sister! Let go of me, I've gotta try!"

Holding him firmly, the officer tightened his grip. "It's too late man. No one could withstand that heat. No one's alive in there. We're too late Sal, I'm sorry."

~~~ Chapter 42 ~~~

It took most of the night for the firefighters to put out the fire and cool the embers to search inside. The barn had been completely engulfed by the time the fire department had made their way down the winding dirt road to the old Carver home, Trista's cabin. The volunteers worked diligently to preserve the cabin as the flames leapt across the yard trying to claim another dwelling. Rebecca refused to go with the EMT's to the hospital until it was confirmed that her sister had perished in the blaze. It had taken the firefighters over an hour to put out the fire, despite the barn's small size. It was in the smoldering rubble of what had been her sister's hobby farm, that her body was discovered; so close to the rear exit, yet not quite far enough to let her escape the inferno and survive. The firefighter's notified Rebecca, Sal and Laverne who'd joined them, of their discovery. The body was burned beyond recognition and essentially disintegrated when they tried to place it in the coroner's body bag. They shielded Rebecca from the body and it wasn't until they were loading it into their rig that Rebecca was allowed to get close enough to what was left of her sister. She asked them if she could have just one moment with her sister before she was shipped off to Utica for an autopsy to determine her actual cause of death, smoke inhalation or if she had burnt to death. Either way, it didn't matter Rebecca thought as she looked down at what was left of her sister's remains. She reached out to touch the body bag holding her sister and best friend. With Laverne on one side and Sal on the other, the three reached out to touch the bag. The second that Rebecca touched the cold hard plastic, she felt it and knew. She smiled, actually laughed out loud, nearly losing her balance. She laughed so hard that she suddenly felt faint and started going under. Sal and Laverne grabbed her under both armpits, and within minutes she was loaded into the gurney and she was transported alongside the remains of her sister to the hospital, one sister heading to the OR and the other to the morgue.

Epilogue

Two months passed before Rebecca felt emotionally and physically strong enough to return to the mountains. Her best friends had begged her to leave it alone and move on. They didn't understand that she needed to return not only for closure, and to thank Sal, Laverne and all of the staff at the ADK Bar & Grill for not only being kind, and great friends to her sister when she'd needed them the most, but also for loving Trista, faults and all, almost as much as she had. So, on a frigid Saturday morning, Rebecca returned to the mountains one last time to say goodbye and thank them in person.

As Rebecca shared a beer with her new second family, and promised that maybe, just maybe, she'd return in the summer to spend a week or two at her sister's cabin. As they laughed and shared stories about the person that they all loved and knew would always be in their hearts; approximately sixty miles north, another straightened her shoulders, made sure that her wig was on just right and walked into the diner after telling her four legged companion to wait in the truck.

"Good morning, my name is Jasmine, and I'd like to speak to the owner about the bartending position that you have open..."

Author's note: I sincerely hope that you have enjoyed Trista's story. No one can condone her actions but I hope that you were rooting for her in the end...

Made in the USA
Middletown, DE
27 June 2017